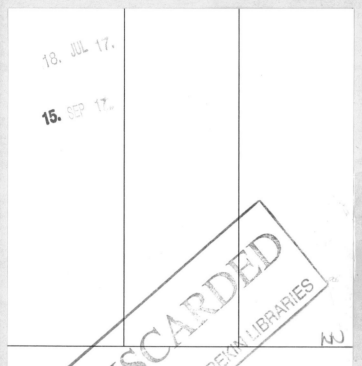

Also by Virginia Ironside

No! I Don't Need Reading Glasses!
Yes! I Can Manage, Thank You!

NO THANKS! I'm Quite Happy Standing!

VIRGINIA IRONSIDE

Quercus

First published in Great Britain in 2016 by Quercus
This paperback edition published in 2017 by

Quercus Editions Ltd
Carmelite House
50 Victoria Embankment
London EC4Y 0DZ

An Hachette UK company

A CIP catalogue record for this book is available
from the British Library

PB ISBN 978 1 78206 935 5
EBOOK ISBN 978 1 78429 240 9

10 9 8 7 6 5 4 3 2 1

Printed and bound in Great Britain by Clays Ltd, St Ives plc

Typeset by CC Book Production

For Kate, Sukie and Christian

JANUARY

January 1

Getting up this morning at eight a.m., I was surprised to find that I hadn't already been woken by my adored grandson, Gene. In the past, when he'd stayed over (which he had last night) he would come into my room very early, demanding a cuddle and a story. But something's happened to him recently. Now he's nine years old, he appears to have had one of those strange growth spurts that has transformed him from a rather grown-up child into a near-teenager. It's all happened in a matter of weeks.

I remember the same thing happening with my son, Jack, Gene's father, at around the same age. One minute he was up for a cuddle and the next positively pushing me – his own mother – away, as if I were some needy lover he wanted to rid himself of. If I kissed him, he'd sometimes even wipe the kiss off with his hand and then try to transfer it, as if it were some piece of slime, to a nearby piece of cloth.

Anyway, struggling into my dressing gown I looked in on Gene sprawled on the spare bed in the room where I work and found him still dead to the world – no doubt because he'd been up so late last night, it having been being New Year's Eve. Seeing him asleep, I suddenly saw exactly the adult he'll turn into. Before you can say 'Jack Robinson' his voice will be breaking and he'll be bringing unsuitable girls round, with lateral scars on their wrists, sinister bald patches on their scalps and rings through their noses. And, no doubt, instead of quietly colouring in drawings of dolphins at the kitchen table, he'll spend his time rolling up illegal substances while staring at his iPhone.

David, my ex-husband who I'm kind of half-back-with-half-not – oh, God, how can I describe this? We'd been really good friends for years but a couple of Christmases ago he suddenly hit on me again and we tumbled into bed and I have to say I found it all rather jolly. So for the last couple of years he's been coming up to London every so often and I go down to his place and we have a nice time and a cuddle and maybe a bit of sex if we're both up for it, and it's the perfect situation. All the security of having a chap around, without any of the 'It was Wednesday . . .' 'No it was Thursday . . .' 'Who's telling this story, you or me?' kind of wrangles that go on when you're married – conversations I remember all too clearly from the days when we were shacked up as man and wife.

Anyway, David. He'd come up from the country for a New Year's drinks party I was having, and he'd brought Gene round, as well. Jack and Chrissie, our son and daughter-in-law, were going out to some bash and it was easier for Gene to come to me than for them to get a babysitter. Rather sweetly David had brought me a book about the Indian Mutiny as a new year present – I felt a bit daunted because history isn't really my thing, but he said it was a compulsive read so I'll give it a go.

I'd only asked a few local people round for drinks to celebrate the New Year – I'd told them to eat first and come at 8.30 – and I'd explained that now we're all so ancient and like going to bed early I'd be happy for midnight to be a movable feast.

But in the circs, even I, early-nighter par excellence, was a bit staggered when Marion and Tim, my old pals from down the road, looked at their watches at one minute to ten and started a countdown, informing us that ten was the new midnight because, even though they'd barely arrived, they had a gruelling journey ahead of them the following day as they were driving to Cornwall to see family.

But when the other guests protested, Penny, my best friend and neighbour, shouted them down.

'No, come on, we can all celebrate at different times!' she shrieked, cracking open one of the bottles of champagne she'd brought (rather generously she'd contributed three bottles). 'One bottle for ten o'clock, one for eleven o'clock and the final one for midnight. Let's celebrate every hour on the hour!'

'And maybe we'll go on till the early hours after that!' shouted Melanie-from-next-door. She'd already kicked off her shoes and was sitting cross-legged on the floor – something that, being sixty-eight going on sixty-nine, I am unable to do any more and, let's be honest, was never that comfortable doing even when I could. She was surrounded by discarded scarves and looking – wearing, as she was, a kind of glittering turban – like a Turkish potentate. 'I love each and every one of you, all through the coming year and for all the many years in the future! I kiss you all! You are my family! My loves! Here's to us!'

I raised my eyebrows at my old friend James, thinking Mel was going rather far, but he was having none of it.

'To us!' he shouted, raising his glass. Leaving me feeling like the bad fairy at the christening, a role that I am trying very hard to shed. After all, as one ages, surely one should become nicer and more charitable, not more and more sarcastic and bitter? Perhaps I'm heading to be a crabby old lady, the sort who, at a bus stop, shoos the people in front of her away with her walking stick and insists on getting on first, shouting, 'I'm eighty! Let me through!'

David, however, caught my eye and rolled both his, so I blessed the fact that he was around to play evil troll to my bad fairy.

But actually, it was a good evening. David arrived with Gene at six, and we worked out where everyone was to sleep – I thought it might be a bit peculiar for Gene to find his granny and grandfather in bed together on New Year's morning when he'd never seen such a thing before, so David slept upstairs in the lodger's room and set up the spare bed in my workroom for Gene.

'I told Mum and Dad I wouldn't see them till next year,' Gene told me when he arrived, looking smug and probably

4

thinking – as I had done when I'd said the same as a child and indeed we all had at some point in our lives – that this remark was incredibly new and amusing. Which of course it always is, the first time round. He had also, at Christmas time, wished us a 'Crappy Hissmas' – another joke that I remember discovering myself at around the same age.

As Gene bustled into the sitting room, wearing, I noticed, surprisingly big shoes, I was struck by how he's filled out and is starting now to get actual shoulders – a masculine shape – which is disconcerting. To add to the adult look, he's even got a new phone, which he was very keen to show me. When I got out my old grey Nokia, he shook his head. And I must say it did look like something one might see in a glass case in a museum of the eighties.

'Granny!' he said. 'You can't have a phone like that. It doesn't even take pictures! You can't get apps on it!'

'Maybe I'll get a new one,' I said – something I've been saying for the last five years, with no intention of getting a new one, ever; as far as technology goes I have reached the final barrier. Email, yes. Skype, just. But an iPhone – that's a bridge too far.

'Yes, get a new one! Get an iPhone 5!' he said. 'Then we can Snapchat and swap Vines, and you can get direct streaming and WhatsApp and synch to the Cloud! I can show you how to use it!'

'He's right, darling – er, Marie,' said David, coming down-stairs. There'd been a fearful banging noise from upstairs as he'd set up Gene's collapsible bed, mingled with the sounds of pre-New Year singing from Father Emmanuel's evangelical church next door but one. ('Oh Happy Day!' they were singing. But I knew that after Father Emmanuel's subsequent sermon on hell and damnation, the congregation wouldn't be feeling so jolly happy for much longer.) 'Honestly, you'd take to an iPhone like a duck to water. Even I've got an iPhone. And Penny. And Marion. And Mel. And Tim, for God's sake. Tim, the thickest man in the world.'

'Is Tim the thickest man in the world?' asked Gene, surprised.

'No,' I said. 'David was joking. Being an accountant, he's just a bit – staid.'

'He's even more of an old fart than me,' said David, in explanation.

'Ah,' said Gene. 'Yes, I see what you mean. Thickest man in the world.'

Jokes! My grandson makes jokes! David and I roared with laughter, not just at the joke and the speed of the joke, but at the very capacity Gene had to make jokes at all. Of course, ever since Gene had, at about six months old, discovered how amusing it was to put a blanket over his head and then remove it, collapsing with laughter, I knew that he'd been blessed with a terrific sense of humour but it's always good to see these things confirmed.

We were all in a very good mood when we sat down to eat the scrappy early supper I'd prepared, and then we put out the glasses and the wine, and buttered bits of brown bread, covered them with smoked salmon and cut them into squares as nibbles – throwing the grey bits of salmon to my cat Pouncer who had suddenly started looking extremely interested in the proceedings – before Gene and I relaxed in the sitting room, talking about New Year's resolutions until the guests arrived.

'I'm not going to make any resolutions this year,' I said as I lay back on my nice green sofa near the fire, sipping at a glass of cold champagne. 'I make them every year and never carry them out.'

'I've got a resolution,' said David. He'd just come into the sitting room having, very sweetly, washed up the supper things. He looked at me, rather meaningfully – and for a frightful moment I wondered if he was going to suggest that he move in permanently. But luckily he glided out to fetch ashtrays – this being very much a smoking-allowed household – and all I could think was: 'I do hope not.' I love the situation as it is too much. Most of the time he's in the country, building flood defences and pruning trees and looking after his orchard and clearing the attics; he's only here for the odd weekend. It suits me perfectly. The moment we get to snapping point, one or other disappears back to their own home and we remain perfect friends.

'What are your resolutions, darling?' I asked Gene, who was now placing pieces of dill on the smoked salmon bits. They were laid out on a very nice decorated plate on the table in the middle of the sitting room – a plate, I may add, that I'd made and painted myself in a pottery class a while ago while I was still teaching art at school.

Gene paused. 'I'd like to get a tattoo most of all,' he said.

'But I'm not allowed till I'm sixteen, but one of my friend's brothers did it with a compass and ink without his mum or dad knowing and there's nothing they can do about it now! It was brilliant!'

'Darling!' I said. 'You can't get a tattoo! It would be ghastly.'

'What's your friend's brother's tattoo of?' asked David, curiously.

'It's of an eyeball,' said Gene. 'He's got a thing about eyeballs.'

David and I grimaced at each other.

'But I want a tattoo of a skull. And I'd like to get a really sick knife,' added Gene. 'All the boys at the big school have got knives. And this year I want to try smoking. Dad says I mustn't ever start smoking but I saw him smoking out in the garden the other day when he thought no one was looking so I don't see why I shouldn't at least have a try. Then I'll stop.'

David laughed, but I was relieved when the bell rang and all the gang started pouring in, stamping their feet, complaining of the cold and moving towards the fire.

Marion and Tim were their usual selves. Marion had forgotten to put on any make-up, Tim's tie was awry, and they were muttering about checking the car's tyres. Penny got out her champagne and put it in the fridge, while Mel arrived waving a present of a weird construction of wire and feathers. She claimed it was a dreamcatcher to stop me having nightmares but I wondered if it wasn't actually some sort of voodoo totem to make me agree with her in residents' meetings.

(She's still smarting because I wouldn't paint my front door the colour she'd wanted a couple of years back.)

James, up from Somerset where he's now moved – to be with a bloke he met on a gay farmers' dating agency on the internet – brought a lovely amaryllis in a pot, still in bud but just about to burst through into a gorgeous bloom. 'Just like all of us,' he said, 'as we approach the coming year.' Then, spotting Gene, he said: 'I say, is that Gene? Quite the young man! You'll break a few hearts soon! I last saw you a couple of years ago . . . and look at you now!'

Gene blushed and grinned and shook his hand.

After about an hour, David insisted on getting out some old rock tapes I'd made in the sixties – yes, tapes! And I still have a machine that plays them! – and after we'd pushed the kitchen table to one side, he and I were persuaded to show off some of our old moves with Gene looking on and saying, 'You're really cool, Grandpa! And you, Granny!' Then Tim started doing the twist, his big bottom wiggling about like one of the elephants in *Dumbo*, and Marion twirled in a dancing-round-the-maypole sort of way, while Mel draped herself over James still trying, presumably, to convert him to heterosexuality – a task as likely to succeed, frankly, as getting a tadpole to learn the rumba.

Next Gene – emboldened by the half-glass of champagne he was allowed – started breakdancing and we all stood at the sides of the room, clapping in time to the music, and it was like that scene out of *Saturday Night Fever* when John Travolta struts his stuff on the dance floor and we hooted and whistled

9

when he finished, flushed and embarrassed but very pleased with himself.

Somehow I managed to hang on till eleven o'clock when I suddenly felt as if I'd been hit on the head with a hammer. After cracking open another bottle of champers and making sure David didn't mind staying up to keep the party going till midnight, and reminding him that Gene shouldn't fall asleep – he's far too big to carry upstairs these days – I staggered up to bed.

Later

Did I mention that David had done all the tidying up after everyone left? Saintly. Anyway, he and Gene woke just as I wrote that last bit and after breakfast we went for a walk in the park where Gene fed several robins, all the while saying, 'If you had an iPhone 5, Granny, you could take a picture of me with the robins.'

This was extremely annoying because I could feel my resolve about never venturing into the land of iPhones starting to crumble, because of course I would have loved a photograph of Gene with the robins. Still, we had a bite of lunch at a café that was open on Holland Park Avenue, and finally David took Gene home before heading back to Somerset.

'I'll come up next weekend, shall I?' he said.

But I'm afraid I rather fudged it, saying: 'Oh, don't bother, I'll be coming down for my birthday on the fifteenth,' and feeling rather bad when he looked so disappointed.

'Well, happy new year, darling,' he said, but I could hear

the hurt in his voice. So I gave him an extra hug and kiss and whispered 'Love you' in his ear, though, to be honest, I'm never sure when I say it to anyone whether I'm pretending or not. It's such a difficult thing to say, even when you mean it. I really do love him but the minute I articulate it, it sounds somehow false. Odd, that.

I missed Gene, as usual, but managed to spend a very nice evening on my own watching a documentary about some teenagers who'd been imprisoned for life in the States for the ritual murder of three young boys and then released nineteen years later after it turned out it was probably the frightful stepfather who did it after all. There were tears in my eyes as I sat there with Pouncer curled up on my lap. Utterly ghastly in real life, of course. And I felt terrible for finding the whole programme so enjoyably cathartic.

Later still

Just woken in the middle of the night, having dreamed that an old school friend of mine had turned into a very small man-like woman and had asked me to marry her. She'd joined a cult called the Church of Scoby and persuaded me to have a baby with her which involved catching a fledgling bird in a suburb of Cardiff. Just at the moment I realised I'd missed the train to Wales, I luckily woke up and, in order to drive all thoughts of the Church of Scoby from my mind, am typing in my nightie.

So much for the dreamcatcher.

January 5

'Ecstasy for the over-fifties! Half of older generation "off their heads", says drugs tsar' (*Daily Rant*).

Turns out that 25 per cent of older people have tried ecstasy, those pills that apparently make you feel all wonderful and loving towards mankind. They take it at raves. (Not fifty-year-olds, obviously, but young people; the oldies take Es in the comfort of their own home after watching *Downton Abbey*.) I've been dying to give it a go for years – E, not *Downton Abbey* – but have no idea how to get hold of it. I suppose, rather sadly actually, that Gene would be the one to ask, even though he's only nine. God, it's rather tragic to think that grannies might be using their grandsons as dealers these days.

But, fortunately, I was just at the corner shop buying some post-party carpet cleaner, when who should I bump into at the counter but Sheila, our local drug dealer known, obviously, as Sheila the Dealer. Not liking to ask her outright because I don't think we're meant to know her trade, I pointed to the headline in the *Daily Rant*, stacked up among the other newspapers on the rack.

'Wish I could try that!' I said, jokingly. 'It sounds absolutely brilliant. Trouble is, people like me have no clue where to get their hands on any. Are you one of those over-fifties on E, Sheila?' I asked. 'You never can tell what people get up to these days.'

'I'm strictly jazz-terbaccer, Mrs S,' replied Sheila, rather prudishly, I thought. 'Don't like this newfangled stuff. Never know what goes into it. But if you really want to try some, I

12

can ask around. You can get anyfink up the estate. But you want good stuff, innit? Not rubbish.'

As I practically have proof that this woman is knee-deep in bags of heroin and sacks of coke, not to mention all kinds of other unspeakable substances such as LSD and ketamine, and her kitchen is probably heaving with those toads that young people are meant to lick and get off their heads on (she's not called Sheila the Dealer for nothing), I'd half-thought she might produce a couple of Es from the pockets of her stained flowered apron there and then. But I suppose if you're a drug dealer you want to keep it quiet and all that 'jazz-terbaccer' stuff was just to put busybodies like me off the scent. (Talking of which, just standing next to her I was starting to reel from her own scent, a heady fragrance of old cabbage, cigarette smoke, paraffin and jazz-terbaccer so strong that I was feeling stoned just inhaling the air around her.)

I made sure she knew I was serious before returning home and found, to my surprise, Melanie from next door ringing my bell, clutching a letter.

'I'm so sorry,' she said, as I let her in. 'This was delivered to me and I opened it by mistake because I didn't even look at the address and assumed it was for me. The postman put it in the wrong door. But,' she added, dramatically, 'I couldn't help reading it – well, a bit of it – and it's from Brad and Sharmie who want you to go to India! So – if you're going, can I come too?'

'Hold on!' I said, shutting the door and taking the letter from her. 'I haven't even read it yet.'

I didn't mind the fact that Melanie had opened the letter because many's the time I've opened letters meant for other people in the house. But to read it! Wasn't that going a bit far? (Or certainly to admit to reading it, anyway.)

She followed me into the kitchen. 'You see,' she said, 'my son lives there and we could go out together and spend a few days in Delhi with Brad and Sharmie and then he could come and pick me up and I could go down to Kerala to see the grandchildren, and then we could meet up together and fly home. It would be brilliant!'

Ever since Melanie moved in next door, after the Americans – Brad and Sharmie – I've often thought she has some kind of psychic plug leading from her which she can insert into an invisible socket on my body and use to drain me of any energy or will of my own. I sat down and looked at the letter.

'Dear Marie,' I read. 'I expect you've been wondering what's become of us!! I hope you remember those two mad guys from the US who had the cheek to come and live next door to you for a year! But, hey, we're still alive, and settled now into this great little house in Delhi – NOTHING like Shepherd's Bush but very comfortable all the same. Brad's loving his new job and I spend half my time looking after Alice – who sends you lots of love of course! – and the other half working at an orphanage just outside the city. We were wondering – would you like to come out and stay with us for a week or so? Even better, bring your paintbrush and sketchbook and do some more of your awesome paintings of trees? We love those paintings of London trees that you did for us, Marie – everyone raves about them – and there are some fantastic specimens out here that are crying out to be painted by you! We do hope you'll say yes! India's a fascinating place if you've never been before and we can show you some amazing sights. Hope all is well with you! All very best, Sharmie, Brad and Alice.'

Alice's signature was in wiggly handwriting and she'd done a smiley-face above the 'i', an icon that gives me the willies when used by adults, but which, from Alice, was completely delightful.

'Well, what about it?' said Melanie impatiently. 'Are you up for it? Let's get out our diaries!'

'I'll have to think about it,' I said, rather grandly. 'I can't decide now. I have too much on my plate.'

'What? Do tell me! Maybe I can help!' exclaimed Melanie, turning over the rest of the post that I'd brought in and put on the kitchen table, and even starting to read a postcard.

'Melanie! I am up to my eyes!' I said. I wondered how I could impress her with how busy I was. 'I'm thinking of getting a new lodger and I have a lot of problems to work out,' I lied. The minute I'd closed my mouth I knew I shouldn't have mentioned anything specific.

'I've got just the man for you! He's a darling! I met him before Christmas when I was on a soul-healing workshop. He's looking for somewhere to live and I was thinking of asking you.'

'Later, later,' I said, feeling rather like some busy Hollywood film director, ushering eager scriptwriters out of his office. 'I'll consider it. I'll consider everything. But not now . . .'

And finally I got rid of her.

But India? It's rather an exciting thought. I never imagined I'd hear from Brad and Sharmie after they'd left because I thought they'd be like most Americans I've ever met – all over you like a cheap suit when you're around but out of sight out of mind. Something to do with the pioneering spirit, I'm told. Because they were always travelling about and conquering new territories in the Americas, they had to be very friendly to fellow pioneers along the way, and that's why they always talk to strangers on buses and form close – but fleeting – bonds with people on trains. All I was, I thought, was another passing pioneer on Brad and Sharmie's journey. But no. It seems they were perfectly genuine in their friendship. Very flattering and nice.

As is the prospect of India, where I've never been before. I have an image of it in my mind as all multi-limbed gods, elephants, women in colourful saris going about with pots on their heads and the Taj Mahal in the distance. Well, either that or wretched children with pot bellies covered with flies of the kind that appear in charity begging letters every week. Or there's the Bollywood India, of course – million-pound weddings, jewels and dark men with flashing eyes singing love songs from a palace balcony. All total rubbish, I'm sure.

Started to feel so excited that I rang Penny and asked her round for a drink.

'Why don't we go together?' she said, as she settled on the sofa. 'I've always wanted to see India. And a long flight's miserable on your own. And I've been feeling really down recently, so it would give me something to look forward to.'

'Why are you down?' I said, rather surprised. Penny's usually on a fairly even keel.

'Oh, I don't know,' she said. 'Partly the time of year, partly . . . well, I think you and David getting back together has made me feel not jealous exactly, but a bit left out. I'm so happy for you, but it does rather throw my own single state into relief. I know we're always saying how nice it is to be single but, to be honest, it's not that brilliant, is it, as you get older? I woke up the other night with my heart pounding, thinking I was having a heart attack, and I suddenly realised how, if I were to be taken to hospital, I wouldn't have anyone to put in the "next of kin" box.'

'You'd have your daughter,' I said. 'You wouldn't be alone, anyway, because you'd have rung me up and I'd have come with you.'

Penny knocked back the remains of her glass and reached for a top-up. 'I know you would, but it's not the same, is it?'

No, it's not the same. I knew what she meant. And I must say, knowing David is around is a tremendous consolation. I felt bad about making her feel bad, but knew there was nothing I could do about it.

'Okay, let's go to India together,' I said. Not only would it cheer her up but also I didn't fancy the idea of wandering about the slums of Delhi on my own. 'But I have to warn you. Melanie's set her heart on coming too and I don't know how I can put her off.'

'Christl!' said Penny. 'Oh well, why not? Let's ask the whole gang. You, me, Melanie, Marion, Tim . . . we could ask James, too.'

Wondered if David wanted to go as well but didn't like to say anything in case it rubbed salt into Penny's wound.

Later

When I rang David and suggested he come too I have to say I was a bit relieved when he said he couldn't.

'I'm not sure I want to go again,' he said. 'And I'm also not sure if you'll like it, darling. It's quite, well – what shall I say? – in your face. And you're quite a sensitive soul. But if you're staying with a couple of rich Americans you'll probably be protected from the worst of it.'

'They want me to go and paint trees,' I said.

'You'd do that brilliantly. And there are some pretty weird trees over there,' he added. 'The banyan's the best, with all its crazy roots, but there's the Indian devil tree, the baobab and the jacaranda, and lovely huge eucalyptuses, of course . . . make sure you get to see a bo tree, too . . . the Buddha was born under one . . . amazing trunk . . .'

'How do you know all this?' I asked. Men's capacity for knowing facts always astonishes me.

'I know everything, darling,' he said. 'I went on a tree tour of India a while ago with Sandra. Don't you remember? That's where she met Ali, when we were in Goa. Oh, by the way, talking of Sandra, will you be going Goa way? Why not pop down there after Delhi? It's meant to be gorgeous. You can have some R and R. And check if Sandra's okay. I haven't heard from her for weeks.'

'R and R? What's that?' I asked.

'Rest and relaxation,' he said. 'Come on, you must know that.'

'Doesn't sound me at all,' I said, hearing the Scottish grandmother coming out in me. 'I don't do rest and relaxation – as you know, I'm compulsively on the go. You'll be talking of spas and a spot of pampering next.'

'Sorry,' said David. 'I just met Widow Bossom' – she's the woman who tried to get her claws into David the moment Sandra left – 'in the street and you know how she witters on about things like R and R. I think I've caught a bit of wittering from her. But I should think Sandra's getting plenty of it, since Ali seems to live on the beach selling beads and fishing or something, when he's not mending tyres. Can you imagine anything more depressing? Anyway, that was the life she wanted, and I'd never make a beach bum.'

Sandra was the young girl that David ended up with after we'd split up – and a couple of years ago she left him to run off with this Goan beach boy who'd promised her a life of milk and honey and mangoes and no doubt billions of baobab trees, and said he wanted a baby with her. After a few unanswered phone calls and emails recently, David's been rather worried not to have heard from her. I frankly couldn't care less what she's doing as I always thought she was a bit of an airhead, but checking up on her would make an excuse for a round trip. So I said that was an excellent idea, and I put it to the gang.

Though who am I, who know nothing of baobab, banyan or eucalyptus trees, to call anyone an airhead? Take the gale out of your own head before you take the draught out of someone else's, to misquote the Bible.

David reminded me that tonight was Twelfth Night.

'The Widow Bossom popped round specially to tell me,' he chuckled, which annoyed me. Will she never leave him alone? I hate to think of her thrusting herself on him still. However, even though I'm not in the least superstitious, I made sure all my decorations were down in time, packing the fake tree in its box like a green mummy, and taking all the cards down from the mantelpiece. Though frankly Christmas seems to come round so quickly now I'm older, I sometimes wonder why I don't just leave everything up, including the fairy lights, all the year round.

January 8

Just found a piece of dried-up holly over a picture that I hadn't taken down a couple of days ago – and one card hiding behind one of my Staffordshire dogs on the mantelpiece.

Does this mean the house is cursed for the entire year?

Later

It was a brilliant day today – winter sun streaming through the bare branches of the trees in my garden – and, because everyone's still on holiday, it's dead quiet in London. Putting on my coat, I ventured out to brush away a few stray leaves along the path. Pouncer was walking up and down the garden wall, like a sentry patrolling his territory, stopping every so often to sit down, lick his paws, then stay motionless, occasionally doing that shoulder-shrugging ears-back thing as if he'd been reminded of an offensive remark someone once made that had just come back to haunt him.

Had to stop because the phone was ringing, so went inside to find Marion gabbling away enthusiastically the other end.

'What's all this about India?' she said. 'Can I come too? Mel says you and she are off in April and you're making plans – it sounds brilliant. I've always wanted to go on the hippy trail.'

'We're not going on the hippy trail, and we're not going for what I gather is called R and R either,' I said, rather sourly. 'I've been asked by Brad and Sharmie to paint trees. Look, I only heard about this a couple of days ago! But of course, sweetie, if I do go and you want to come, let's all go together.'

Had to end the conversation then, because there was a banging on the door and Mel gushed in, clasping several maps and picture books of India, in a great cloud of patchouli oil. Out of her pocket she produced two little plaster models, one of the Buddha and one of the repulsive Kali, all arms and legs and painted blue.

'We must have them looking over us as we plan,' she said. 'They will bring great fortune.'

I'd looked at her Facebook page that morning. On it she'd written: 'The heart has it's [sic] own language. The heart has a million ways to speak', which didn't make me feel very well disposed towards her since one way her wretched heart could have spoken was by ringing up and asking if it was conven-ient before she barged in. I'd actually been looking forward to seeing if my 'rads', as heating engineers call them, needed bleeding, and going round the house with my special key feeling like a master craftsman as I let the air hiss out and felt the warmth of the boiling water surging in. No such luck.

'We'll get a flight to Delhi on the second of April,' she said. 'I've found really cheap fares. And then you can stay with Brad and Sharmie while Marion and I – and Penny too, if she wants to come – can stay in this brilliant guest house I've found. You look into the jabs because you're good on the medical stuff,' she said, 'and I'll do . . . I'll do the flights and the visas.'

By now she looked like one of those Victorian women explorers. Having kicked off her shoes and settled cross-legged on the sitting-room floor there was something rather charming about her enthusiasm. She finally looked up from the map.

'And Mar, you know I told you about that guy looking for a room? I met him again yesterday, at a shamanic workshop,' she said. 'What say you at least meet him to suss him out?'

It turns out this character is called Robin, around sixty, a bit of an old hippy, who owns the Alt Bookshop on Golborne Road up near Portobello (Alt being short for Alternative, obviously). He's got the lease for the shop and the flat above, where he lives. But as the rents are going up he wants to relocate further west to a cheaper place by the end of the year, and it would suit him to let his flat for a fortune in his now-trendy street, while he looks for a new home near here.

Melanie seems rather keen on him. She says he is v. intelligent, not fooled by 'default reality' and very well read. And, she added, he could keep an eye on both our houses while we go to India. She promised to bring him over tomorrow.

'As long as he doesn't try to convert me to Vedic medicine,' I said. I'd had a particularly grisly encounter with Vedic medicine a year ago. The doctor made me stick out my tongue, made a few notes, prescribed some pills which made me feel terrible and left an enormous hole in my bank account.

January 10

'Former Royal Marine choked to death in a pickled egg eating competition at his local pub after stuffing three in his mouth at once' (*Daily Rant*)

Reading this I made a mental note not to bolt my food. I've been finding recently that being old and therefore busier than I ever have been and, I suspect, in need of less sustenance than I did when I was young, I often eat lunch standing up in the kitchen, frequently popping things into my mouth before I've swallowed the last bit, Royal Marine-style. More than once I've had to rush to the sink for water to prevent myself choking – and I'm not even in an egg-swallowing competition.

I'd asked Melanie to bring Robin round so that I could give him the once-over and tonight she rang the bell. It's odd – it takes me much longer than usual to get downstairs these days and frequently, when the door goes, I'm at the top of the house. So first the bell rings, then I start tottering down, hanging on to the banister rail and, just as I get to the front door, the impatient caller rings the bell again, very long and loud, frightening the daylights out of me, and then I open the door immediately, frightening the daylights out of him. I have taken, I'm afraid to say, to shouting: 'Coming! Coming! All right! Keep your hair on!' as I descend to prevent this unpleasant drama on the threshold. Just like a mad old lady.

Anyway, my bad temper dissipated the moment I met Robin, accompanied by Melanie. He is one of those old Etonian hippies – the very best – tall, slightly stooped but with bright blue eyes and a twinkly smile. He stood on the doorstep, making a flirtatious appraisal of me before stepping over the threshold and I was smitten – until, at least, he stopped on the front step and started muttering to himself and making curious movements with his hands, reminding me of Joe Cocker singing 'With a Little Help from My Friends'.

'He's doing the Ritual of the Entering,' whispered Melanie.

'Does he have to do it every time he goes in any house?' I whispered back, alarmed.

'No, only the first time,' said Melanie. 'It's to bless the house and give him protection against any sad or malevolent spirits who might be here.'

'I hope he doesn't think I'm a sad . . .'

'No, of course not,' said Melanie. 'Anyone who might have lived here in the past. Come on, Robin – this is my friend Mar!'

'Marie,' I corrected, as I shook his hand.

'I do hope you don't mind,' he said, laughing amiably. 'Half my friends think I'm crackers. But I say, it can't do any harm and who knows, it might help put some poor souls to rest! Well!' he added, taking a deep breath in the corridor and looking around him. 'I can tell already! This house has the most wonderful, peaceful and serene atmosphere! I can tell you, it's not every house I enter that I can say that about! It's full of warmth, laughter, creativity and love!'

Considering it's inhabited by little old me, who spends her life gibbering with anxiety about ludicrous things like whether forgetting Churchill's first name means I am getting dementia, I couldn't quite agree with him. Still, it was a terrific compliment and I started to forgive him his Entering Ritual.

We sat down to a small salady lunch and when he got out his inevitable pill supplements, at least he had the courtesy to hand them round like cigarettes – probably the old Etonian politeness kicking in – rather than keep them to himself. Melanie tucked in, but I wasn't about to accept a strange pill from anyone.

'Ah, I can see, you don't need them,' said Robin, throwing me a dazzling and knowing smile. 'I can tell. You are an Old Soul.'

'Not too old,' I said, slightly prickly.

'The older you are on the inside, the younger you appear on the outside. Yin and yang,' said Robin, not missing a beat. 'By the way, you don't have to show me the room. I know already that I'm going to love it. But I don't want to put any pressure on you. Mel's explained the situation. I only want to be here till I find somewhere else – a few months, perhaps – and I always pay by banker's order. By the way, I'm certain we've met in another life, you and I . . .'

Later

Oh dear, I feel rather silly, but I caved in and gave him the room. I usually insist on all potential lodgers having a cooling-off period, but Robin was such a sweetie that I couldn't resist him. He's rather attractive, too. I mean, I know I've got David, but it's quite nice not being with David all the time so at least I'll be able to have a good old twinkle with Robin now and again. Nothing like a little flirting to boost the old ego. And anyway, as he says, he won't be here for ever. But as he passed by a bookcase, he was so taken by the authors he saw there – 'Anna Kavan! Arthur Koestler! Julian Maclaren-Ross! Jocelyn Brooke! Denton Welch! What a strangely eclectic and esoteric collection you have. My favourite authors!' – that I could hardly believe we hadn't met in another life.

Not, I must add, that I believe in other lives.

January 13

I'm typing, on my laptop, in my dressing gown in front of the fire. Pouncer is clearly dreaming of something extremely distressing as his ears are right back. Perhaps I should try Melanie's dreamcatcher on him – though knowing Pouncer, he would think it was a bird and kill it.

Just had Penny round for supper who's got really keen on this India lark. I have to say there are moments when I wish I hadn't mentioned it to anyone because it's going to be dreadfully 'Four Old Ladies Go on an Indian Adventure'. The idea is that we'll go for three weeks, which seems a horribly long time, but it's hardly worth going that far for a fortnight. Delighted, however, that Penny is coming because what with Melanie going round doing that hands-pressed-together-in-front-of-her thing and bowing pose while saying 'Nastase' wherever we go, and Marion bleeding-heart over all the poverty, I can't imagine that they'll be much fun as companions. But there won't be too much to drink over there, I imagine, which will be good for Penny (because, I hate to say it, she does seem to be rather tucking into the booze these days).

Still, I'll make up for that tomorrow when I drive down to see David. He's taking me for a birthday supper, but if there's time we're going to drive over for drinks with James first. Having been left all that money by his boyfriend, Hughie, he only drinks the finest champagne now and no doubt he's gulping it down by the bucket-load since he's moved to freezing Fakeley, to set up with Owen. (While Owen farms, apparently, James has decided to turn himself into a 'land artist' on the lines of Derek Jarman and Andy Goldsworthy, so I'll have to hone my lying skills when I actually see what he's got up to.)

I'm rather looking forward to meeting Owen again. He seemed like a very nice bloke when James brought him to London once. And when I say he's a nice bloke I'm not lying because I don't lie to my diary. Well, sometimes I do when my thoughts are just too mean; it would be awful to die and have everyone read my diary and realise what a slimy old creep I REALLY am.

Rather longing to see David again, actually, as though we've spoken on the phone I haven't actually clapped my eyes on him since New Year's Day.

Later

Robin has just arrived – rather later than he thought. I felt a bit awful welcoming him in in my dressing gown, but since he's obviously going to see me in it quite a lot, he may as well get over the shock now. Not that it isn't a very glamorous garment. I spend so much time in it, I wear a kind of opera coat in the hopes that its rich embroidery and intricately worked collars and cuffs will draw people's eyes away from my distinctly frowsty early-morning or knackered-at-night face. (And when I say early morning, I mean anything up to midday.)

I was rather surprised that he had only a few things to move in. He says he's left most of his stuff in storage, or back at the flat for a new tenant to use, but he did bring a mandala rug (so-called because it's got a circular pattern on it, all to do with psychic geometry). He also brought a load of ancient books, lots of paper and pencils and geometric tools and, rather oddly, a wand. When I saw it in the box I thought it was an old twig, and said: 'I'll chuck this, shall I?' But Robin looked appalled and seized it from me, saying that it had been given to him by a tree in Glastonbury on the day of the solstice and it had strange powers.

'Given to you by a tree?' I asked nervously.

'Yes,' said Robin. 'It's a very good friend of mine.'

And there we left it.

Slightly maddened by the whale music that he's playing at the moment, but no doubt I'll get used to it.

Even later

Robin's just been down to ask what the Wi-Fi code is. When I gave it to him he did a quick calculation on his phone.

'What are you doing?' I asked.

He looked up, his eyes twinkling. 'Oh, just a bit of numerology. But don't worry. This number looks safe enough. Don't want to find we're invoking the lizards.'

Lizards?

January 14

Before I had a chance to ask Robin about the lizards, he announced that this weekend he was off on a mind-expansion workshop in Hastings so wouldn't be around. I was a bit put out because I always like having a lodger around when I'm away – to discourage intruders – but Robin assured me he would do a smudge ritual with burnt sage before he left and that would ensure the house was completely protected. I wasn't entirely happy about this, as it sounded rather grubby, but he assured me it was completely symbolic, foolproof and not to worry.

Later

Haven't been out in my lovely Fiat 500 for days now, and was hoping it hadn't seized up in the same way I sometimes do when I haven't had a walk for a while. Looking at it from my window it looked normal enough, bright blue and sparkling (though covered, I noticed to my dismay, with bird poo since I'd rather stupidly parked it under a tree). But would it be all right inside? Would the battery have given up hope of ever being used again and, like a dog on its dead master's grave, simply have died, waiting in vain for him to come home?

No problem, though. I chucked the suitcase in the car, remembering to include the birthday present from Penny to open on the day, hopped in the front seat and it started like a dream.

It was absolutely lovely seeing David again, though he seemed very disappointed when I said I wasn't staying more than two nights.

'I thought we could go up Glastonbury Tor the day after tomorrow,' he said. 'Do you remember when we went up before we were married?'

I certainly did remember. And I remember he actually proposed to me at the top. In view of that memory, I was particularly keen *not* to go up Glastonbury Tor.

'Another time,' I said, rather briskly. Despite a slight atmosphere for five minutes, we managed to forget this hiccup by trying to char an aubergine to make some *baba ganoush*. Neither of us have ever been able to char an aubergine properly and now was no exception. As usual we ended up with a watery mush that tasted like decaying frogs' tongues.

January 15

My birthday! We had a cuddly night together and both woke up in a very good mood.

David gave me a DVD about a forgotten New York photographer called Vivian Maier which looks good, with a card that read: 'Today you are twenty-five thousand, two hundred and ninety-eight and a half days old!' and Penny had given me some home-made damson jam – God knows where she'd bought it from but it was delicious. She'd given me a card bearing the words: 'Age is like underwear – it creeps up on you!'

Before lunch, Jack rang to say happy birthday and Gene came on the line hoping I liked the card he'd sent me.

'I haven't got a card!' I said.

'But I sent it to your mobile, Granny!' he said.

'Oh darling, you know my mobile's an old Nokia. I can't get things like that!'

There was a silence at the other end. 'It's very funny,' he said. 'Are you sure you can't get it?'

'I'm sure,' I said, rather disappointed. 'Still, perhaps I should get a new phone as a birthday present to myself. How about that?'

'Yes, great, and then I'll send it again,' said Gene.

I had to lie. I can't tell him that I will never in a million years get an iPhone. And anything that has a name that starts with a lower-case letter, followed – even worse – by a capital, is, surely, the last straw.

Later

I have to say I had a brilliant evening. We had to cry off James and Owen – with the driving and the drinking and a reservation to turn up for, it didn't make sense. But David took me to the Old Fire Station, the talk of Shampton – which used to be a perfectly normal country town and now for some reason has attracted the sort of people who live in Notting Hill. Gone are the old butchers and greengrocers and shops selling bits of string. Now everywhere sells lifestyle: cushions, spindly lamps and those pictures of a single aubergine or quince against a black background.

Just outside town is a large square art gallery – no doubt the Old Shoe Leather Factory or something – surrounded by frightful gardens laid out by a Swedish designer. These comprise a patch of grey grasses, next to a patch of brown grasses, with greenish grasses waving nearby, next to some black grasses. And after a lot of gravel, you come across a whole bank of beige-coloured grasses. There used to be an obsession with lavender and now it's grasses. Can't see the point of them.

We were given a table right in the middle, the one with the pole going down it.

'Sorry about this, but it was the only one I could get,' he said. 'At least it shows it's a genuine Old Fire Station.'

'Oh well, you needn't worry that I'll start dancing on it,' I said. 'Too old at sixty-nine. Golly, to think that I've made it this far. No wonder people say "congratulations" to old people.'

'You'll never be old to me,' said David.

'That's because you're so old you can't see me properly,' I said, putting my hand over his. 'Funny, isn't it, this obsession with old buildings? I had dinner last year in an Old Vinegar Factory.'

'And there's the Horse Hospital,' said David. 'And the Mortuary Cellars . . .'

'When Gene's sixty-nine, do you think he'll be going out to dinner in the Old Nuclear Power Station or the Old Climbing Centre?'

'Is it your birthday?' A woman leaned over from the next table. It turned out this was the predatory Widow Bossom, David's stalker. 'May I wish you many happy returns?'

I smiled graciously and said thank you.

'Don't the years fly by!' said Widow Bossom. She wore dark glasses on top of her dyed blonde hair – even in the evening! – and her tight shirt blouse was open rather too far down for someone of her age. Glancing under the table I saw she was wearing suede boots into which shapely leopard-skin-printed jeans were tucked. She wasn't exactly slim, but she had a strange look as if all her flesh, boobs especially, was just waiting to burst out of her clothes. She had a husky, conspiratorial voice as if she'd drunk rather too many G and Ts in her time.

'How very jolly that you're still such good friends, you two!' she added amiably. Though I wasn't sure how amiable she really was. 'And getting friendlier every day, I hear! Get me into a room with my ex and I wouldn't answer for the outcome! Bloody shit! Excuse my French!'

She then gave me a penetrating stare – wondering, I imagine, what David saw in me – before flashing a charming smile. 'Why don't you two come over and have a drink with me tomorrow?' she said. 'Of course I know David very well – we're old friends, aren't we,' she added with a conspiratorial nod to David, and reaching out to pat his arm, 'but I would so like to know you better – his ex-wife. Any friend of David is a friend of mine!'

'I'm afraid Marie is leaving tomorrow,' said David, swiftly. 'But thanks so much, Edwina. Really nice of you. Another time.'

He turned back to the menu, while I smiled at her apologetically.

'Leggets eggordegger,' said David, smiling broadly, 'beggefeggore sheggee eggengeggagegges eggus eggin egganeggy meggor ceggonveggerseggateggion.' I felt very fond of him all of a sudden. He was speaking 'egg language', something that he'd learned at his school – a language the boys spoke to each other so that the teachers couldn't understand. He'd taught it to Jack, and we'd spent many giggly afternoons chatting to each other in it.

'I thought she was a widow,' I said in a whisper, finally.

'Her first husband died but she's still smarting over her ex. Poor woman,' he added, unnecessarily, I thought.

I made a face.

34

'Oh, she's not bad,' said David. 'She's still attractive, don't you think? And deep down she's very kind.'

Attractive? Deep down kind? Very deep indeed, I'd say, but I kept my thoughts to myself.

Like all restaurant food in the country, dinner was over-priced and overproduced. I don't think they realise that towers of vegetables topped with a couple of chives went out decades ago in London. Still, we had a good time and to be honest, I'm sorry I have to leave tomorrow. I don't have to, but I just don't want to get too sucked into the old domestic routine. It's so perfect as it is with me and David that I just can't bear risking us settling back into the same old ways that made us split up last time.

Even later

While I remember, Widow Bossom, before she left with the rather brazen horsey friend she was dining with, stood behind David and kneaded his shoulders in what I thought was an overfamiliar way, before giving him a smoochy kiss goodbye and waving warmly at me.

January 16

The most frightful thing has happened. I drove back feeling blissfully happy, thinking sixty-nine wasn't such a bad age to be, listening to *Gardeners' Question Time* on the radio, the most comforting programme known to man, all about putting out seedlings and whether rhododendrons can be grown in clay or sandy soil and suddenly looking forward to India. I parked the car, unloaded the artisan bread and various goodies I'd bought at a farm shop on the way back, opened the door and found I'd been burgled!

So much for Robin's smudging technique!

The moment I got into the house I knew something was wrong because it was so bitterly cold. I thought that maybe I'd left a window open, but it turned out someone had smashed the glass in the garden door, and helped themselves to various bits that took their fancy. I felt so shaky I had to sit down. I was terrified the burglar, whoever he was (or, as Jack would probably have it, being very politically correct, whoever he or she was), might still be in the house, so I immediately went round to Melanie's and burst into tears. Rather silly, I know, but I was just so shocked.

'What's the matter, Mar?' she asked, putting her arm round me. 'Nothing Robin's done, I hope? Did you have an accident?'

'I-I've been burgled!' I said, through my sobs. 'I've just got back from David's and . . .'

'Let's go round right away and make sure he's not there any more!' said Melanie, grabbing an enormous brass Tibetan bowl that she uses to make weird humming noises when she's feeling stressed. 'This'll fix him!'

We went back and Melanie was, I have to say, a real trouper. She went from room to room, flinging open cupboards and shouting: 'Come out of there, you piece of scum!' She looked under the beds, and even insisted on going into the garden and checking behind all the bushes. I was still, I'm ashamed to say, shaking like a jelly so I sat in the kitchen breathing deeply.

'Did he take your jewellery?' she asked when she came in. 'You'd better check. And have you called the police?'

It turned out that no, he hadn't got my jewellery, not that he would have found a great deal. The only things I have of any value are a brooch that belonged to my mother, a pearl necklace that my godmother gave me for my christening, and a couple of earrings that David had given me when we'd got married. No wedding ring, though. After David and I divorced I'd got a temporary job in a china shop; I'd lost so much weight with the stress of it all that one day my wedding ring simply dropped off as I was wrapping up someone's cake-stand and was never seen again. But the burglar had taken all kinds of little knick-knacks that he could carry easily.

I called the police who said they would send someone round tomorrow. Tomorrow! What bloody use is that? Then I got an emergency glazier in to repair the glass, and Penny and Marion very sweetly came round for supper to keep me company. Penny arrived with an air freshener thing, a special room spray she'd got for Christmas.

'I don't usually like these things, but it would be good to get the smell of that man out of the way, wouldn't it?' she said, canister in one hand, glass in the other, taking sips between sprays. At the first whoosh, Pouncer, who had hidden under the sofa during the entire drama and only just reappeared, zoomed off again. If only cats could speak, then he could have been a crucial witness. I think he thought Penny's spray was some newfangled tomcat who was marking its territory – as, indeed, now I came to think of it, it was, in a way.

January 17

'Very common, this sort of robbery,' said the twelve-year-old policeman who finally deigned to drop by. 'They used to be in it for the electronic goods. But now we've been more successful with our marking process, they often take little things of small value that they can sell down Portobello Market.'

I'd made a list: a clock, a new toolbox, two Staffordshire dogs that I'd bought years ago for 6d when I was about fourteen, a small silver ashtray and, worst of all, a lovely photograph taken by Cecil Beaton of my gorgeous friend Hughie, dressed as Lawrence of Arabia at the 1965 Chelsea Arts Ball. I doubt they wanted the pic, just the frame, but it was particularly sad because after Hughie died, James, who was then his boyfriend, had given it me to remember him by. I doubt there's another copy.

Anyway, I'd expected the policeman to get on his hands and knees with a magnifying glass and dust the place for fingerprints and take DNA samples from us all, but he did absolutely zilch beyond saying that it might be worth going down to the Portobello Road to see if I could find my stuff there.

'You can try giving us a call,' he said, casually, 'but you'd probably be better off just buying it back.' Ridiculous. And what's worse, I've been in touch with the insurers who have kindly told me there's a £500 excess charge on my policy. So there's no point in making a claim because I doubt what's been taken amounts to five hundred quid's worth.

January 18

'Caught on camera! Thieves use iPhones to record floor plans' (*Daily Rant*)

Dear David. I don't know why I didn't call him sooner. But the moment I rang him he came up like a shot. He seemed really angry about the situation. Funny how men get so furious. I was feeling all feeble and tearful and David was stomping around in a rage. I know I shouldn't say this but sometimes it does seem to me that men and women are incredibly different.

'This man Robin, what did he do? You say he smudged the house? What on earth made you believe that that would have any effect?'

'Oh, he's very convincing,' I said, smiling. 'You'll like him, I know you will. He's a sweetie!'

At this point Robin walked in, apologising the moment he saw David was there.

'Oh, I'm so sorry, Marie, I thought you were alone,' he said. 'I'm Robin, by the way,' he said, holding out a hand to David.

'And I'm David,' said David, rather warily, I thought. 'I'm really upset to hear about this burglary! Weren't you here? Couldn't you have stopped it? Marie's a woman on her own, you know!'

'I was away on a mind-expanding weekend,' said Robin.

'Well, it's no use having your mind expanded if the house

is going to get burgled while you're having it expanded!' said David, his anger obvious in his tone of voice.

Robin looked very taken aback.

'If Marie had been here she might have been attacked!' added David.

'But, David, she wasn't here,' said Robin, understandably puzzled.

'Exactly, that's why I was burgled, David,' I said. 'Anyway, Robin's not here to guard the house. He's here as a lodger.'

David sat down, opened the paper, stared at it and didn't speak.

Robin was about to ask me something but then said, 'Don't worry – I'll ask tomorrow' and disappeared.

David put the paper down and shook his head. 'You've got a funny idea of a sweetie,' he said.

'Oh, come on, darling,' I said. 'It's not his fault.'

'I suppose not,' said David. 'Sorry I was a bit rude to him. I suppose I was just upset about the idea of your being burgled with no one here to protect you.'

I changed the subject by telling him about the *Daily Rant* headline and he pooh-poohed it at once.

'Darling, much as I love you, I don't think anyone would want to record your floor plans,' he said, looking around at the slightly chaotic sitting room. 'I mean it's clear that you haven't got anything of real value here. Except, of course,' he added, pulling me down next to him and putting an arm round my shoulders, 'you yourself. And you weren't here.'

'Stop being such a weasely old flatterer,' I said, pushing him away with a smile, 'but thank you anyway.'

Later, after supper, we watched telly and unbelievably – according to some dreadful statistic on the news – if you've been burgled once you're ten times more likely to be burgled again because the burglars know the weak spots in your security. I gave a little moan.

'What you need,' said David, turning to me seriously, 'is a man around the house. Don't you think?'

I felt the hair on the back of my neck rise at this, so I said: 'But I've got Robin.'

'He's not a man!' said David. 'He's ... he's some kind of weird magician. And not a very good one, I'd say. That smudging thing probably alerted the burglar to the house rather than put him off.'

'Oh, he's okay,' I said. 'I rather like him, actually.'

David looked even more livid than he had done before and just said 'Hmph!' very loudly.

FEBRUARY

February 1

Haven't been writing my diary for days now. The truth is that I was so freaked out by the burglary that I was immobilised. Every time I returned home after being out, I burst into a cold sweat at my front door and found myself starting to shake. And when I got into the house I was overcome with a strange terror. Mad as it sounds, I had to go through every single drawer in the house, and every single cupboard, all over again, just to check the burglar hadn't been anywhere I hadn't noticed because I was so scared that one day I'd be looking for something and find it gone and the whole experience would come rushing back to me.

In a way I wish the burglar had just come to the door with a small list of objects he wanted, allowed me to go inside while he waited, and then let me hand them to him, said thank you and taken them away with him. That would have been fine. But it was the violation, the feeling that I wasn't in control

– that any time someone could just smash his way into my house, my home, my very self – that made me so upset.

Robin was horrified, of course. And although he, the burglar (or perhaps it was they, the burglars), hadn't taken anything of his, he clearly felt dreadfully responsible.

'Marie, I smudged everywhere,' he said. He'd come into the sitting room and stood in the doorway, long and gangly, twisting his hands. 'But I didn't do the garden door. I can't think why. I only did the windows and the front door. It's all my fault. One can never be sufficiently protected against evil. I will do it all over again tonight, so that there is absolutely no chance of anyone else getting in and, if you don't mind, I will perform, later, a small exorcism to rid the house of any trace of bad spirits and karma that the invader might have left behind.'

Later
Tonight Robin returned home with some special essence that he sold at the shop – it came from the Amazonian jungle, of course – and made up a potion. He claims that the reason his smudging didn't work was because of the lizards nearby and naturally I asked him what these lizards were. Turns out that they're not lizards like you see in London Zoo, with hooded eyes, who stay motionless for hours on end and who, weirdly, grow new tails when you pull them off but, rather, the sort of lizards discovered by David Icke, who apparently believes the world is run by them. Tear off the face of the Queen, the Duke of Edinburgh or any Rothschild (particularly a Rothschild) and

you will find behind it an alien being, in the form of a giant lizard, one of a lizard elite which rules the world.

Cripes.

Anyway, Robin put the potion into a lantern-type thing, lit some oil he'd put on top, and went round the whole place swinging it and chanting – 'to get rid of the negative energy'.

Frankly, I don't know how anyone could have lived in the house after that, let alone an evil spirit. Every room absolutely stank. I was going to suggest that I just go out and get some fresh air but I didn't dare mention it because then Robin might think that I was an evil spirit, driven out, so I retired to my bedroom, opened the window and sat by it for a while, breathing deeply into the dark, damp air until I thought I might die of cold.

February 2

However, it has to be said that this morning I woke feeling miles better and wasn't overcome with those horrible feelings at all when I returned from getting some pomegranate molasses from the local Middle-Eastern supermarket – molasses which, I might say, is on sale in the neighbouring posh Notting Hill Gate for £6.50 a jar and here for only £1.59.

There can't be anything in the exorcism stuff, surely. Or can there?

After breakfast

I'd just run my bath and since I noticed I'd run out of loo paper in the lavatory next door, I got some loo rolls out of the cupboard in the bathroom. On the way one of them fell into the bath. Soaked.

I was then left with the ghastly choice. Do I throw it away, at a loss of approx 50p, or do I put it on top of the radiator to dry, constantly turning it over for the next few days? Stinginess won and my loo roll is now sitting on the radiator, looking more like a piece of deformed sponge each time I pass. I'm hoping that in a few days it will have turned into something resembling a statue of the Madonna and I will be able to put it on Facebook.

And talking of Facebook, when I last looked at Marion's page she'd reproduced the whole of the 'Footprints' poem, the gist of which is that the writer always saw two sets of footprints in the sand – hers and the Lord's – except when she was low. She asked why Jesus had forsaken her in her hour of need. He apparently replied that it was because when she was low he'd been carrying her. Typical bloke excuse, say I. I think he'd just buggered off, terrified, as are most men, at the sight of tears.

Except, of course, good old David.

Talking of low, I always remember, when my darling friend Archie died, wondering if I could find any solace in going to church. Not only did I find zilch solace but, worse, I felt like C.S. Lewis, who wrote that when he looked for succour from above and knocked at the door of God, not only did he not get

45

a reply but he could hear the sound of the door being bolted on the inside.

February 3

'Stool down the hazel, cut back the mahonia and mostly importantly make sure you've got plenty of pyracantha to brighten up February' *Daily Rant*'s gardening columnist.

?????

Anyway, I must recap on the events from the January days I missed.

Whatever Robin said about resmudging I wasn't going to rely on burning sage to keep me safe. I rang up the burglar alarm people and was soon talking to their representative, a man who stood on the doorstep with a lanyard round his neck on which hung an identity card with his photograph which, needless to say, looked nothing like him.

I'm very suspicious of those lanyards. I always think that if you reach forward to examine the picture, the wearer will cunningly slip it over your head and then threaten to strangle you until you tell them the code to the safe, just like the dreadful tribe in India in the nineteenth century who I'm reading about at the moment who went around garrotting people wherever they went. Thuggees. From which the word 'thug' derives. Oh, stop being such a pedant, Sharp!

Anyway, back to the burglar alarm man. I was horrified by his report. What with putting special locks and grilles on all the windows and heat sensors in every room, and chopping down the bushes in front of the house ('Excellent cover for burglars,' said the man. 'Houses with hedges in front are burgled twenty-five per cent more often than houses with an open frontage'), the bill would come to around £2,000. Luckily I mentioned the existence of Pouncer and he said that every time I went out, Pouncer would have to be locked into a single sensorless room, so by refusing this option I soon cut the cost down quite a bit and he agreed that some rooms could be left unguarded. I also said I would cut down the bushes myself, so they wouldn't have to subcontract that job out, and before I knew where I was the estimate was down to only £1,000. I say 'only'. Made my hair stand on end, but still, I thought getting myself barricaded up electronically would make me feel safer.

'There's been a spate of burglaries in the area recently,' said the alarm rep as he left. 'And chummy has taken the same sorts of things in all cases as your policeman said – not things of great value but things that can make a difference to people's lives. One photo that was taken recently was the only photograph a couple had of their baby girl, only a day old, taken the day before she died, poor mite, the only memory they had of her and it was gone. Just because of the frame. And there was an old lady, and her simple gold wedding ring, the only memory she had of—'

'Thanks,' I said. 'I don't want to know any more. I feel sorry enough for myself, frankly, without having to feel sorry for anyone else right at this moment.'

Later

Felt rather awful because when I was showing the alarm rep Robin's room to see if any future burglar might have access through there, I accidentally stepped on a carefully constructed circle made up of dried leaves, in the middle of which was a pile of ash – not, I hoped, the remains of some wretched spirit who Robin had invoked and disposed of one night.

The place absolutely reeks of joss sticks so I got an instant migraine just by standing there, and Robin seems to have made some kind of shrine on the dressing table, with a small nightlight burning in a saucer of water in front of a jam jar with a flower in it against the mirror on which was drawn the star of David. Petals were strewn around the table and various little brass bells were lying around.

Must warn him about leaving candles on during the day. Couldn't bear to be burgled *and* have the house burned to a crisp.

February 6

Drove off to babysit Gene yesterday down in Brixton because Jack and Chrissie are going out. Chrissie was upstairs dolling herself up and as he put the kettle on, Jack said: 'What's the situation with you and Dad, Mum? Are you back together or not?'

I hummed and hawed and said sort of but not sort of and although we were extremely good friends and loved each other very much, I felt it was better we should live in separate houses because I didn't want to get back together with him and then break up again. Whereupon Jack said I was mad and surely David must feel very confused, and I said that was his problem, and Jack said 'Hmm', and I said, 'Why, has he said something?' and Jack said, 'Not exactly' – which meant he had – and at that moment Gene came down, phone in hand, eager to explain the extraordinary workings of his machine.

'It's got a voice, you see, Granny,' he said. 'You can ask it things. Look. Do you love me?' he asked it – rather an odd question, I thought.

'I do not understand the question,' replied a voice from the phone. Whereupon we all burst out laughing.

'And look,' he added, fiddling with it. 'I can take a photograph of you and me sitting here on the sofa' – and sure enough there it was – 'and now with this app, it can tell you exactly where you are.'

Weirdly, it came up with our address.

'But you've put that in,' I said, 'surely.'

'No, it just knows. We could go anywhere and it would know!' he said. 'It's amazing.'

'But I always know where I am!' I said, rather muddled. 'Why do I need it to tell me where I am as well?'

'Well,' said Gene, wrinkling his brow. 'Let's say, um, you were in, say, the middle of the Amazonian rainforest and being eaten by bears – no, not bears, they don't live there – being eaten by crocodiles. It would know where you were!'

'So?'

'So we could come and rescue you, Granny!' he said. 'We'd

know where to find you. Though it would probably be too late, but at least we could find your remains so we could give you a proper burial.'

'Thanks, darling,' I said, drily. 'That's what I've always wanted. A proper burial!'

He also showed me how we could talk to each other face to face, if only I could get a phone like his, and said we could Snapchat in future.

'No trail,' he added, mysteriously.

He very kindly let me fiddle about with the phone when he'd gone to bed – he no longer wants a story, which is rather sad – but it wasn't much good because I couldn't even turn it on. I fiddled with a few buttons, but nothing. But as I was making myself some coffee in the kitchen, a voice came wafting up from the sofa. 'Do you love me?' said Gene's voice.

Oh God, I must have activated some terrible thing that repeated the phrase back to me. All through the evening this voice kept coming through at half-hourly intervals, so I shoved it under a cushion and tried to watch some telly. Luckily there was a very good documentary about Elvis Presley, a man who, even at my great age, I still worship like a god, so I could forget about the pitiful murmurings that occasionally filtered through the cushions during 'Jailhouse Rock' and 'Hound Dog'.

When Jack and Chrissie got back, Chrissie laughed when she heard the voice and turned it off by magically sliding her finger across the screen. 'You must get one of these, Marie,' she said. 'You'd love it.'

And I thought, well, maybe, just maybe, I'll go along to the

Apple store tomorrow and just have a look. Nothing more, of course. Just a look.

February 7

When I was in my teens, I went along to a Billy Graham performance. It was stirring stuff. Although not in the least religious, I had to exercise great self-control not to rise from my seat and sign up to the Lord. The man was mesmerising.

Similarly, when I'd been feeling particularly low, I'd considered joining a cult called the Process. I knew some people who were in it and – despite the fact that they roamed London in cloaks, pulling enormous Alsatians and producing magazines devoted to Aleister Crowley – they were funny and I liked them. So I went for an initiation meeting in a room in a house in Park Lane. With the aid of a clock, a particularly good-looking member of the Process demonstrated it was no use constantly fixing the hands if it continually went wrong. The only way you could make it right was to get inside the works. He then said: 'If you want to join us, this is your moment! We want all your money and your commitment – NOW!'

I chewed my lip and dithered, but finally shambled out of the door, to cries of abuse and warnings that I was now doomed.

I mention these moments because I want to remind myself how difficult it is usually to convert me to anything. But at that point, I hadn't visited an Apple store.

I went today, just to have a look. And that's what I told the smiling man at the door of the Apple store as he welcomed me in. The problem was that, as he ushered me in with one hand, he was at that very moment signalling a friend of his to meet me a little further into the store.

'Andrew will take care of you!' he said. And Andrew turned out to be very nice indeed. He led me over to a set of iPhones and asked which colour I'd prefer and I said, 'Silver, but I'm only looking . . .' whereupon Andrew signalled another member of the team, who turned out to be an extremely smiley girl called Greta who took me to a table and sat me down.

'Just waiting for your model to appear,' she said. 'It won't take a minute.'

'You do realise,' I said firmly, 'that I don't want a new phone. I just want to look at one. There is absolutely no question of my buying anything today.'

'Of course,' she said, but she looked as if she was just humouring me. 'Many people feel fearful of buying a new phone. But there is nothing to be alarmed about. My mother has one of these and she loves it.'

Not very reassuring since her mother was probably about as old as Jack, but still.

At this moment, a bundle of charm appeared – Gary. He was immensely tall and good-looking and had a groovy beard and a ring through his ear. He looked as if he'd just stepped into the store from the Australian outback, fit, brown and confident. Not a man it would be easy to say no to. Gary was holding a small box which he placed on the table with the same reverence and delicacy as a magician handles a pack of cards. He asked to see my Nokia. Even he was rather taken aback when I produced it from my bag.

'Well, I haven't seen one of these before!' he said, with all the astonishment of a man with a metal detector who has just unearthed a hoard of old Roman coins in a field of marrows. 'Good little machines. I think my grandmother may have had one.' At this point, an elderly customer who was queueing up for some app or something spotted us and at the sight of my Nokia she leaned over and said: 'Oh look! How sweet! I had one of those once! But you're in for a treat with a new phone!' she added. 'Your life will be transformed!'

I couldn't help wondering if she was a plant.

'I am not buying one!' I said firmly. At which everyone exchanged rather patronising looks as if I were a child refusing to drink up my milk.

While this conversation was going on, Gary had opened my Nokia with one hand, extracted the SIM card and asked for my credit card. 'Now let's get a PIN number for you,' he said, his eyes twinkling, 'and at the same time, put your bank PIN number in here.'

'But . . .' I said, 'I want to think about it first!'

'Of course,' he said. 'Let me introduce you to your new iPhone.'

And before I knew it, the box had been opened and my Nokia had been replaced by a strange shiny silver rectangular object which needed swiping and fondling – I even open it with my personal thumbprint, for God's sake – and slowly, after a brief lesson, I was led to the door. As I left, I had the impression that a whole crowd of Apple employees were waving me off with their handkerchiefs. 'See you soon, Marie!' they said. 'We love you! We're always here! Enjoy!'

Now I feel distinctly wobbly. They did give me my old Nokia back, but it's just a grey husk. It's like a dead body. I try to turn it on and nothing happens. Golly, those people at the Apple store. They could take over the world. I feel I was just sucked in, like some wretched cow on its way to the abattoir, pushed along a ramp, stunned and then slaughtered without so much as a by-your-leave. I mean I wasn't slaughtered but I feel completely changed.

When I got home I couldn't stop fiddling with the wretched gadget, turning it on and off and seeing what happened when I pressed various symbols. It even registered how many steps I'd taken from the Apple store to home! It knows my name! And when I texted Gene to tell him that I'd bought a phone, it predicted nearly everything I was going to say!

After I'd written 'D' it immediately suggested 'Dear'. And as far as I can see I only have to write the first letter of every word and the message just magically appears as if it can read my mind. I ended up by typing 'l' and it came up with 'lots' and then it gave me 'love' without my even having to do anything at all. And the moment I put in 'M' it supplied 'Marie'. In one way it's marvellous but in another I feel rather diminished, as if what I write is so predictable I don't even have to bother to compose it. In other words, that while I'm criticising Widow Bossom for wittering, I am just as much of a cliché-ridden witterer as her. We are all witterers, in Apple language.

Wonder if Tolstoy had been writing *Anna Karenina* in a text he would just have had to type 'A' and it would have come with 'All' and then 'h' and it would have come up with 'happy' followed by 'families' then 'a' and it would come up 'are alike', and so on until after only a couple of strokes he would have been given the first sentence by a machine. He'd probably have finished the entire work in half an hour.

Have just tried 'It is a truth universally acknowledged, that a single man in possession of a good fortune, must be in want of a wife' and my phone did pretty well on that, too, immediately providing 'acknowledged' after the word 'universally'. We do just speak in clichés, clearly. There is nothing new under the sun. Unfortunately I sent the Austen quote off to David by mistake. It just suddenly turned green and shot off making a weird whooshing sound. Hope he didn't see it as some sort of hint. I immediately rang him to explain. He said he was touched to think I might have thought he had a fortune though, he added, he was sorry that it wasn't a hint. Felt very slightly uncomfortable.

Later

Loo paper finally dried out so I tried to use it this evening. Unfortunately, the whole roll seems to have coagulated into a huge white lump and it is immensely difficult finding the beginning, rather like trying to unpick a roll of Sellotape. And when you do find the beginning of a sheet, it comes off rather stiff and peculiar, all misshapen. And the loo is covered with bits of white fluff where I've been scraping away to find the right spot to start unpeeling. Oh, God, it's going to take me weeks to finish this up. And all for the sake of saving 50p.

February 9

Stomped angrily onto the lawn this morning as it seemed to be covered with bits of loo roll, though God knows how it got there, only to find the specks of white were actually snowdrops. My mood immediately changed from murderous to sentimental and enchanted. As I was out there, swooning over the little chaps, there was a cough from the open door and it was Robin, in the process of rolling a joint. Well, I imagine it was a joint. I asked him to come out and look and he joined me in a bit of marvelling. But when I told him about my plan to cut back the bushes in front to make the house more secure, he seemed extremely concerned. We were now indoors, having a cup of coffee at the kitchen table.

'Do you have to cut them down?' asked Robin, taking a long drag of his joint and blinking slightly.

'Yes,' I said firmly. 'Apparently they're absolutely ideal cover for burglars. I suppose you wouldn't help me, would you?'

Robin looked extremely alarmed. 'I'd rather not kill a living being,' he said. 'But if you're getting it done anyway, I suppose I'd rather it were me than some insensitive brute who'll just come and hack away at them. At least I can apologise to them before cutting them.'

'Apologise?' I said. 'What for?'

'For cutting them down,' he said. 'You wouldn't like to be hacked down, would you? No, don't worry. I'll just say a small prayer and it'll be fine. Do you want to do it now?'

Which is how I came to be stuffing huge quantities of old branches and dead leaves into bin bags while Robin, having bowed down in front of the bushes and said that he was 'honouring' them, got to with gusto, and before long the whole of the front garden was cleared. What is brilliant is that the sitting room is now so much lighter, and Robin assured me that while the surplus bits of bush were sorry to leave, the friends they'd left behind would be in a much better position to flourish since all their water wasn't being sucked up and they'd have more sunlight.

I have to say, he may be sixty but standing there, rather flushed with hacking, and covered with bits of old leaves, there was something of the Tarzan about him. I wonder: does smoking lots of dope and meditating keep you incredibly thin? Robin looks, sometimes, like a noble sadhu.

When I told him we were going to India, he was wildly envious but luckily he didn't insist on coming with us. I was absolutely determined that someone should be left at home to look after the house. He promised to make us a list of holy sites to visit, including a trip to a shrine which contained an invisible god.

'But aren't all gods invisible?' I asked, feeling rather out of my depth. 'Anyway,' I added, before he could explain, 'you should tell all that to Melanie. She's much more into it than me.'

'The thing about this that is so interesting,' he added, with a mysterious smile, 'it's not just the god who is invisible, but the shrine itself. But you can just feel its presence.'

Sounded a bit Emperor's New Clothes to me but what do I know?

February 10

Very funny thing happened to me today. I was round at the newsagent getting some milk when the Indian guy, Mr Patel, who runs the shop said: 'You are looking very well today, young lady!' And I heard myself replying, 'Thanks so much! So are you! And do you know, I'm nearly seventy?'

Now why on earth did I say that? Is it just the sort of thing that pops out once you're older, whether you like it or not? Is it brazen advertising of my facelift? The worst thing is that if some old person says to me 'Do you know, I'm eighty!' I never know what to say. 'Congratulations!'? Or 'Well, not long for this earth, then!'? And here am I doing exactly the same thing – putting other people in the same excruciating position without even wanting to.

It's such a childish thing to do, too. I can just understand Gene saying he's nine and a half (though even now, I notice, he's old enough to have dropped those halves and quarters that were so important when he was younger). But older people? It's as if they have nothing else to recommend themselves except their longevity. What's going on? 'I'm nearly seventy?' I am cringing as I think of what I said. It's not even as if seventy is that old these days. I mean, I wasn't expecting Mr Patel to burst out into a round of applause.

Oh God, I feel like such a total idiot.

Later

David rang up for a gossip, but when I told him how brilliant Robin had been with the bushes, he became rather frosty. There was a long pause before he said: 'But I should be doing that! Why didn't you wait for me to come and I'd have cleared them away in a moment without all that idiotic honouring stuff. For Chrissake, they're only bushes!'

Very tricky all this, of course. Because although I'm basically with David on my views of bushes, I can see Robin's point of view about honouring all living things.

Oh dear! Blokes! Freud was always banging on about 'What do women want?' but what about 'What do men want?' It's certainly not just 'one thing'.

Sometimes they're total mysteries to me.

February 12

All us India-goers have just been to the Nepalese restaurant across the road. Have to say the food is fairly disgusting – very much old-style Indian – but the guy who runs it is so sweet and makes us feel so at home it doesn't really matter. Too few restaurants realise that the food is only one aspect of eating out. It's the nice little touches – the pulling-out of the chair, the napkins folded into waterlily shapes, the chatting as you choose from the menu, the giving of a bit of cut-up orange at the end without you asking for it, the smiles and the warmth of the place – that's nice too. And the Nepalese is so big on atmosphere, the food is almost incidental.

Tim had brought a huge atlas and we moved the plastic flowers and the candle floating in water in a brass dish, and set it out across the table. Then we started, like real explorers, to map our route, getting out pieces of paper to make lists, looking in diaries and pencilling in possible dates. Unfortunately the atlas was one Tim had had since school, so the whole of India was coloured in pink, part of our gigantic empire. Seems totally incredible that even when I was tiny, we owned, it appears, almost half the world. Penny was a bit woozy but she said that was because she'd been out to lunch, but she did have a huge bottle of Tiger beer to go with the supper. I'm starting to worry a bit about her. Awful when you start checking on the amount your friends are drinking. I feel a bit like a policeman.

The idea is that when we get to Delhi, the other three girls – girls, ho ho – stay at the cheap and cheerful, I stay with Brad and Sharmie for about a week, and then Melanie goes off to Kerala to see her son while Penny, Marion and I go down to Goa to lie on a beach and find Sandra, and then we all meet up on the flight back.

Melanie insists we buy some salwar kameezes because she said we've got to keep covered up and blend in with the locals, and when in Rome, and I said we weren't going to Rome, and she said why was I being so literal, and I said wild horses wouldn't get me into a pair of trousers. I have a phobia about trousers and was just about to say it was almost as big as my phobia about scarves when I stopped myself because I remembered that Marion was always giving me scarves for presents. Luckily Penny changed the subject by asking about malaria pills and jabs, and I said I'd deal with that, and Tim said he'd organise the visas if we gave him copies of our passports (don't think he trusts Melanie), so it all looks as if it's coming together.

Later

Got home feeling rather jolly and almost looking forward to the trip. But just as I'd got into my nightie, the phone rang. Thinking it was David, I picked up, but it wasn't – it was Penny, crying.

'I've been burgled!' she wailed, through hysterical sobs. 'They've broken in! Will you come over?'

Hitching my nightie up with an old dressing gown cord and flinging on my coat and shoes (I'm quite used to this outfit since I'm always getting into it to go round to the newsagent's for bits and bobs before dressing), I rushed round and found almost the same scene that I'd experienced myself last month. The only difference was that nothing had been broken and it looked as if the burglars had just walked in through the front door. Didn't like to say so but had an awful feeling that Penny might actually have left it open, because she was pretty pissed when she got to the restaurant. Whatever, I thought it would be almost certain she wouldn't get anything back on insurance because there was no sign of a forced entry that I could see.

Penny's jewellery had been taken – and she was beside herself, weeping and shaking. This time the police came round straight away, but they thought there was evidence of a forced entry. Though she might have closed the door, as there was no deadlock it could have been easily opened with a piece of plastic. This made us both remember how easy it had been, a couple of years ago, for Sheila the Dealer to get into the back garden of the house across the road to rescue Chummy, the Alsatian – but that was another story. The police gave us the numbers of several locksmiths and suggested that she put her door on the chain for the night. They thought there was a link to my burglary and confirmed what the burglar alarm man had said – that there'd been a couple of other similar ones in the area.

After they left, Penny poured herself a huge brandy to steady her nerves and I said, rather prudishly: 'Are you sure you haven't had enough?' at which she made rather a face. And then I offered to stay with her till tomorrow.

Sometimes I think I am a SAINT.

February 13

Bloody Nepalese restaurant! Can't think what I was on about, saying who cared about the food as long as the service was good! I was up half the night at Penny's, being sick and rushing to the loo, obviously having been thoroughly poisoned by the chicken biryani I'd had last night. Felt absolutely frightful and it was even worse being in someone else's house because I was terrified I might be leaving horrible traces behind. I thought it might be safer to sleep in the loo itself to avoid any kind of ghastly accident, but as it was I went down to Penny's kitchen to find a bowl to keep by my bed. As I couldn't find a bowl, I carefully poured the pot-pourri from one in the sitting room and tiptoed upstairs with it. Fell at last into a deep sleep and woke feeling far, far better, though still rather nervous about even having a cup of tea with Penny at breakfast. Said nothing about my dreadful night because Penny was still shattered about yesterday and I felt it was a bit selfish to interrupt with stories of being ill.

I clearly *am* a saint.

Later

When I got home, Penny rang to say she'd discovered that not only had the burglars taken her jewellery, they'd also stolen a priceless Chinese bowl from the sitting room. Found it rather embarrassing to explain that, thinking I'd be sick in the night, I'd removed that priceless object myself to use for throwing up in, but had left it in my room.

Luckily Penny roared with laughter, and when I asked how she was feeling she appeared to have completely got over it and said: 'Fine! It's only jewellery!' I asked if she could have said that a few years back, and we agreed that, when you're older, you don't mind about losing things quite so much.

'Partly because we can't find anything anyway and always

63

imagine it'll turn up one day,' she said, 'and partly because we know that "stuff" doesn't really matter that much.'

Sort of agree with her. Maybe it'll all change when I am actually seventy. But at sixty-nine I still do prefer my possessions around me and not in some burglar's bag of swag.

We decided to have a residents' association meeting to discuss these robberies and then Penny suggested we go down the antique market in Portobello Road tomorrow at the crack of dawn to see if we can find any of our stuff – something I rather wish I'd done after my robbery, because presumably anything of mine will have long gone. We decided to pop in on Robin in the Alt Bookshop at the same time because I wanted to show him off to Penny.

Must remember to make jab appointments by end of the month.

February 14

God, I hate getting up early! I've learned to operate the alarm on my new phone but can't get it to stop something called 'Snooze' so even when I've turned it off and am halfway through cleaning my teeth, it still buzzes away, telling me to get up.

The idea was to make the market at eight in the morning, before the antique dealers had time to sell anything. It was pretty grey as I drew up outside Penny's house and, rather than get out of the car and ring the bell, called her on the mobile to say her taxi was waiting outside.

Immensely pissed off to find that she hadn't even got up. She asked me in for a cup of coffee to wait while she got ready. I was furious because if I'd known I'd have had to wait I could have had half an hour extra in bed. Slight chilliness in the air – and not just from outside – as we drove to the market. Not improved by the rather sour smell of Penny's breath, which means she'd obviously downed an enormous quantity of wine last night. I'm starting to feel like the leader of a temperance society.

When we got there it was getting lighter, some of the market people were still setting up their stalls, heaving great sheets of tarpaulin over metal struts, while others were already sitting in chairs, swathed in blankets, clutching Starbucks coffees in mittened hands. Since I had no idea what Penny's jewellery looked like – why do we keep it, I wonder, since none of us wears it now? – I couldn't really help her look for her stuff, but I certainly kept my eyes peeled for my two Staffordshire dogs and the lovely silver frame with Hughie's photograph in it. We looked so interested in each stall that most of the owners thought we were professional buyers and kept offering us deals on things like Coronation cigar boxes, or miniature cars made in the 1950s. Who buys that stuff, anyway, I wonder?

Just as we'd searched all the stalls on one side of the road and were sitting down outside a café on the corner of Golborne Road with cups of coffee to get our strength back, what looked like a small shed beside us started to shake and crackle. Then out of it proceeded to blare the most overwhelming rap music and a beat so loud that it made me fear that my eyeballs might simply pop out and roll down the pavement, into the gutter and down the drain. Signalling to Penny that I couldn't stand the noise, I downed my coffee and crossed to the other side of the street. And there, on a rather seedy stall selling cracked mugs, old watches and bits of damaged costume jewellery ingrained with grease and dirt, were a couple of Staffordshire dogs.

As I stopped to examine them, an unpleasant-looking man emerged from the shadows behind the table on which they were displayed. He wore a dirty white scarf around his neck and when he spoke he revealed a tooth missing at the front of his mouth.

'Lovely pair, aren't they? Don't see many like that these days. Not in that condition anyway. Usually got an ear missing. But these are beautiful. Very rare. I remember in the old days of the market you used to be able to pick these sort of things up for sixpence – now you're lucky to see them at all. Or only reproductions. But these are the real McCoy.'

'I can tell,' I said, turning them over. Yes, sure enough, there were exactly the same details as had been on the bottom of my Staffordshire dogs. But then, in Victorian days these bits of china were churned out by the hundred, so how could I be sure they were mine?

Then I remembered. About fifteen years ago, when I was very much into crafts, I'd noticed that the tail on the left-hand dog had got chipped, quite severely. I'd mended it with a magic quick-setting clay-like stuff called Milliput, moulded it to the right shape, painted it and then varnished it. You couldn't tell the difference by looking at it – it was virtually invisible. But you could feel it. And when I ran my hand over it, and felt the slight abrasiveness of the Milliput under my finger, there was no doubt about it. It was mine.

'How much for the pair?' I asked as casually as I could. Penny had crossed over by now, and I gave her an almighty kick, while getting out my mobile phone and handing it to her.

'Fifty quid,' said the greasy man, confidently.

'Fifty quid?' I said, amazed. 'Why, that's ridiculous! I wouldn't pay more than a fiver for the two of them! Do go ahead and make your call,' I said, nodding meaningfully to Penny. 'Where did you get them, by the way?'

Penny slunk off to call, I hoped, the police, while the stall-holder put his two hands on the dogs' heads, in a proprietorial way. 'Picked them up at an auction in the country,' he said glibly. 'Old lady died. Come on, give us a sensible price, I don't like time-wasters. I'll do you fifteen quid apiece. Thirty quid. Couldn't be much fairer than that.'

'Twenty,' I said. And much to my surprise he immediately started wrapping them up in old copies of the *Daily Rant*.

'I suppose you didn't get anything else at that, er, "auction"?' I said, as casually as I could.

'Got some lovely stuff, but it all went. Just them dogs left. Why d'you want to know?'

'Because,' I said coldly, as I took the roughly wrapped dogs from him and stuffed them into my bag, withdrawing the offered note at the same time, 'those dogs happen to belong to me and were stolen from my house last month. My friend

67

has just rung the police and they will be arriving shortly to question you!'

The greasy man looked furious, and starting cursing me. 'You're mad, you are! Stealing from my stall! I'll give you police!' But all the while he was gathering up his manky wares, shoving them into boxes and hurriedly piling them into the back of a white van parked nearby. I stood waiting for Penny. But she had barely returned before, uttering dreadful expletives, he'd bundled everything into the back, got in and put his head out of the window to shout 'Fuck off!' to us as he drove away at great speed. By the time I'd got my wits together to think about taking the number of his van, he was long gone.

'Well, are they coming?' I asked Penny, urgently.

'Are who coming?' asked Penny.

'The police! Those were my dogs!'

'I didn't know you wanted me to call the police!' said Penny. 'I thought you just wanted me to call Robin to say we'd be coming over later! Why didn't you say?'

'I said it with my eyes!' I said, exasperatedly. 'Surely you could put two and two together? Why would I give you my mobile, stare at a couple of Staffordshire dogs, and say "Make that call!" if I didn't mean you to call the police?'

'I'm sorry,' said Penny. 'I just thought you were behaving rather oddly. I'm awfully sorry!'

'Oh well, understandable,' I said. 'Do you think there's any point in calling the police now?'

'Hardly think so,' said Penny, 'unless anyone can tell us who he was.'

But all the other stallholders said they had absolutely no idea where he'd come from. They were either lying their heads off, part of a great Band of Robbers, or honest traders who'd never seen him before in their lives.

'Oh well, I got the dogs back, I suppose,' I said, though oddly now I'd got them I rather wondered why I'd bothered. I'd never really liked them and a bit of me had been rather relieved to have seen the last of them.

We then walked up to Golborne Road, past the Portuguese shop where we bought some rather delicious chorizo, and past the vintage clothes shop on the left where I'd once bought a very pretty skirt with a net petticoat which I'd only worn once. We bought some Portuguese custard tarts to take to Robin and, after a bit more mooching, found his shop by bumping into a sign on the pavement which read 'ALT BOOKSHOP'. Decorated with blue stars and silver moons and geometric patterns, there was a large arrow pointing upstairs.

The shop was much as I'd expected. Booklined walls and, in the centre of the room, ramshackle old sofas covered with Indian bedspreads. I have to say that everything smelt a bit, of old tobacco smoke, joss sticks and ancient books. The books were arranged in categories: 'Astrology', 'Inner Peace', 'Buddhism', 'The Seven Ways', 'Psychic Geography', 'Lizards', 'Soul', 'Angels' and so on. ('It looks like a bad set for *The Hobbit*,' I whispered to Penny. She giggled and then pointed: 'Phone home!' she said in a squeaky voice. 'That was ET, you banana,' I said.)

'Can I help you?' A girl, who looked distinctly like one of

Melanie's daughters, or what I imagine Melanie's daughters to look like anyway, approached with her hands in the usual palms-together-pointing-upwards position. But I'm afraid Penny and I couldn't stop laughing. God knows what she thought of us, giggling away and unable to speak.

Finally Penny managed to blurt out: 'Is Robin here?' and then we both collapsed again.

'I'm his landlady!' I said. And at this, Penny and I clung to each other, helpless with laughter.

She pointed upstairs and, pulling ourselves together, we tottered up a flight of rickety stairs at the back. There, on a small balcony, with a blue silk scarf tied round his neck, was Robin, smoking a joint.

'How lovely to see you!' he said, extinguishing the joint and tucking it into a small wallet to finish later.

As we drank herbal tea downstairs, we told him about our find.

'I have to say that guy sounds very familiar,' said Robin. 'Did he have a ring in his ear and a leather thong round his neck with a little elephant on it?'

'He did!' said Penny. 'You're quite right. And a tattoo on his hand.'

Blind old me had missed all of this, of course.

'He came in here once. Tried to sell me a copy of *The Golden Bough*. A first edition. But quite honestly, I didn't like the vibe around him. He said he'd got it at an auction but I didn't believe him. So I said no. Had to do a lot of rituals after that to get rid of his vile presence from the shop. He's always around.'

70

'His karma's doomed,' I said, giving Penny a slit-eyed look.

And then, I'm afraid to say, we both started to giggle again and eventually had to excuse ourselves because we were starting to look rather rude and bad-mannered.

Is this what's meant by entering a second childhood? Or was it shock? Or just the dope fumes? I don't normally behave like that. But there was something really creepy about actually confronting the man who must have seen the inside of my house. Gives me the willies.

'I see what you mean about good-looking,' said Penny in the car home. 'You always seem to get dishy lodgers.'

Later

Got back to find the postman had been and there were two Valentine cards for me. One was from David – not difficult to guess because it was postmarked Shampton and the envelope was written in his handwriting. The other, which featured an angel and smelt rather of joss sticks, was from – who knows? Couldn't read the postmark so felt jolly irritated. Hope it wasn't from Robin. That would be too embarrassing.

Also felt very guilty because I hadn't sent David a card myself. Must ring him later.

February 16

Daily Rant: 'Smartphones cause dementia!'

Of course I could barely read that headline because I'd just lost my glasses, and when I made it out by narrowing my eyes and peering, my heart started to race with anxiety. No good getting a new phone to make my life easier if the minute I start using it, it sends out dreadful electronic waves which make me incapable of comprehending it because I'm going gaga.

Later

Found my glasses (which were dangling off my neck by the arms) by praying to St Anthony. What a guy! All the more extraordinary because I don't even believe in him!

February 18

Gene's half-term. I was hoping he'd be coming to stay a couple of nights but it turns out he has a diary so packed that I suspect I will soon be asked whether I can fit into one of his 'windows'. In the event, he and Jack came over for lunch, and while Jack went out to look for a particular kind of chain for his bike, I was left with Gene for a few hours. Not quite sure what to do as it seems rather embarrassing to ask what seems a near-teenager whether he'd like to make gingerbread men or play snakes and ladders, but luckily Gene was eager to continue his iPhone lessons and showed me how to take videos and panoramic photographs and how to switch on the torch and record conversation, and even how to turn the whole thing into a mirror. Is there anything this amazing machine won't do? He downloaded a Kindle app so I can now read books wherever I go, without carrying a great big paperback around.

Very odd moment when he checked the number of steps I'd done by looking at the Health app and said, 'Granny! You don't walk anywhere! Do you just drive all the time?'

'No, it's just that I'm always walking around but don't always take my phone with me,' I said defensively.

'You must take more exercise,' he said. 'You're too sedentary.'

The word 'sedentary' came flying out and hit me like a thunderbolt. Surely this wasn't the sort of word a nine-year-old would use? Curiously, it was. He'd just learned it from some word list he'd been given at school. It seemed only yesterday that I'd had him on my knee and was showing him a cloth book with a fish in it, and he'd said, excitedly, 'P!'. I remember taking this as a sign that he was 'reading' at only one year old. A genius.

Because I'd got a wizard new phone which opens just by the feel of my thumbprint I don't need a number code, but Gene's is 7555. He explained that it is his name in code, if you gave every letter of the alphabet a number. The 'n' became '5' he said, by adding 1 and 4 together. Golly. It sounded to me like one of Robin's numerology tests. He's forever trying to persuade me that Marie Sharp is a holy name because if you number each letter from 1 to 26 and add them up and then add the numbers of the total together, you get 3, the holiest number in all the world's religions. Haven't yet told him that my middle name is Jocasta which would, I bet, screw the whole thing up. Let sleeping holy numbers lie, say I.

Rather sweetly, when Jack rang to say he was just having a drink with an old friend and wouldn't be picking Gene up for an hour, Gene looked around and asked if there were any jobs he could do for me. I mentioned that the gutter that runs along the roof of the conservatory was clogged with leaves and was causing ghastly dripping when it rained. Even though it was by now pretty dark, Gene insisted on getting out the ladder and, wearing a pair of oversized rubber gloves, and a large apron of mine that made him look like a French waiter, did an amazing job by clearing all the leaves which I collected in a bucket. It eventually got so dark I had to use the torch on my phone to light everything up. Gene came down looking very pleased with himself, saying: 'You wouldn't have known how to use that torch if I hadn't shown you, would you?'

'Do you remember,' I said, when we were having a cup of tea and a biscuit, 'how when you were tiny I used to make an apron for you out of an old plastic bag, just cutting holes in the side for arms and a slit at the bottom for your head?'

Gene grinned. 'Shall we try it now?' he said rather sheepishly.

'All right,' I said, surprised. 'We'd have to get a big bag, though.'

Eventually, bursting at the seams, Gene dressed up in a giant plastic bag that I'd got when I'd been to Argos and bought a toaster. He stood there roaring with laughter, begging me to take a picture of him on my phone which, without his help, I was able to do. It obviously was a kind of comfort for him to go back to those old days. Then, with an embarrassed smile, he ripped it off.

'That's probably the last time I'll ever do that,' he said, a rueful sadness in his voice.

And I thought: he's aware now that he's got a past. My grandson has a past. How strange.

February 24

David came up, which was lovely. I haven't seen him for a while. Though I'm slightly worried as I think he might be going deaf. I've been wondering this for ages actually, but haven't liked to say anything, but when, last night, he insisted on turning the BBC news up to ear-splitting levels, I couldn't help saying something.

'You don't think you're going deaf, do you?' I said, yelling above the din of the commentator who was telling us of some harrowing murder involving five little boys and a grandmother kept in an underground prison in Dartmoor. Some maniac had kept them chained up there for years. Frightfully depressing. Didn't really see why I had to yell since we were cuddled up next to each other on the sofa, but I couldn't make myself heard above the racket.

He didn't respond at all. And after I'd repeated it several times, all he said was 'What?'

In a fit of irritation, I turned the television off.

'Deaf!' I shouted. 'Do you think you're going deaf?'

'You don't have to yell, darling,' said David. 'Of course I'm not going deaf! I can hear you perfectly well.'

'Why do you have to have the television on so loudly, then?' I said.

'Is it too loud for you? You should have said,' he replied,

amiably. 'Anyway, it was a depressing story, wasn't it? How can we cheer ourselves up after that?'

We soon found a very good way of cheering ourselves up by going upstairs to bed, and afterwards he put his arm round me and said: 'I wish I could be with you every night like this,' and I said: 'I know, but it wouldn't be as nice if it was every night,' and he said, 'I suppose you're right' in a sad kind of way, and then we went to sleep.

February 25

Melanie's Facebook page has a new post: 'Things turn out best for the people who make the best of the way things turn out.'

Plan to remember that and spring it on her when she starts whining.

Later

Melanie, Penny and Marion insisted I accompany them to the local Shepherd's Bush Market to buy salwar kameezes, so David came too. Against my better judgement I was persuaded to try one on, but David laughed so much and said I looked like someone from a Women's Institute amateur dramatics production of *Aladdin*, particularly as my skin, having not been near the sun for months, is about as ashen as cold putty, not to mention my spectacles which don't look good with an Indian outfit.

Melanie insisted on entering every shop we visited with her hands pressed together saying: 'Nastase' until David gently pointed out that Nastase was a Wimbledon tennis champion and the correct word was 'Namaste'. Hope she remembers when we get to India.

Marion looked like a strange transvestite, Penny kept saying, 'But haven't you got a black one? Haven't you got black?' and it was only Melanie who carried it off, insisting on donning Turkish sandals with curly toes to finish off the look, covering her head with a bit of sari and ending up so swathed in Indian silk that she could hardly be seen at all.

I said, rather primly, that if it came to covering up I'd wear longer skirts and a light cardigan, and if they wanted me to cover up more I'd got a scarf I could put over my head, but no way was I going to draw attention to myself and look like an idiot. I was considered a terrific spoilsport and everyone returned home with masses of bags of saris, trousers, bangles and slippers, not to mention all kinds of Indian vegetables and peppers and herbs and spices, while I came home with nothing but a catnip mouse for Pouncer from the market pet shop, which I always go into staring at the ground lest I witness the pitiful scene of birds in cages and rabbits in hutches far too small.

Melanie said she was going to fry up her beedies for her supper and David said didn't she mean bhindis, because weren't beedies Indian cigarettes, and Melanie batted her eyelids at him and said he was so clever and wasn't I a lucky woman, and I felt crosser than ever.

Even later
David left in a bad mood, having noticed the anonymous Valentine on my mantelpiece.

'Who's that from?' he said, rather brusquely.

'I have no idea,' I said. 'I just put it up because I thought it was rather pretty.'

'Looks suspiciously to me as if it's from Robin,' he said sourly. 'When's he moving out?'

'Don't be so stupid,' I said.

And we parted not on the best of terms.

MARCH

March 2, evening

'OAP now stands for "Old And Pissed", claims liver specialist'
(*Daily Rant*)

Oh dear. Rather reminds me of Penny. We've always both liked a glass of wine, but she's really going a bit far these days. Oh well, maybe India will sort her out, because I guess it won't be flowing with booze. Masses of yoghurt drinks and rosewater, I imagine.

Was driven mad today by the burglar alarm constantly going off and had no idea why until I discovered that Robin had left his window open (I don't blame him; his room is so stuffy and smells of dope and joss sticks) but of course a burglar alarm immediately senses a crack in its armour and thinks someone's sneaked in. I was just wandering about shouting, 'Oh God, I wish I'd never been born, I wish I were dead!' to myself having finally fixed it, when I was aware that Robin had returned, having forgotten something, and had come into my room hearing my melancholy complaint, and immediately walked over and put his arm round me.

'What's happened?' he said. 'You mustn't say you wish you'd never been born! Life is wonderful! Let the light shine in! Look at all you've got – a lovely house, lovely grandchild . . . a lovely lodger!' he added, rather sweetly.

Took me ages to reassure him that I go around the house saying this sort of thing all the time to myself and it doesn't mean I wish I'd never been born or I wish I were dead; I just say it to let off my frustration with life. He gave a wan smile, but then said: 'It's best not to say those things, though, Marie. Whenever you say something like that your subconscious hears and it might actually believe you and do something about it. Or a bad spirit might slip in, and take over your soul. And you wouldn't like that.'

'Fiddlesticks!' I replied, remembering that excellent word, last used, I think, by my grandmother. And he laughed.

Glad, anyway, that he hasn't spotted the myriad bad spirits that are sneaking around my soul already.

March 6

Went off with Penny today to Boots in Westfield, the huge shopping centre at the top of the road, to get our jabs for India. We were asked whether we were going to 'swampy areas' and I said I had no idea, so they gave us everything, as far as I can see, and we came out with tingling arms and great holes in our bank balances. We are apparently protected against typhoid, yellow fever, hepatitis, rabies, Japanese encephalitis and God knows what else so we feel like superheroes. I'm longing to meet some Japanese encephalitis germ down a dark alley and beckon him on and challenge him to a fight, secure in the knowledge that he could do me no harm whatever and that I could resist his attacks with a light 'tra-la!'. The only thing we have to be wary of is malaria, of course, and instead of a jab we need pills. We were given some rather sinister stuff called Lariam which we have to start taking now. Terrible bore. Bet Penny won't remember to take them.

We had a cup of coffee afterwards, feeling rather light-headed and sore about the arms, and Penny asked if the police had made any progress with the robberies.

'Haven't heard a peep,' I said. 'But perhaps we should ask Sheila the Dealer at the residents' meeting?'

Penny went home while I prowled around trying to find something that would be a nice present for Alice, Brad and Sharmie's little daughter. Finally decided on a manicure set with lots of different coloured varnishes and an instruction book for making patterns on your nails. Suitably girlie, I thought. I'd have loved one when I was young. Better than the usual book token that people used to give us as children.

March 8, morning

Daily Rant: 'Booze is Better Than Beta-Blockers!'

Better hide that from Penny.

David came up and we went to see a play because he's got

some friend who's directing it. It was a production of *Hamlet* set in an underground car park. Hamlet was the parking attendant, his father was the man who ran the building above (I think) and Ophelia was the cleaning lady. I couldn't work it out at all. Most peculiarly, Claudius was dressed as a Nazi officer. David sighed as we made our way backstage.

'I'm so sorry, darling. You were Trojan to sit through it. What total tosh. And the sound was so bad! I couldn't hear a word! Anyway, why can't they just do it normally? What are we going to say?'

'An unforgettable performance,' I said. 'That's true.'

'Okay, you say that and I'll lie. It's easier.'

So David told his friend he was stupendous and that the whole thing really worked, and was incredibly moving and so on.

I was terribly impressed. 'Are you sure you didn't enjoy it?' I said as we walked down Piccadilly towards the Underground to go home. 'You really sounded as if you meant every word.'

'If you're going to lie, lie properly,' said David, taking my arm as we crossed the road. 'No point in doing anything by halves. Now, darling, where can I take you for a late supper before we go back?'

I must say, sometimes I do rather love him.

March 9

The residents' meeting was livelier than usual, understandably, because high on the agenda was the spate of local robberies. Father Emmanuel was there, the 'vicar' from the evangelical church next door, predicting that the perpetrator would go straight to hellfire and damnation when he died, while Sheila the Dealer took a more indulgent view saying it was probably just 'local lads up to no good!'

'Boys will be boys!' she said, as she slurped tea into her messily lipsticked mouth. 'Got to 'aver bit of fun before they settle dahn.'

'Fun!' said Penny, indignantly. 'They took all my jewellery! It belonged to my mother!'

Sheila wasn't fazed at all. In fact, when she heard what the robbers had taken she actually broke into a rather admiring smile. 'Jewellery!' she said, somewhat in awe. 'That's clever! I 'eard they just took knick-knacks. Didn't realise they'd got into the big time. They'll have a problem floggin' that, though. Gettin' more difficult these days, floggin' 'ot stuff.'

'Well, I hope they get caught!' said Penny, choking on her glass of Beaujolais.

'So do I!' I added.

'But you have got your dogs back, darling Mar,' said Melanie.

'Dogs? What dogs?' said Sheila the Dealer.

'Mar and Pen went up to Portobello and they tracked down this guy who was selling her dogs, and said he'd bought them in an auction!'

'Did 'e now!' chuckled Sheila. 'Same old story!' she added, as if she were reminiscing.

'Anyway, how are we going to stop them?' I said, feeling that S the D knew a lot more than she let on.

'We've got to get the council to put in security cameras,' said Tim, who looked up from taking minutes on his laptop. 'That's the only way.'

'No, that's so *1984*,' put in Melanie. 'I've got a tremendously good idea. Why don't we ask them to put in twenty-four-hour piped classical music on our street? Apparently surveys show that there's nothing like Mozart to calm down a criminal. Bach and burglars, Verdi and villains – they just don't mix.'

'Well, I'm not a villain and I don't want Verdi blaring down our street at all hours of the day or night,' I said.

'Though *La Traviata* is a wonderful piece of music,' said Marion. 'Tim and I saw a production in Ghana when we were there in 1984.'

'Yes, yes, yes,' I said. 'And no, no, no to classical music.'

'Tell you wha',' said Sheila, 'I've got a young friend, Terry. 'e'd 'elp. You get 'old of 'im and I bet you'd find the burglaries moved on somewhere else in no time. At least if 'e listens to 'is old auntie Sheel. 'e's a good boy, loves 'is mum. Not that 'e's got one, of course, but you know wha' I mean. And 'e can sort you aht wiv some Es an' all,' she added, nodding to me.

Before anyone could really take in what she'd just said, I hastily moved the agenda on to the subject of flower baskets on the lamp-posts, a topic introduced by Melanie who is dying to muck up the street in any way she can. First trying to get us to paint our doors the same colour, and then classical music and now bloody flower baskets. What a thought.

'We are living in Shepherd's Bush, not the Cotswolds,' said Tim unusually impatiently.

'Hanging baskets are so naff,' said Penny, forgetting that Melanie has one outside her front door, and helping herself to some more wine. And with that, the meeting fizzled out.

March 10

Was just reading a lovely email from James when Robin burst into the room. 'What's all this I hear about cameras?' he said, anxiously. 'Mel tells me you're thinking of putting cameras up in the street! You do know, don't you, that it is not only a gross invasion of our civil liberties, but also that the cameras exude rays which are extremely harmful to unborn babies and dogs? And I've heard that they not only leak out this toxicity, but they also destroy our souls at night. Souls need peaceful environments to regenerate themselves during sleep, and they can't do this if the air is full of electrical waves. And cats,' he added, noticing Pouncer, curled up on the desk beside my easel. 'Yes, cats. Very dangerous to the feline species. Makes their whiskers fall out.'

'Don't worry,' I said. 'There'll be no cameras while I'm in charge of the residents' association.' I waved him away and he shuffled out of the room, leaving me to James's email.

'Darling Marie,' it read. 'Haven't heard from you in an age! How are you? Are you Somerset bound soon? Longing for you to come over and see my, though I say it myself, spectacular garden. Derek Jarman would eat his heart out. Owen and I are happy as bees, though it's bloody cold here. I wouldn't mind one of those burka things, actually, preferably made of sheepskin. I could wander all over the countryside and become a mysterious monster and be featured in the local press.

'Come soon, darling! Longing to catch up on your news! All my love, James.'

Much as I like 'lots of love' and 'much love', 'all my love' always seems a teensy-weensy bit excessive. I mean, what does he write to anyone else if he's given all his love to me? But I made a plan to pop in for lunch when I next go down to see David, in a couple of weekends' time.

March 11, evening

Had rather a weird experience today. The bell rang, just as I was on the phone to Penny, and who should be standing there but Sheila the Dealer, dressed in a pinny with her manky hair done up in an old scarf. Telling Penny I'd ring back, I welcomed Sheila in and made her a cup of tea.

'I've the answer to all your problems,' she said. 'Terry.' She got out a packet of tobacco and expertly rolled her own cigarette. ''e's this lad I was tellin' you abaht. If you come along wiv me, 'e's waitin' at the top of the road.'

Anyway, after I'd checked that Robin wasn't in, put on my coat, changed my glasses, seen that all the windows were shut, got my key and set the burglar alarm (getting out of the house takes AGES these days), Sheila and I walked up the road to that little patch of green at the top where only a few years ago the council were trying to build a hotel. When Penny and I'd been canvassing support we discovered that the whole place, though we presented it as a haven of rural wildlife in a sea of concrete, was actually awash with drug dealers and criminals with Rottweilers. Sad to say, it hadn't changed, and a couple of dealers even hailed me as an old mate from their negotiations under the two trees we'd also saved. They looked rather wary when they noticed I was with Sheila. No doubt she was on their patch, or they were on hers. They're like cats, these drug dealers – they've got their areas all marked out. I expect at night they go round urinating on their territories just to make sure no Albanian or Romanian drug dealers try to muscle in and steal their pitch. Just like Pouncer.

While we were waiting, Sheila expounded about Terry. ''e's 'ad an 'ard life, 'as Terry,' she said. 'Lived wiv 'is bruvver and then turned out 'e weren't 'is bruvver arter all and 'e was 'is farver all along! 'is sister'd gorn orf wiv this drug dealer and the baby she'd 'ad by 'er grandfarver – not Terry's grandfarver, no, 'e was in jail doin' life – and the council said the flat weren't fit for purpose, so 'e came to live wiv me for a while.'

'You said he loved his mother . . .' I said, helpfully.

'Figure of speech. No, 'e never 'ad a muvver. Would 'ave loved 'er if 'e'd 'ad one, but no. No mum. Never. Not even when 'e were born.' There was a pause. 'They do say 'is muvver was his uncle, but that was before the sex change and by then 'e'd been murdered by 'is pimp.'

Before too long, a scrawny figure appeared through the bushes and introduced himself as Terry. He was only about 5'5" with a very white, feral face and a couple of acne spots on his cheek. When I say 'feral' I wasn't sure whether he looked more like a fox or a rat. Apparently, you make a judgement of any person you meet within the first five seconds but it was very difficult with Terry because in the first two and a half seconds I recoiled, deciding that he gave me the creeps, but then he smiled, and I immediately warmed to him. His face changed completely. All his suspicion and menace dropped away and you could suddenly see what he must have looked like as a little boy – vulnerable, eager to please, rather weak, but not actually bad. It's an odd thing about being old – the capacity to see other people as young children. I don't ever remember doing this when I was actually young myself, in my twenties or thirties, which is so peculiar.

'Well, say 'ello!' said Sheila.

Taking the hint I stretched out a hand and said: 'Hi!'

He looked at my hand rather warily, obviously not used to this ritual, but after a couple of seconds' pause, took it and gave it a hesitant shake.

''ello, missus,' he said.

'Marie,' I said. 'I'm Marie.'

'Now, tell Marie what you know about them robberies,' said Sheila, briskly. 'And don't forget wha' I told you about you know wha'.' And she tapped her nose. Then she shuffled off, leaving us together.

As I didn't particularly want to ask him to the house, we found a rather grimy cafe nearby and I explained about the robberies.

'What they take?' asked Terry, who was drinking Coke. An enormously fat woman nearby with an equally enormous child strapped into a pushchair, was feeding it alternately crisps and some kind of sugary juice. Chrissie would have a fit, always having been very strict with Gene when it came to sweets and junk food.

I explained what had been taken – including Penny's jewellery – though adding I'd got the dogs back from the Portobello Road.

'Yeah, I 'eard abaht that,' said Terry. ''e was right pissed off!' And he laughed in such a way that it was difficult not to join in.

'You know the guy, then?' I said.

'Well, I don't know 'im as such,' said Terry. 'But you know, veeze fings get arahnd.'

'The saddest thing I lost was a photograph of one of my best friends, who'd died, and it's the only photograph I had,' I said. 'He was dressed up as a sheikh and it was taken at a ball by Beaton.'

'So 'e was an Arab geezer, was 'e?' said Terry, draining his Coke. 'Fair play. My mum used to go out wiv a Moroccan. Nice bloke. Not me real mum, of course.'

'No, he was dressed up,' I said. 'It was all rather silly.'

'And 'e didn't win?' said Terry. 'I mean, wiv 'im being beaten an all?'

'Not "beaten". Cecil Beaton was the man who took the photograph. It was perfectly normal. At a party. Anyway, the thing is someone's burgling houses round here and they're not taking all the things you'd expect like laptops, which can be replaced on insurance. Just little things, things that really mean something to the owners.'

89

'You mean they'd rather they took cameras an' stuff?' asked Terry, obviously rather surprised. I wondered how many things he owned that actually held a sentimental attachment for him. If, indeed, he owned anything at all, come to that.

We parted, with me shoving a twenty-pound note into his hand in exchange for the couple of Es he promised to get me, and I came away feeling rather sorry for the poor boy. He'd obviously had a hard life.

Later

Robin very suspicious when I told him of this mysterious encounter. He said he thought Terry must be a lizard, and not to trust anyone.

'I don't think Terry's a lizard,' I said. 'He couldn't be a member of a powerful elite if he tried!'

But Robin had already gone upstairs and was out of earshot.

March 18

Just come back from a visit to David. I wish I knew what was going on. I keep feeling I have to hold him at arm's length because there's no doubt that he wants to get closer while I want to leave things as they are. Funny, isn't it, this societal change? In the old days I would be absolutely desperate to get close to a man, any man, but now I've lived so long on my own I feel very wary of sharing my life with anyone again. It's a hard-won situation, this lone-living, and it's been achieved with pain and difficulty, and the idea of slotting back into a partnership isn't as easy as it seems. For David, of course, it's quite different because until she went to India, he'd lived with Sandra since we broke up, and so he's never known what it's like to be on his own. I think men find it harder to be on their own than women. I suppose they always want to be mothered.

But why don't women want to be fathered? Some women do, I know, but not all. For all her chat about going out on the pull, I don't think Melanie would really be happy with a partner. Of course Penny is completely different. She's always been unhappy without a husband – she even went on the internet to try to find one once, with disastrous results. She can't understand why I don't welcome David back into my life with open arms.

Anyway, staying with him. It was lovely. We pottered around and I admired his flood defences which seemed to be mounds of earth like giant molehills springing up everywhere (Somerset is incredibly liable to floods, apparently). He's even got his name in the local paper because he's the only farmer who's doing this. I asked him if it wasn't rather dangerous, but he laughed it off, and said it would be far more dangerous if the water were to come into the farmhouse and drown him.

We chomped our way through some lasagne which seemed rather good at the time, but when I asked if he'd made it, David revealed that no, Widow Bossom had dropped it round.

When I looked rather astonished, he said: 'Oh, she often pops round with meals and things. She's very kind, Marie. Takes pity on a lonely old bachelor!'

I have to say that after that the lasagne didn't taste nearly so delicious. Too many carrots.

Afterwards, he briefed me on Sandra.

'I last heard from her before last Christmas,' he said. 'She was just about to have her baby, but since then, nothing.'

We were sitting in front of the fire in his cosy sitting room, the wind whistling outside. In ten days the clocks will go forward, so the evenings will be far lighter. Can't wait, as this perpetual gloom is getting me down.

'Do you have an address for her? Email? Text?'

'I've tried everything but she never answers. I'm starting to get really worried. I mean, obviously it's her life, and perhaps she's just drawn a line under our time together and decided to start anew with Ali, but she promised she'd keep in touch. She even asked if I'd be godfather when the baby arrived. It's very odd.'

'What Ali like?' I asked. 'Does he have another name?'

'Not that I can remember,' said David. 'He's nice enough. Good-looking if you like that sort of thing' (I love the way men can be just as bitchy as women when they're jealous!) 'and apparently he makes a reasonable living in some kind of tyre shop in a resort called Mandrem, selling jewellery on the beach at weekends. They were going to live with his mother until they'd saved enough money to lease a bar.'

'Aren't her parents worried about not hearing from her?' I asked.

'No, they're both dead, and her only sister's schizophrenic and in a home. That's partly why I feel so responsible for her.'

I promised we'd go and look for her, though I imagine it'll be like looking for a needle in a haystack.

Later

Have to say David really is getting deaf. I got rather fed up with shouting all the time though he got very cross when I suggested he should get a hearing test.

'It's not me who's going deaf, it's you who's losing her voice. You speak too softly all the time! You mumble, Marie, and you always have done!'

Being congenitally insecure I always think I'm in the wrong in the face of any criticism so I was surprised to find myself on firm ground here, because I'm rather renowned for the clarity of my speaking voice – having honed it in years of teaching in noisy classrooms – so I felt a bit cross, but didn't say anything until, after a pause, he said: 'I can hear everything Edwina says, so I don't know what's wrong with you!'

'Widow Bossom – or "Edwina" as you call her – has a voice like a foghorn!' I snapped back. Very loudly.

Men are absolutely weird about their being deaf. A friend of mine's husband was going deaf and refused to believe he was until she pretended a friend of hers had asked if he was getting Alzheimer's because he was so hopeless at following conversations. After that he scampered off to the hearing aid place like a greyhound out of the slips and is now the life and soul.

On the way back we planned to drop in on James and Owen. We took both our cars so I could drive back alone. Rural or what! James told me that before he moved in, Owen's idea of interior design was little more than an outside loo, a bed, a table, a chair and a tin and bottle opener.

James has changed all this completely, and insisted on installing central heating, curtains and sofas, showers and loos, not to mention an Aga. And though Owen resisted at first, he soon found he rather liked living surrounded by chintz and flower arrangements. He's a relaxed sort of chap who basically lives in his gumboots and a thick jerkin, so, as long as he isn't required to do the housework, he's more than happy with the transformation.

They have a dog, naturally, and James insists on Owen being called 'Mummy' and him being called 'Daddy' which is all rather embarrassing, but it's a nice enough Jack Russell, even if it is yappy.

James had rustled up a delicious lunch made entirely from things he'd foraged from the garden – sorrel soup, ducks' eggs, dandelion salad, blackberries frozen from last autumn and unpasteurised cream from a local farm – along with home-made bread. Owen sat down to eat with us, still wearing a bobble hat. It was one of those ones that aren't properly pulled down over his face but have a pocket of air at the top, so he looked like someone who had an extra brain attached to his scalp. Rather unnerving, that – particularly as Penny always refers to them as 'condom hats'. Still, the lunch was all very yummy. And then James showed me his pride and joy – the garden.

I put my foot in it straight away because he led us outside to a patch of apparently barren ground and then he said: 'Ta daa!' and opened his arms wide, and I could see absolutely nothing.

I said: 'But where is it?'

'This is it, darling,' said James, rather put out.

'What is it?' I asked, genuinely baffled. I couldn't see anything but stones, a bit of gravel, some patches of what looked like weeds, and a few teasels.

'This is it ... this is the garden ... look at the flint-based gravel, the different grasses, the elegantly laid out wood-chip paths ... it's based on the work of the internationally renowned landscape designer from the Netherlands, Piet Oudolf.'

'But where are the flowers?' I asked. 'And the trees? And the bushes? And the pond?'

'No, no, you don't get it, Marie!' said James. 'It's the subtle change of grasses that's the thing. You see the pale ones here, and the darker ones here, and these have very interesting seed-pods ... and then you've got the bamboos to add height ...'

Oh, God! He'd copied the garden at the Old Fire Station! I hesitated but before I could become even more perplexed, good old David waded in. 'Magnificent!' he said. 'James, you've really triumphed! And I just love the lavender over there, to contrast with the ... the ... red grasses over there. And I'm sure the wind through them makes a fascinating noise, too.' (Not that *you* could hear it, I thought, rather sourly.) 'It has a positively ethereal quality about it.'

Then I remembered how David had pulled it off with the ghastly *Hamlet* set in a men's toilet or whatever it was. 'If you're going to lie, lie properly,' he'd said. So, 'Do you know, it's growing on me,' I said, as if I'd reached the conclusion after much consideration. 'It's not like a normal garden, true, but it has a magical . . . it's not so much a garden, James, as a work of art!'

That seemed to satisfy him and we were allowed, then, to scuttle inside and warm our hands at the fire over a couple of crumpets.

'Well done, darling,' said David, just before we got into our separate cars and James was out of earshot. 'I mean, what's the point of arguing with him about his ghastly garden? It was more like a bomb site, wasn't it? And nowhere to sit down, no real grass to have a picnic on, no pond full of goldfish, no bird table or sundial, or roses, for God's sake. That's the kind of thing we like, isn't it? Do you know what I think would have perked it up?' he added. 'A gnome. Fishing, preferably.'

Trust David to get the point. There aren't many men who could understand how, in certain circumstances, a gnome is the only answer.

March 19

Great drama this morning, back at home, because the people opposite have now been burgled! I heard about it from Father Emmanuel who was just slamming shut the door on his enormous people carrier which he uses to transport the faithful from all over London to his wretched church.

'Yes, it's very bad,' he said dolefully. 'There are many bad people around here. I hope they don't think my lowly church has any valuable things in it. Of course,' he said, correcting himself, 'my church is full of valuable things, but the valuable things in it are things you cannot steal – faith and love and forgiveness and the wrath of the Lord,' he added, confusingly.

I don't know the people opposite because they don't speak English – though we wave to each other occasionally and make friendly signs when we meet – so I have no idea what was stolen, but I bet it was done by the same gang as the ones who broke into mine and Penny's houses.

March 21

Had ghastly nightmare last night. I dreamed that Melanie had got her way and classical music was blaring out all over the street, and Hughie was in Arab dress, breaking into someone's house, and stealing the photograph of himself. I turned round and it was Father Emmanuel who was conducting the orchestra from where the music sprang, and when I looked back, Hughie had transformed into David and, however much I shouted to him, he couldn't hear.

Later Terry texted me: 'Got something for you. Meet me up the grass at 4.30.'

I assumed 'up the grass' meant on the same patch of land where we'd met before, so I rolled up feeling really fearful because I'm not used to doing drug deals. I felt I was walking in a frightfully guilty way, head pushed down, a wary look in my eyes, obvious to any passing copper that I was Up to No Good. So I tried to unbend and walk with my head held high, as I'd been taught in school deportment classes. 'Pretend there's a string attached to the top of your head that is holding you up,' our teacher used to say. Of course, now I come to think of it, that's exactly the look that someone assumes when going to do a shady deal so probably police watch out for ludicrously confident-looking people with invisible strings coming out of their heads, and not the usual devious, skulking people we see in comics.

When I arrived, head still held high, I was surprised to see Terry was bearing a parcel. 'These Es must be enormous,' I thought. 'Elephant pills!' But he encouraged me to look inside, which I thought was rather unwise until I found the contents. Bound in cardboard and bubble wrap was the photograph of Hughie in his Arab costume!

'Oh, Terry!' I said, beside myself with pleasure. 'I can't tell you what this means to me! But where did you get it?'

He put a finger to his nose. 'Let's just say it fell orf the back of a lorry. Someone owes me a favour. Couldn't get the frame back, of course – that'd been flogged. But fort you'd like this anyways.'

I felt like hugging him – though something prevented me from actually clasping him to my bosom. Probably the fact that he was looking a bit skinny and smelly. But then I wondered if he'd remembered my other commission.

'Er, did you have any luck with the, er . . .' I stammered. And he hit his forehead and said: 'Corse! Forgot! 'ere you go!' and bundled a tiny packet into my hand which I immediately stuffed deep into my bag. 'Don't 'ave a drink wiv it, but lots of water,' he said, suddenly sounding a bit like a doctor. 'Might make you a bit, er, friendly, so watch out 'oo you take it wiv!'

March 24

Over to Jack and Chrissie's for Easter lunch. I'd brought a bag of tiny Easter eggs to hide in the garden, but according to Jack, Gene is no longer interested in all that, so I had to keep them hidden in my bag. Felt very sad as I remembered all the Easters we'd had in the past with fluffy chicks on the table, and daffodils floating in bowls, not to mention so many chocolate eggs, some even rattling with other chocolate eggs inside, that it was like the sweets department in Fortnum and Mason.

They were very excited about the India trip and Gene asked if I could get him some nunchucks, at which point Chrissie gasped and said what was he thinking of.

'But I wouldn't use them, Mum,' said Gene, smiling slyly. 'I'd just like to have them.'

Apparently they're the sort of thing those thuggees used to use – two bits of wood separated by a metal chain and very good for murdering people with – but luckily it turns out they're only available in South-East Asia.

After lunch I washed up and we all had a snooze in front of the fire while Gene watched an old cartoon on telly, and I stayed for a cup of tea before heading home.

As I was drinking my tea, Chrissie was putting away the dishes and pans I'd left to drain and to my horror I noticed she was washing nearly everything I'd done again. Obviously I hadn't been as thorough as I'd thought. I blushed down to my feet because I remember so well old people doing the washing up when I was young and they always left smears and bits of food on the plates and saucepans – and now I was one of those! Felt terribly humiliated and decrepit. Found myself, on the way home, consuming all the tiny eggs I'd brought for the Easter egg hunt in a desperate attempt to comfort myself and got back feeling terribly sick.

March 27

Daily Rant: 'OAPs: Online And Plugged-in!'

You wouldn't guess it from the latest issue of 'Grey Matters', which is one of those free product magazines that comes unbidden through the door. It advertises all kinds of strange items for old people, like special constructions that help you put on your socks, and weird gadgets you wear to separate your toes when they've become pushed together with arthritis. They were selling not only new record players to listen to your old vinyl on, but new-minted typewriters, with ribbons in them.

Hardly plugged in.

APRIL

April 1

Nasty moment on way out to dinner with old friends from art school tonight. I'd been given some amaretti biscuits as a little present by Penny when she came to dinner a couple of months ago and because I can't stand the things, I thought I'd recycle them and take them to my friends. Halfway there I suddenly thought: I wonder if the biccies are still within the sell-by date? I pulled in at the side of the road and looked. They were out of date on March 25! So I had to spend the next ten minutes prising sell-by date sticker off, which made a ghastly mess, and then suddenly wondered if any of these friends knew Penny and what would happen if they took the biscuits round as a present to her . . . It all got so complicated that eventually, seeing a bin nearby, I hopped out of the car, dropped the biscuits inside, and arrived empty-handed and half an hour late. I suppose that is God's idea of some kind of April Fool joke.

April 2

This morning I was in the kitchen when I heard a strange scratching sound and, looking up, I saw it was a pigeon wandering about on my glass roof. It was a very classy-looking bird, and it had on those rather fashionable pigeon-trousers, made of feathers, and a little crest on the top of its head. Going up to the bathroom I stared at it through the window – which overlooks the glass kitchen roof – and noticed it had a green tag on its leg.

Must be some kind of homing pigeon just having a rest on its way somewhere exotic. Rather charming. Took a photograph of it (on my phone!) and sent it to Gene, hoping it would amuse him.

Later
Slightly perturbed to see that the pigeon is still there, looking extremely anxious and bemused. It hasn't left the roof and I'm worried that it might be hungry.

April 3

Pigeon still here. I'm starting to panic. I've got quite enough to do with preparing for India and doing last-minute packing without a bird to worry about. But I rushed up to the pet shop – where I still have to keep my eyes closed so I don't see all the cruelty – to buy some corn, having discovered (via Google) that this is what pigeons like to eat. I asked if the man who

runs the pet shop would like a fancy pigeon (having also discovered that this is how my type of pigeon is described) and
he said he'd got quite enough pigeons already, and anyway
there wasn't much call for pigeons these days, thanks.

Put the corn in a bowl on the windowsill with some water
and when I next looked, the whole lot had been polished off
and the pigeon was sitting on a nearby pipe looking very full,
but very sad.

Later

I rang the RSPCA but they were totally uninterested, and
then I tried an outfit called the Bird Fanciers' Association. A
croaking little voice answered. I wasn't sure if it belonged to
a man or a woman or, indeed, a talking bird.

This voice explained that my pigeon was probably a bird
rejected by a breeder. Apparently if their birds are not up to
scratch, breeders often chuck the poor creatures out of the
window and into the wild, hoping they'll be able to fend for
themselves. Most die, said the voice. It would be best to see if
the bird would fly away, which it would eventually, in search
of food.

'But I've already fed it!' I said.

There was a cackling laugh at the other end.

'Well, you've made a rod for your own back, I'm afraid,
dear,' said the voice. 'He'll expect you to feed him regularly
now! You can either harden your heart or keep him as a pet.'

'But if I keep him he'll be so lonely! He doesn't seem to
be able to socialise with other birds! He hasn't got a friend!'

103

'Oh, yes, he has got a friend!' said the voice, with a chuckling menace in his tone. 'You're his friend now, dear!'

April 4

In a complete panic, as I'm leaving tomorrow. Actually, I've been in a panic all week wondering what on earth I'm doing going to India. Penny and Marion say they're feeling just the same and Marion says she must have been mad to agree to come on the trip, and how will Tim cope, and we'll all get dreadful diseases. The only person who seems to be looking forward to the jaunt with unalloyed joy is Melanie – but then she's got her son and grandchildren to look forward to seeing.

Is it something that happens when you get older? Feeling panicky when you leave home for a holiday? Though the whole idea of a 'holiday' now seems mad anyway, since I'm not exactly working, despite my days being completely packed with events.

Later

Have spent the entire day leaving notes for Robin and discussing everything from the burglar alarm to the pigeon. I've even got Terry on board, since he's looking for work, and he says he'll mow the lawn and clean the windows, water the plants and feed the pigeon on the days Robin forgets or can't make it. He promises he'll fix a broken lamp and repair one of the banisters and do any other little job he sees that needs doing, so I feel I've definitely got my fifty quid's worth

– which is what I'm paying him. Luckily Robin has given him the once-over and now declares he is completely free of any lizard characteristics.

'He's an honest lad, one of nature's gentlemen,' he declared.

Jack rang to wish me goodbye, and put Gene on the line who said he wished he was coming.

'I wish you were coming too, darling,' I said. 'It's "were coming", by the way. Subjunctive in a conditional clause.' (Why do I bother?) 'I'll send you lots of texts and photographs, I promise.'

'And don't get eaten by tigers,' he said. 'Or crocodiles.'

David arrived late because he's going to come with us to the airport tomorrow and help us with our bags and checking in and so on which is very sweet of him. We had a scrap supper, and he said he'd miss me terribly. I said I'd miss him, too, and he said: 'What?'

Oh dear.

Spent the rest of the evening doing last-minute packing, remembering to take not only paper, brushes, and paints (gouache as well as watercolour) but pastels too.

April 5

Just typing this on flight. Absolutely shattered and it's only eleven a.m.. We had to get up at four thirty in the morning which is so early it's more like late at night. To think I used to stay up sometimes till four thirty when I was young and thought nothing of it. I haven't seen four thirty in the morning in the last twenty years, and it's not, I can tell you, a pretty sight. Pitch black, freezing cold, eerily quiet. Anyway, this giant people-carrier arrived with Marion inside it – she'd ordered it – and David and I piled in, with Melanie from next door, and we went off to pick up Penny. We were all pretty bleary-eyed and then Marion started up an argument with Penny about whether her hand luggage was too big or not and Penny said she'd taken it on a trip to France and Marion said but France wasn't Delhi and they have different rules, and then Melanie thought she'd forgotten her passport but hadn't and David just said: 'Calm down, girls, everything's fine,' which made me want to hit him it sounded so patronising. We were all totally frazzled, and staggered out at Heathrow cross-eyed and bandy-legged with tiredness.

Luckily David, who is the only one among us who can see properly, directed us immediately to the correct check-in desk, where we waited in a giant queue which seemed to consist of enormous Indian families with great cling-wrapped suitcases and cardboard boxes done up with string with big addresses scrawled on them in felt-tip. Finally we tottered into Departures, leaving David at the gate.

For a moment I really did wish he was coming with us, because he appeared to be the only one who knew what was what, and I was starting to feel rather scared. So incredible to feel frightened of going abroad! When I was young, I went to China and South America and even drove across the States on my own – and yet here I was with a bunch of jolly old girls absolutely panic-stricken at the idea of going so far from home. Very peculiarly, for me, once we were in the departure lounge and sitting in a cafe in an area curiously called The Village, I suddenly got an attack of the miseries over an enormous hot chocolate. Penny put her arm round me and asked what was up and I couldn't explain that I was missing David and Jack and Gene and Robin and the pigeon and suddenly didn't want to go away at all.

Anyway, she recommended a stiff drink, and after a glass of wine I felt so woozy at that time in the morning that I didn't have a minute to feel sorry for myself any more and we staggered onto the plane. Penny's hand luggage was the right size which clearly made her feel rather smug and she looked at Marion meaningfully and Marion looked very disapproving in a 'well, you've got away with it this time, but wait till the flight coming back' way, and we settled down for hours and hours of flying.

Penny, who was sitting next to me, insisted on ordering champagne while I, rather cleverly I thought, slipped myself a Valium and am just starting to feel the effects. Hope to sleep all the way to Delhi.

April 7

Which I did. Arrived totally starving as I'd missed out on all the meals, I'd been so conked out. However, I could hardly move I was so stiff. Sitting for over nine hours doesn't do the old joints any good.

Crikey! What a place! Even though we were at the back of

the queue to get out of the plane, the moment the doors were opened, the heat, dust and smell was like a punch in the face. The airport itself was fantastically modern and glam, but the moment we got through Customs we were surrounded by the terrifying sound of yelling and bells and roaring and very thin Indian men all around us seizing our luggage and pulling us one way and another shouting, 'Taxi! You want good hotel? Come with me . . . my cousin . . .'

But in the corner of the airport, through the rush and scurry of everyone greeting and unloading and yelling, I saw an Indian woman huddled with a small baby, begging, and I thought: 'I wonder if I'm going to like this?' Luckily, before I could decide I didn't and turn on my heels to take the next plane back to London, Marion spotted Brad and Sharmie waving and we fell gratefully into their white air-conditioned car – a gigantic affair, with a driver – and sped off. As we pulled out of the airport, children with snotty noses and flies in their eyes tapped on the windows making pointing signals to their mouths as if they were hungry, and I felt horrified at the poverty.

'They're always like that!' said Sharmie, cheerfully, seeing my face. 'That's India for you! Anyway, great to see all you guys!'

'Isn't this just amazing!' said Brad. 'Here we all are together – just like old times! Pity you couldn't have brought Father Emmanuel as well!'

'I'm glad you left what-was-her-name, that Sheila woman at home,' said Sharmie. 'Alice, have you given Marie a kiss?

She's been looking forward to seeing you for the last few weeks!' she added.

Alice, their daughter, by now a shy eight-year-old, turned to me from the seat in front and gave me a smile. I wouldn't have recognised her.

'Oh, darling, I've got something for you, but I hope you won't think it too silly,' I said. 'How lovely to see you!' and I gave her shoulder a big squeeze and leaned forward to kiss her cheek.

We dropped Marion, Penny and Melanie off at the 'cheap and cheerful' hotel that Melanie had booked. The path up the hotel was too small for the car to get to – it was hidden in the blackness behind some scrubby trees. A couple of the thinnest stray dogs I've ever seen sniffed around, and I noticed one was covered in sores.

'Yes, ma'am, many dogs in India!' said the chauffeur cheerfully. 'Many dogs.'

I tried not to look too hard and eventually, after Brad had helped the chauffeur get out the cases and see the girls into the hotel and arranged for them to come over for dinner, he got back in the car looking rather grim. 'I wish they'd let me recommend a place,' he said, as we drove away from the 'hotel' they'd ended up in. 'It might be cheap but it's certainly not cheerful.'

Thank God, when we arrived the first things we were given were the most scrumptious plates of samosas and bits of paratha with breathtakingly delicious chutneys and dips of coconut, tamarind, mangoes and mint, so I was able to stuff myself to the gills as I hadn't eaten for about twenty-four hours.

Brad and Sharmie live in a little bungalow in the residential part of New Delhi. You can tell it's the posh part because all the houses nearby are surrounded by trees and it rather reminds me, the whole area, of Esher in Surrey – except for the stupendous heat, of course.

The bungalow had apparently been designed by Lutyens, the English architect who built half of New Delhi, so that's another reason it feels so familiar – and my room is delightfully cool, with a four-poster bed surrounded by a mosquito net. It's painted in a pale green colour, with modern copies of Indian miniatures on the walls, exquisitely executed with brushes that must have had only one hair. As a painter, I was baffled and impressed by their detail. The furniture is old colonial and my room looks out onto a patch of lawn.

There is a bathroom attached, and slices of pineapple and mango set out on my dressing table for me to snack on whenever I like.

'Dilip is our servant – well, butler really!' said Brad, as he showed me around. He pointed to a small hut in the garden, that I could only just make out from the glimmer of the security light at the gate. 'He lives there with his mother, father, wife and three children.'

'How do they fit in?' I asked.

'Heaven knows,' said Brad, rather dismissively, I thought. 'Anyway, he is incredibly lucky to have a position here – working for Americans is one of the best jobs that can be got – so he's very happy, and we never see the children.'

My eyes bulged rather. True, they may not actually have

bulged so that Brad would notice, but I could feel them bulging inside me, if that doesn't sound too odd. How could three children live in that tiny space and never be seen unless they were all rolled up together in a carpet and kept, drugged, in the dark?

'We don't have to lift a finger,' said Brad. 'Dilip does everything. He's absolutely marvellous. And his mother does the ironing and his father, who you've just met, is the chauffeur, and his wife, of course, does all the cooking, so everything's great. When we arrived we found they were paid a pittance, so we doubled their wages at once – and now they get $700 a month which is a fortune in India.'

My internal eyes were bulging fit to burst at this news, but of course I didn't like to say anything.

Later, I was about to unpack when there was a discreet knock on the door. Opening it, I found a man who I presumed, rightly, was Dilip himself.

'I will unpack for you, ma'am,' he said.

'Oh, how kind of you,' I said, 'but don't worry, I can do it myself.'

'No, no,' he said, looking rather distressed. 'Is my job. I will unpack for you, very good unpacking.'

Having got rid of him, I got halfway through my unpacking, spreading all my clothes on the bed before putting them away – and had hoiked out the oil painting of a plane tree that I'd done for Brad and Sharmie, to remind them of their travels. I also got out the manicure set I'd bought for Alice, but just as I was about to put my clothes away there was another knock on the door. It was Sharmie.

111

'I'm so sorry, Marie,' she said. 'But I'm afraid Dilip has just been to see me. He's very upset because you won't let him unpack. He's in tears, actually. He thinks you suspect him of being a thief, and anyway, he says that this is his job. Would you mind very much if he helped you? Well, when I say "help", I mean . . . if he could do it for you? Things are very different here, Marie. I'm sure you didn't mean to upset him. I should have explained.'

Of course I was horrified and said Dilip was welcome to do what he liked though secretly I'd have preferred to unpack myself, partly because I'd have known where I'd put everything, and partly because some of my clothes are pretty scuzzy, as Gene would say. For instance, I've got a particularly nice old silk skirt which has a very cobbled-together tear at the top, but no one notices it as I wear a top pulled down over it. Still, I had no wish to upset Dilip.

I asked if I could have a quick shower first, and once I came out of my room, all refreshed and feeling like a new woman in new clothes, I discovered to my horror that Dilip had been waiting all that time for me to emerge.

'I'm so sorry!' I blurted out. I was carrying the presents of the picture and the manicure set. 'I didn't mean to keep you waiting and it's terribly kind of you to unpack. I hope you didn't think I was rude!' Whereupon he seized my parcels and insisted on carrying them for me to the veranda, where everyone was sitting having a delicious cold mint drink and more eye-wateringly spicy home-made snacks.

'Golly, it makes one feel rather powerless, doesn't it?' I said as I sat down, thanking Dilip as he put the parcels down beside me. 'Don't you find it odd, being waited on hand and foot?'

'Oh, you get used to it very quickly,' said Sharmie, cheerfully.

'When we get back to the States, she won't even be able to make a bed!' said Brad.

'Make a bed?' said Sharmie, rolling her eyes. 'I can no longer even wash my own hair! How do you make a bed?'

And everyone laughed, though I felt slightly uncomfortable.

Later

The picture went down a storm and Alice was enchanted with the manicure set. I said I hoped she'd be allowed by the Dilips to apply her own nail varnish and she said 'Sure!' but I had a feeling that she wasn't getting quite as used as her parents to having everything done for her.

The girls, as everyone insists on calling them, arrived much later, having found it extremely difficult to get a taxi from their hotel, and the moment they came in the door I noticed that they looked rather desperate. Clearly no Dilips at the cheap and cheerful.

Penny hurled herself on a drink and gulped it down. And after exchanging a bit of chit-chat with the two Americans, it all came out.

'It's ghastly!' she said. 'The beds are just bits of old foam sitting on planks of wood. God knows how I'll sleep. And I saw a cockroach in the loo . . .'

'Loo!' said Marion. 'You can hardly call it a loo! And the water from the taps is brown-coloured . . .'

'And they said there were bathrooms, but they're just ordinary rooms with a plastic stool and a tap and a jug and you're meant to chuck cold water over yourself for a bath!'

'And there's only one light!'

'And you can hear the rats scuttling across the roof!'

'I even got an electric shock from the bathroom wall!'

'And there's no air-conditioning except these big fans going round which don't do anything!'

'And the man who runs it – you know what we caught him at?' said Penny, by now almost in tears. 'He goes around with an upturned broom trying to kill cockroaches who happen to come into the hall. He just squashes them with a horrible crunch!'

'And he actually said to me, with a creepy leer, that he'd show me paradise tonight,' said Marion, pop-eyed with horror. 'And somehow I don't think he intends to show me a view!'

'It's very real,' said Melanie, defensively. 'I mean, come on, this is India! You can't expect the Hilton!'

Brad immediately became decisive.

'No, you can't expect the Hilton but this is quite ridiculous!' he said, getting up. 'I'll get you somewhere else to stay, near here. Dilip!' he cried. 'Can your father collect these ladies' luggage from the hotel they're staying in – he knows where they are – and take them to Amitsa's . . . I'm sure he'll be able to put them up. Can you check they have rooms?'

'My father will be ready very soon. At present he is sleeping but I will wake him,' said Dilip. 'My father he say very bad place you stay. Not clean. Dirty people. Jungle people.'

114

'That's fine,' said Brad. 'As soon as he can.'

So poor Dilip's dad had to be woken from his sleep – at nine in the evening, no doubt shattered from a long day working – and drive off again. Poor bloke.

Dilip appeared with mosquito spray and more candles. A bit later we all filed into the dining room for another wonderful supper served, in complete silence, by Dilip's wife. She just shimmered in and out as if she were on wheels, rather like Jeeves, and at about 10.30 Dilip's dad reappeared with the luggage collected in the car, and took the girls off to a much nicer place down the road. By that time the cicadas were setting up a terrific racket, and the tree frogs were croaking like mad, and what sounded like a thousand dogs in the area howled and barked.

'Many dogs,' said Dilip's father when he dropped off the girls, looking at me and smiling benignly. 'In India we have many dogs.'

I think it might be the only thing he can say.

April 8

Woke to the most wonderful dawn chorus of tropical birds and chattering of monkeys – but slightly embarrassed to find that all my clothes had been ironed and folded perfectly and laid in neat piles in separate drawers. Made me feel rather strange – and particularly strange when I found there was no sign of the silk skirt I'd been eager to wear that day. Still, I can't say anything or Dilip will think I'm accusing him of stealing. No doubt he's thrown it away, thinking it was an old rag.

Brad and Sharmie had organised for all of us to have a tour of Delhi today, so Dilip's dad was ready and waiting to take me off to pick up the girls.

'Whatever you do,' said Sharmie as she waved me off, 'don't eat any of the street food! You'll get dysentery. It's not worth it. I did once and I was in bed for three weeks afterwards.'

Well, of course the Lutyens government buildings in New Delhi were absolutely fabulous – and Connaught Place was like Regent's Park but laid out in crescents and reeking of the British Raj. All particularly odd because in the arcades underneath, there were the poorest of shops selling spices and electrical equipment, all of which made the whole thing appear even more romantic and decadent.

The roads were jam-packed with traffic. There appeared to be no order at all and cars were constantly scraping against each other to get past. I felt terrified most of the time, since Dilip's dad just seemed to drive without any consideration for pedestrians or other cars.

'Very bad drivers in Delhi,' he said. 'Many deaths.'

'Well, if you'd go a bit slower, we'd appreciate it,' said Marion nervously from the back. 'You must remember we're from England.'

I got the feeling that he didn't like taking correction from women. He frowned and he put his foot even further down on the pedal. 'Driving different in India, ma'am,' he said. 'Fast driving good driving. Slow driving bad driving. Many deaths.'

So after that we gave up.

Finally, after much hauling us round the huge Birla temple

where we were each garlanded with strings of marigolds – much to my embarrassment as we were clearly expected to pay huge sums for them and none of us had any idea what was appropriate – we persuaded him to drive us to the Chandni Chowk, the big market in Delhi. After a lot of arguing he agreed to let us go it alone for the time being. He kept saying we'd prefer the Delhi Haat, but Melanie said that was ghastly and touristy and full of designer shops and McDonald's, and the Chandni Chowk was much more real, so we believed her. Dilip's dad was very unwilling to let us go, and insisted on having a time to pick us up, but we finally persuaded him and managed to get out into the boiling streets. And was it boiling.

'It must be over forty degrees,' said Marion, gasping. 'Why on earth did we come at this time of year?'

'Well, it's very India,' said Melanie. It seems to be the only thing she can say.

'He's probably going to tail us like we used to do with our children on their first weeks going to school on their own,' said Marion.

Melanie was consulting the map. It was a great mistake, because we were immediately surrounded by a crowd of people eager to help us, all tugging at our clothes and talking about carpet shops, and holding up little statues of elephant gods and saying: 'You like? You like? Very cheap. Arsenal fan? You like Arsenal? Or Chelsea?' Then they started chanting what sounded like 'Kimmun ewers! Kimmun ewers!' and it was only after a lot of discussion that Penny said: 'Do you think they mean "Come on you Rs?"'

Don't think they've quite got the message about it being blokes that tend to like football, not elderly English women, and Melanie kept saying 'Ham paise naheen hai hi', which she told us meant 'We have no money,' but it didn't make any difference.

After a while having fun looking at the silver, spice stalls, fabrics and clothes and getting the hang of shaking off the touts, we came to a rather pretty temple. I was dying to go in and the others seemed game so we walked up the steps. But before we could do anything we were sucked into a jogging line of men and women in saris who were all chanting. We tried to escape, but a woman in a sari pulled me back, smiling and pointing, so we bobbed on.

'Isn't this fun!' said Melanie and she pranced along. 'So India!'

'Hope we're not all in line to become Hindu nuns or something, and have to go through an initiation ceremony and are never seen again,' I said.

Marion looked a bit nervous but there was no way out, and now tablas started drumming and pipes were playing and we danced on and on, through pillared rooms and past golden shrines, until finally we shuddered to a halt and everyone put out their cupped hands. When we didn't do the same, the lady in the sari smilingly showed us what to do. 'Like this!' she said. And before we knew where we were, we'd passed some kind of monk who had poured a ladleful of the most disgusting-looking lentils into our cupped hands.

'Eat, eat!' said the lady with a sari, but of course with Sharmie's words ringing in my ears I just couldn't. Nor could anyone else. So we four just danced out of the temple, our hands full of lentil sludge, until we came to the street.

'What can we do now?' wailed Penny.

'Let's pour it into the gutter,' said Marion, chucking her lentils down.

'Oh, don't be so silly!' said Melanie. 'When in Rome! They can't do you any harm!' And she started dutifully sucking her way through the stuff. But even though she ate hers and the rest of us chucked our lentils, our hands were covered in grey gunge. Luckily we found a tap by a wall a little further down and were able to wash.

'But don't put your hands anywhere near your mouths,' added Marion, anxiously. 'That water's probably full of dysentery germs.'

We all felt a bit silly after that and were extremely glad to pile into the car where we wiped and laughed until we got home, utterly shattered.

Later

I was so embarrassed when I looked in my cupboard, before I went to bed, to find that my silk skirt had been returned to me, with no sign at all of the tear. Someone – and I only hoped it wasn't some wretched child who was ruining its eyesight – had done the most incredible piece of invisible mending on it: there was absolutely no evidence of any damage at all.

Even later

The girls came over for supper. We were, as usual, served plate after plate of curries, sauces, different types of rice, followed by a selection of Indian sweetmeats all, apparently, made by Dilip's wife. She must spend her entire life slaving in the kitchen. What wouldn't I give for someone like her back home, filling the house with yummy smells of cumin, black mustard seeds popping in ghee, cardamom and the tangy fragrance of freshly chopped coriander! We all drank lassi – a lovely cool yoghurt drink – except for Brad and Penny who, I noticed, was downing the cold beers rather too quickly for my liking.

Sitting back, after they'd gone, and having a chat with Sharmie on the veranda under the stars, I felt as if I might burst. I was worrying that I might nod off suffering from a mixture of jet lag (still present), a surfeit of food, mint tea and a pause in the conversation, when Sharmie dragged me back from incipient slumber by saying: 'There's something I must mention, Marie, I hope you don't mind.'

'What?' I said, springing into action like a guilty child. Oh, God, I did hope I hadn't offended yet another member of Dilip's family. I'd been so careful all day.

'Your Penny, is she okay?'

'Yes, fine,' I said. 'Why?'

'It seems to me,' said Sharmie, obviously choosing her words carefully, 'and don't get me wrong now – but she seems to be, er, drinking rather more than she used to? Or is it just the anxiety of being on holiday? I mean, I hope you don't mind my saying?'

Mind? I was relieved that someone else had noticed.

'No, you're right,' I replied, sighing. 'I've noticed it, too. I've got to say something to her. Thank you for reminding me. I'm glad you did. It's made me realise it's not just me who's worried. I must have it out with her. I promise. I will.'

April 9

Woke this morning having had another frightful nightmare. I say 'another' because I have been absolutely plagued with them since we arrived. I dreamt that I had arrived back at my house one evening to find a removal van outside it, and all my furniture and pictures being loaded into it by a very sinister-looking gang. When I said they couldn't do that, they just laughed at me and drove off. When I got inside, I found that my house had been half stripped. Only half, thank goodness, but when I looked around I found a note on the kitchen table saying they'd be back the following day to take the rest. I woke feeling absolutely terrified and completely violated.

I'd got up especially early because we were making a crack-of-dawn trip to Agra to see the Taj Mahal. On the way in the car, we saw a terrible accident by the side of the road, and Dilip's dad said that apparently five people had been killed the night before in a pile-up. Marion hid her eyes, but I couldn't help noticing that the mangled cars were still there, and blood was drying on the road. A stray dog was trying in vain to lick it off the tarmac.

Melanie started banging on about how death meant nothing

to Indians, they have a different view of it from us because of their religion. I got very stroppy and said I was certain that losing a loved one was just the same whether you were a Hindu, a Muslim, or good old C of E. She said rather loftily that I couldn't apply Western standards to India. After twenty minutes of wrangling, with me getting more and more het up and her saying I was a blinkered European, I realised that unless I shut up we'd be having this argument every day, so I did. But underneath I was buzzing with outrage.

Thank God I can at least sound off to David, who writes me constant emails and texts and says he's longing to have me back. He quite understands how sad it all is, and that I'm quite right to say that you can't just declare that people are perfectly happy living in oil drums on the sides of the streets and so on. He also said he'd been frightened I'd react like this which was partly why he hadn't been sure about my going. I so wish he were here! I know he'd be on my side. Penny is quite sympathetic, as is Marion, but Melanie is just revelling in the poverty and quaintness of it all, as if the whole thing is some kind of film set and after we've gone everyone goes off to have hearty meals in civilised houses with running water and proper beds.

Talking of film sets, the Taj Mahal – well, of course I was fully prepared to be disappointed. It's just the sort of thing I usually can't bear, built up to be one of the Wonders of the World and invariably failing to deliver. But once we'd got out of the car and I caught sight of it, with its white minarets, shimmering in the sun, my breath was taken away. There was something about the lake, and the perfect symmetry of the delicate towers around it and the glowing paleness of the marble against the deep blue sky that can't fail to make your heart leap – despite the fact that there is a virtual village of touts that you have to go through before you get into the grounds themselves. The building exudes a sense of peace, to an extent that I felt tears coming to my eyes and I could hardly breathe. It was the sort of architectural gem that makes me feel that there is actually a golden mean, a moral perfection about a work of art.

When Melanie shouted at me to come and look at the fish and started jabbering on about the history of the place, I almost felt like pushing her in the pond and had to leave her, just to be on my own with my feelings as I stared, spellbound by the dazzling proportions of the mausoleum.

It was sensationally beautiful.

April 10

While Penny, Marion and Melanie had gone off to watch some ceremony outside Delhi which involved chickens being sacrificed (thank you very much!) and then look in on Sharmie's orphanage, I finally took my courage in both hands and went off with my easel and paints (and, I have to confess, my camera) to look at trees.

Dilip's dad was deputed to transport me around to various sites and wait for me in the car while I painted and sketched. He drove like a maniac (scattering dogs, chickens and children) until, after hurtling down a dusty road, we arrived at a grim village just outside Delhi. My heart beating, I got out and set up my equipment in the middle of a market square, in front of a banyan tree. It was a great knotted affair with the most splendid roots, which looked like something out of an Arthur Rackham drawing. I had barely made myself comfortable when what seemed like the entire village appeared to watch me at work. To make it even worse, several boys started climbing the tree and striking poses and I was terrified they'd fall.

All the time I was sketching, crowds hovered at my shoulder pointing, touching my hair, smiling and bobbing, and though they all seemed friendly, I was a bit overwhelmed. I felt so self-conscious! Every mark I made on the paper was greeted with cries, either of dismay or applause, and it was so hot I had to keep wiping my wrist on a piece of tissue to stop the sweat getting on the paper. After about an hour I'd had enough and went back to the air-conditioned car for a rest. No sooner did I pick up again than a whole line of villagers, by means of signals and pointing, demanded that I paint their portraits. Because I felt so sorry for them, I tried, at the end of the session, to portray some of them in a group. The result was greeted with shrieks of laughter and delight.

Just before I left, I asked if I could take photographs of some of them, because they were dressed so prettily. After I'd snapped them, I was astonished when several of them produced phones and demanded to take a photograph of me!

I suppose I was a rather strange-looking sight in their village, with my black tights (never take them off, however hot!) and old Vivienne Westwood skirt!

Dilip's dad was clearly quite appalled by my taking any time over them, saying they were 'dirty village people'.

'Jungle people,' he added, disgustedly, as we started on the journey back.

Easy to disapprove, but it's only comparatively affluent people – like we privileged Westerners who are so distant from the 'dirty village people' – who have the luxury of being able to see them as decent human beings.

April 11

Saved by the bell! While I was out painting trees, Marion, Penny and Melanie had all been taken to see Sharmie's orphanage just outside Delhi. I say 'Sharmie's orphanage' – it's the one that she has a special interest in. The girls came back absolutely grey-faced at the sights they'd seen, and Marion was in tears.

I don't think I can actually bear to write down some of what they described. As I'm the sort of person who would break into a stranger's house simply to water a dying plant if I'd glimpsed it wilting through the window, I think I would have had a nervous breakdown. It was bad enough seeing the pictures they showed me. The wards were filthy and some of the children were chained to the walls. Rows and rows of abandoned babies lie in cots and are rarely picked up. When

VIRGINIA IRONSIDE

the girls left, three of the children clung on to them and begged to be taken home with them.

Sharmie is trying to raise funds for better treatment but it's difficult because the people who run the orphanage are very hardened to the situation. When you take toys in, the staff tend to put them in cupboards. Sharmie is trying to put in place a policy whereby as many children as possible are adopted into family homes, and she's been pretty successful so far. She's also instigated a plan that no new children should be accepted until every possible chance of them being looked after by their families has been exhausted. As a result, the intake is getting smaller and it will, if Sharmie's got anything to do with it, eventually close down completely. The problem is that the people who run the orphanage obviously don't like their business being taken away, so she has to compensate them. But with extra money she estimates they can close the whole orphanage down in two years and turn it, instead, into an agency that rehouses unwanted children into family homes. But it's the 'extra money' that's the problem.

'We must do something!' said Marion, her normally happy face contorted with anxiety at what she'd witnessed. 'I want to get back home as soon as possible and I'll do anything – fundraise, sell things. Tim and I will do our utmost, Sharmie, I promise.'

'Perhaps you could sell my tree paintings for something,' I suggested. 'I mean, I know you want them, but you've got a lot of my trees already.'

'Why don't you get them reproduced as a calendar? We

could sell the calendars in England. Then you can keep the paintings but still make something out of them,' said Penny.

We were sitting on the veranda under the pretty red and blue awning, and at last there seemed to be a proper purpose to our all being here together. We toasted each other in lassi – Penny soon moved on to beer – and resolved to make it our mission to raise funds when we get back to England.

Later
Text from Terry saying pigeon is fine but still not going any-where, and that he's fixed the cupboard door in the kitchen that always sticks, and the burglar alarm has only gone off once, but he seems to have got the hang of the problem.

Relief!

Even later
Just woke from terrible dream that Terry and Robin had cut down all the trees in my garden and had made a huge bonfire and were dancing around it. To make things worse, they had roasted the pigeon and were eating it, and they'd got Pouncer in a cage waiting to be next on the spit.

April 12

I've spent the last couple of days solidly painting trees, which has been absolutely brilliant except that I am absolutely cov-ered in mosquito bites. However much DEET I apply, it doesn't seem to make any difference. Alice came with me one day and she is quite a nice little artist – but she did seem to be particularly anxious when the villagers started clustering round. She made a retreat to the car, leaving me to soldier on alone. Can't really blame her, being only eight years old. No doubt she's had the daylights scared out of her by her over-anxious American parents.

Yesterday Melanie's son came to take her away to Kerala, and Melanie brought him round proudly to introduce us. I was expecting a neurotic lunatic – couldn't imagine anyone who'd been brought up by Melanie to be remotely sane – but instead he seemed like a perfectly normal guy. He runs some kind of phone-answering network, training Indians to answer calls from London and give the illusion that they're actually in Britain and not five thousand miles away. He says he instructs them to say: 'And what about this weather!' And it always reassures the people at the other end, whatever weather they're having.

Marion's left, too, to go back to London – she felt she couldn't leave Tim for too long – and, since she's a sensitive soul, I could see that she'd rather had her fill of India. We had to persuade her not to pay thousands of pounds to take back a stray dog, who seemed to have adopted her. The vet and quarantine bill would have been astronomical. Luckily Sharmie and Brad promised to keep an eye on it, but to be honest I'm not sure they'll do anything about it.

So it's just me and Penny left, and we're off to Goa – on our own! – tonight.

April 15 night

It was horrible saying goodbye to Brad and Sharmie. They'd looked after us so well, and we've been so sheltered from the outside world that it's frightening to be off on our own. We've even grown rather fond of Dilip and his family – I managed to have a conversation in sign language with his wife at one point – and gave them a gigantic tip when we left.

'Come again,' said Brad, 'if we're still here! We loved having you!'

'You must come and stay with me in London if you're over,' I said. 'I'm sure I can squeeze you all in!'

Sharmie and I became a bit tearful as we said goodbye and Alice showed me her nails that she'd finished at last – all kinds of brilliant patterns on each one. I remembered dressing her as a princess when she was little, and was glad to see she still enjoyed showing off her girlish prettiness.

'Oh dear,' said Penny, as we waved goodbye to Dilip's dad at the airport. 'Hope we're doing the right thing.'

On the plane down to Goa we both agreed we'd had enough of India. I know we've only been away ten days, but it's such an intense experience, I hardly think I can cope with any more of it. Quite honestly, being in India is like having *Daily Rant* headlines blaring out at you every minute for twenty-four hours of the day. As far as I'm concerned it's just horror, horror and more horror, and makes me, at least, feel permanently guilty that I live such an incredibly pampered life in London. Melanie says that it's the Indian way of life, that they're used to poverty and disease and this is what's so wonderful about the Indian people, they're so fatalistic, but Penny and I think she's living in a dream world. Who would want to live like that when they can see people driving around in fast cars and having wonderful lives on Western television programmes and the internet? At least, though, they do all seem to have mobile phones. Not sure that that makes things any better, though.

We've been assured that Goa is blissful, however, full of gorgeous golden beaches and nothing like India, but, well, it *is* India . . . so how can it not be like India at all?

April 19

It's not like India! It's like Russia! We've arrived in Mandrem, which is a weird kind of hippy beach resort, and all the signposts are in Russian and the place is packed with oligarchs and oligarchs' beautiful daughters. Or perhaps they're mistresses. Or prostitutes. We can't work it out at all.

There aren't nearly so many beggars here, which is a relief, but everywhere is curiously dirty – there's rubbish all over the streets and in the gutters. But the beaches are, it has to be said, absolutely amazing.

We're staying in a wooden beach hut, which is part of a posh hotel complex. We go to a communal breakfast place in the open air every morning and help ourselves to the most amazing dishes of papaya, mango, kiwi fruit . . . as well as wonderful fruit drinks and even delicious coffee. Some of the guests are rich hippies from around the world – Australia, the US, Holland – and the others are these rich Russians. It's all very strange.

Anyway, after a day's lazing about and lying on the beach, we decided to go and see if we could find Sandra.

We started off by asking at the hotel reception. Was there a local tyre shop with someone called Ali working in it? But we drew a complete blank. So we took a taxi – a baked bean can on wheels known as a tuk-tuk, powered by a sputtering engine which spewed black smoke from the back – and headed for town.

We managed to enquire in four tyre shops – smelly, oily places all squished together in the same part of town – until I remembered that David had said it was a tyre shop by the beach and that Ali sold bits of jewellery as well. Language was a problem but finally I drew a picture of a man banging a tyre and selling necklaces and jewellery on the beach and yelled, over the sound of tyre rims being banged and wrecked cars being wheeled in and out, 'Ali!'

Finally one man – desperately thin and bare-chested, covered with oil, with white, staring eyes, came up to us and smiled charmingly. Yes, he knew him. 'Ali,' he said. 'Ali.' Then he looked serious and shook his head. 'No Ali. Ali gone.'

'Baby?' I said. 'Mother.'

'Baby, mother, yes.' And he gave us the name of a street not far from the hotel we were staying at. By heaping paper money into his hand we persuaded him to come with us in a tuk-tuk to drop us off at the right place, and when we arrived, he dropped us off but then he insisted on walking back, keeping the return fare, presumably for himself.

'I wonder what he meant by "No Ali",' I said to Penny. 'Surely he can't have done a runner?'

'I'd do a runner if I lived here,' said Penny, surveying the dusty street, full of concrete shacks. 'What a dump.'

It was a very modest residence, down a dirty track. The door was answered by a rather grim-looking Muslim woman, who looked like an Indian version of Sheila the Dealer.

'No English girl,' she said firmly. 'No baby. No Ali.'

As we were arguing with her, a young woman appeared at her shoulder. She started talking to her mother in Hindi and they appeared to be arguing. Far away I could hear a baby crying.

'There is a baby here!' I said rather sharply. 'Do you know where Sandra is?' I asked the girl. 'What's going on?'

'No baby, no baby!' said the mother, trying to shut the door on us.

'My baby, my baby!' said the girl. 'Is my baby!'

Before the door was slammed on us, I just managed to yell out the name of our hotel, saying we were there if they wanted to be in touch. Then we trailed back, feeling very sad and gloomy.

'There was a baby,' said Penny, firmly. 'And it wasn't that girl's. She was hiding something.'

'I know,' I said. 'But I wonder where Ali is? Sandra's husband? Why were they so against us seeing her? We're only visiting to see she's okay.'

Turning down a track, we made a detour to get away from

the dusty slum we'd come from, to walk back to our hotel along the beach. It was a complete contrast. There was silence as we scuffed along the sand. Dusk had already come – it comes down so quickly here, like a curtain dropping, accompanied by the most amazing purple and blues of the changing sky – and stars were starting to appear. We heard the sound of young boys shouting as they splashed in the warm water in the gathering darkness. Far away there were the wails of Indian pipes. The smell of fish and hot spices grilling wafted through the air. I kicked aside one of the many plastic bags that were piling up in the shallows.

'Perhaps she's not okay,' said Penny.

April 20

'So what are we going to do?' I said to Penny, as we lay on the beach. She'd insisted on smearing me with sun cream even though I assured her that I never burn. Hate the horrid white, lardy stuff. 'I don't fancy a midnight raid on the house, do you?'

'I suppose we'll have to go back and just snoop around,' Penny said, rather doubtfully. One of the hotel's many servants passed by and she ordered a cocktail, even though it was only midday.

'Look, Penny,' I said, filled with a sudden courage to tackle her on the subject. 'I'm sorry to nag, but aren't you rather overdoing the alcohol? I hate to sound like a fussing mother, but honestly, it's not just me who's noticed. You are drinking an awful lot these days. I know it's nothing to do with me, but I'm worried about you.'

'Oh, don't worry,' said Penny. 'I know I'm drinking more than I used to. I'm trying to cut down, honestly. I don't know what it is, but I just feel desperate for a drink most of the time! It kind of calms me down.'

'But don't you think that if you stopped for a couple of months, you might feel calmer anyway?' I suggested. 'I mean, alcohol can relax you, but it can also make you feel terribly edgy.'

'I'll see how I go with cutting down,' said Penny. 'To be honest, it's just that I get so lonely sometimes, and I feel life's so pointless. A drink makes everything more bearable.'

'You need something to occupy you,' I said. 'Perhaps when we get back to London and start trying to raise money for the orphanage you'll feel there's more point. I know I will.'

'It's like I've said before,' said Penny. 'Everyone seems to have someone and I don't. I know not everyone needs a man, but I think I'm one of those people who just does. Yet every man I'm interested in seems to run a mile. It's a vicious circle. I'm sure I exude a kind of psychic desperateness and they flee. I'm sure if I felt secure, the psychic desperateness would go. I wish I appeared more happy and self-contained. Perhaps I should change my name to Penni with an "i" to make myself appear more fun-loving?'

'Don't do that,' I said. 'You'll be adding smiley faces to your emails at this rate. God, no. You don't want to be a Penni. Like Jenni or Judi or Jodi or Nikki. Think if I were called Mari? You wouldn't have me as a friend, would you?'

'No, I wouldn't,' said Penny. 'It's the same sort of pose I used to affect in the sixties. If I wore a rose in my hair I thought people would think I was interesting.'

'Me too,' I said ruefully, remembering the puffy *Jules et Jim* hat I used to wear in the hope that I would look fascinating and kookie.

We were chattering along like this, looking at our books occasionally – I've moved on from the Indian mutiny book (not a very tactful choice for here anyway) and am rereading *Midnight in the Garden of Good and Evil*, a brilliant book about Savannah, Georgia in the US. I read it only ten years ago, and yet I can't remember a word of it. It's just as good the second time round.

Anyway, we were just mooching, when Penny sat up and stared around.

'I thought I heard someone calling!' she said, adjusting her sunhat and looking out across the beach. I hitched myself up on one elbow and stared across the sand.

And there, in the distance, was a figure, running towards us. As far as I could see, it was a girl, clutching a bundle, and as she got close, I realised.

'It's Sandra!' I said to Penny. We both jumped to our feet and hurried towards her. The baby was yelling its head off and Sandra was crying, too. She rushed into our arms and then looked behind her fearfully.

'I'm sure they'll come after me!' she said. 'Here's my passport – take it! I've only just managed to get hold of it, and that's what they're after. Where can we go?'

We hustled her into the shade of the hotel veranda, and sat her down.

Penny went back to collect our things from the beach, while I tried to calm Sandra. I put my arm round her shoulder, and found a tissue to dry her tears. Then I took the baby on my knee and started jumping him up and down, and soon he was smiling and giggling and pulling my hair.

Sandra managed to gulp out the story of what had been happening.

'My husband, Ali, died a couple of months ago – he was crushed under a car he was repairing. I wanted to come back home, but the family wouldn't have any of it. They wanted to keep my son, Gangi, here. They said I could go back, but Gangi was theirs. So I've been kept a virtual prisoner and I haven't been allowed to go out, except with one of the family. They've even taken away my mobile . . .' Here she broke down again. 'Oh, Marie, I couldn't believe it when I heard your voice yesterday. I managed somehow to give them the slip today and here I am. What can we do? How can we stop them coming and taking Gangi away? He's not on my passport . . .'

'We'll get hold of David and he'll sort everything out with the British consul,' I said, decisively. I had no idea whether this might be possible, but there was no point in worrying her. 'You'll be safe here. I'll explain everything to the hotel and they won't let anyone come to take Gangi away. I'll get you a room – no, you'd better share mine . . .'

And that was how I now find myself stuck in this wretched hotel with David's ex-squeeze, her child, and Penny who seems to be taking advantage of the cheap cocktails as if there were no tomorrow.

April 21

God, what a nightmare! I just seem to spend my entire time on the phone to David. He has been totally AMAZING, I must say. He's been in touch with the British consul and with Brad and Sharmie, who are somehow getting Gangi's passport to us from Delhi – God knows how they've managed to rush everything through – and we're all booked on the flight back to London in three days' time. I can't wait to get away from this horrible place. Far from R and R, we're all creeping about in disguise, in case Sandra's mother-in-law sends Ali's brothers over to kidnap the baby. We've decided it's too risky to go out onto the beach. Penny goes off and suns herself and visits the bar but I feel I should stay with Sandra to keep her safe.

But I have to say that Gangi is absolutely adorable. He reminds me so much of Gene when he was a baby that I'm quite goofy over him. He has lovely pale brown arms and tiny brown hands and brown fingers, his skin is like silk and he has a smile that makes you melt.

But the result is I hardly get any sleep, and when I do I continue to get the most awful nightmares. Last night I dreamt that Penny was keeping a poodle in a big bottle and it was getting no exercise and you could hear it whimpering and see it dying through the glass.

'You were crying in your sleep,' said Sandra yesterday morning, as she fed Gangi. 'Are you okay?'

What's most odd is that Sandra is completely kitted out in

my things, as all her Western clothes were taken away from her. Sitting on the side of her bed, she looks like a young version of me. It's like one of those ghastly films that Marion and Tim are so often trying to get me to see at the art house cinema in Notting Hill Gate. Really eerie.

And the fact that she, too, had lived with David, for a while at least, makes the whole scenario even more odd. I've never really thought of her as a person until now. Years ago she was just David's new squeeze, and I was very relieved, after we got divorced, that he found her so quickly. I was pretty sure it wouldn't last for ever, and she was always pleasant enough when we met – but so young I always thought of her more as a daughter than a rival.

'I'm plagued by nightmares,' I said. 'I dread going to sleep these days.'

'You're not taking Lariam, are you?' said Sandra, looking up in horror.

'Yes, as it happens, I am,' I said. 'It's for malaria.'

'Not Lariam!' repeated Sandra, wide-eyed. 'You've got to stop taking it at once! That's what's causing your nightmares. You know they've driven some people completely mad, those pills. For God's sake, don't take any more.'

Feeling very guilty, because I know you're meant to take them even after you get home, I chucked the rest down the lavatory and crossed my fingers I wouldn't get malaria. Very irresponsible, I know, but I can't stand being tortured by these dreams any more.

Later

Just had a text from Robin. Apparently everything's cool back at the ranch. Terry's grown very attached to the pigeon and is round every day mowing the lawn or sorting out the garden, which is brilliant. The only bad news is that Pouncer's not too hot. Robin's tried some healing on him, but it doesn't seem to have worked.

Texted right back and insisted that though 'healing very nice, thank you', could he please take Pouncer to the vet at once. I gave him the address and phone number and said I'd pay.

April 25

Finally on the plane! The last few days have been complete hell. I've felt really trapped – a prisoner – in the room with Sandra, as I didn't like to leave her on her own. Gangi has been crying all night and I haven't had a wink of sleep. Sandra has been crying, thinking about Ali, and despite stopping the Lariam I still have the ghastly dreams – presumably because the wretched drug is still in my system. A couple of days ago I dreamed that Gene had been kidnapped by ISIS terrorists and they were threatening to cut off his feet, ears, eyes and everything, bit by bit, and show it all on video. Woke crying myself at that point. Again.

Penny has been getting browner and browner and drunker and drunker. I made a chart of the hours left before we got on the plane and we solemnly ticked them off one by one.

Brilliant reunion at the airport with Melanie, who was in the middle of a tearful farewell to her son, but otherwise she seemed extremely well and happy. Slightly unpleasant moment at the airport when some guy, presumably one of Ali's brothers, waylaid us and tried to talk to Sandra and persuade her to stay, but otherwise it all passed without incident, thank God. So far on the plane Gangi has been an utter angel and we all feel very excited and relieved to be going home!

Later on plane

Can't help it, but am amused to see Melanie endlessly staggering up the aisle to go to the loo. She says she's got a tummy upset. I bet it's dysentery! That'll teach her to say India is so safe and wonderful and we should eat everything and not fuss! The revenge of those lentils, no doubt!

April 27, night

Golly! Never have I been so relieved to get back to see the good old cloudy skies of England. The greyness was such a relief after the glaring, gruelling days of Goa. It wasn't that warm either, definitely nippy, but it all felt like a refreshing salvation for us. Seeing David at the barrier was wonderful, too, though I politely allowed Sandra to rush into his arms first, because I thought she needed more comfort than me. I know she's no threat now. As for the M4 coming home – a road I usually regard as one of the eyesores of the English landscape, edged as it is with the most hideous examples of contemporary architecture if indeed it can be dignified with the name 'architecture' – it seemed familiar and welcoming to me.

I noticed David was slightly miffed to discover that Robin, too, had slogged down to greet us, by train. Of course David was obliged to offer him a lift back with us. As there wasn't room for all of us in the car, David seemed delighted to force Robin into the dog cage at the back, where he had to crouch until we arrived at Shepherd's Bush.

Gangi poked his tiny fingers at Robin through the bars and seemed utterly enchanted by him – as did Sandra, I noticed, who kept saying: 'David, are you sure Robin's okay? I could swap places with him. I'm worried he'll do something to his back, squashed up like that!'

David just revved the engine and drove on impassively.

I have to say, fond as I am of Sandra and the baby, it'll be great to have some time on my own. David's whisking them straight home where he's found some accommodation for them in Bath. But first they'll stay in the farmhouse to get sorted.

Got back just in time to see the last of the cherry blossom in the streets round my home, and the house seemed in perfect nick. Funny how pretty it always looks when I've been away for a time. It makes me realise how lucky I am to live in such a charming place.

MAY

May 1

Golly, am I glad to be back in my own house! And in my own country! Everything that seemed grim about Shepherd's Bush before I went now seems absolutely magical. Huge friendly rubbish collectors hoovering up all the yuck day and night; fat people instead of thin people; no one begging. And on top of that, Waitrose, my own bed, rain, (which is bucketing down), the garden, the stocks just coming out, being able to iron my own clothes and make my own cups of tea, Pouncer . . .

Oh, dear! Pouncer! Robin was right – he's not well, and I don't think he's been improved by Robin putting him on a vegetarian diet. The moment I could get to the shops, I got him thin strips of raw chicken, which he absolutely adores. But after a meal, he just slinks to a corner and curls up. And he purrs. Having always thought that purring is the sign of a contented cat, I've now discovered, thanks to the *Daily Rant*, that purring is actually a way cats in pain comfort themselves. In other words, purring is a sign of great discomfort.

Talking of the *Daily Rant*, I forgot to cancel it so there were twenty-one days of horrible news all piled up, waiting to leap on me and make me feel ghastly. Half-closing my eyes so as not to be seduced by any catastrophic revelations, I tied them up in four separate bundles and put them out for the bin men. No doubt I'll live but let's hope the bin men don't glance at them by mistake. To read twenty-one *Daily Rant*s all in one go would make most people fit to be hauled off in a straitjacket.

I'm still suffering terribly from jet lag but at least I'm well. Melanie put her head over the wall at the front today, looking like one of those sadhus covered in ash she tells me she made friends with in India.

'It is dysentery,' she said. 'So don't come near me! I'm on super-strength antibiotics.'

When I offered to make her some light soup, she was extremely grateful, so I expect I'll be providing for her for the next few days. Poor girl. She's going to be seventy next birthday (as indeed am I). Will we be able to call ourselves 'girls' even in joke? There must come a limit.

Jack said he'd bring Gene over at half-term on May 17, and I was just starting to wallow in the pleasure of seeing them again when he rang back and said sorry, he'd got football and a party, and then a painting course, so maybe 'another time'.

Felt totally crushed and disappointed though naturally didn't say so on the phone.

'It's fine!' I chirped happily. 'Any time!'

One of the problems is that I live so far away from them. If only I could be nearer I could pop over or they could pop over. It's such a production getting from here across the river to Brixton.

Wonder if I shouldn't think about moving nearer to them? It's certainly an idea . . .

Later

Frightfully worried about the pigeon. He just sits on this pipe and doesn't move or fly except when he comes down to the bathroom window for food. He stares at the wall all day, like one of those sad single suicidal men I keep reading about, who just look at the internet from dawn to dusk. My heart aches for him. I wish he'd go away. I wish he'd never arrived on my roof. I wish he'd be happy. I wish he'd die.

Even later

So good, too, to be alone for a while. I can't do twenty-one days of being with other people all the time. It's exhausting.

Just watched a documentary on why people are fat. Apparently it's nothing to do with greed – they can't help it. Put them on a diet and get them down to a normal weight feeding them the correct number of calories and they can exist, true. But if you give them a brain scan they're in a constant state of near-starvation. Feel very bad about jeering at fat people in the past, and condemning them for having no self-control.

May 3

David rang to say he was coming up to stay for a few days.

'I must see you!' he said rather wildly. 'I missed you so much while you were away!'

Considering it was only three weeks, I think it's a bit odd that he's missed me quite so much. After all, we've been divorced for at least twenty years and there were periods when we weren't in touch for months! Anyway, he's settled Sandra in and everything's fine. The whole village is besotted with little Gangi, so let's hope she can sort herself out.

Asked David to give me her new address because, oddly, Robin has been nagging me for it. He says he needs her email to tell her about some amazing natural cure for babies' eczema, not that Gangi ever had eczema as far as I know.

Maybe he fancies her? Who knows.

Later

Marion and Tim came over tonight to talk about setting up a bric-a-brac stall in the market in aid of the Indian orphanage.

Melanie, who seems slightly better, insisted on coming over later to give us a slide show of all her Indian pics. Which was good because it got me out of going round to Marion's. I just couldn't face the usual supper of halved barely ripe tomatoes, coleslaw from a Sainsbury's tub and sinister slices of something called, mysteriously, a 'chicken roll' (what do they do to the poor birds?) topped off with Hellman's mayonnaise. So I persuaded them round here and made a delicious dish of smoked haddock on a bed of spinach in a creamy sauce. Tim, rather annoyingly, had three helpings which put paid to my idea of freezing it and keeping it for supper for Penny later in the week.

Anyway, he's going to ask around if there's anywhere we can set up a 'pop-up shop' which is a shop between lets. Excellent idea. The idea is to collect clothes, toys, crockery, whatever from local residents and sell the stuff in the market. A kind of permanent car-boot sale. Marion says she's going to put notes through everyone's doors and get them to deliver all their stuff here, because I've got a bigger hall than hers. Oh Lord. I'll just have to grit my teeth. All in a good cause.

Melanie, looking whey-faced, did pop round later, by which time we were all exhausted and not really up to watching an interminable slide show. But luckily it turned out that she had, unsurprisingly, kept her camera in 'selfie' mode the entire time, so she had taken a hundred pictures of herself taking a picture, so it was all over very quickly.

May 4

This afternoon I took Pouncer to the vet in his cat basket. When I say I took Pouncer to the vet in his cat basket, I mean, of course, that I took Pouncer in his cat basket to the vet. Pouncer would far prefer it to be the vet in his cat basket because the moment he hears the rustle of the wicker, he goes into panic mode, however ill he's feeling. He can be lolling around looking like *The Death of Chatterton*, but the merest sound of the cat basket and not only has he shot off, but he's managed to squeeze himself into half his normal size and wedge himself under the lowest sofa in the room. When I look, all I can see are two saucer-like eyes peering out at me accusingly.

With the help of Robin and a broom handle I managed to get him out and somehow put him into the cat basket. Eventually I heaved it into the back of the car and off we went.

Poor old Pouncer. He yowled all the way there. The minute we got into the vet's waiting room – I go to rather a posh one in Notting Hill which smells of pet disinfectant – he went rigid with fear. More so than usual, because two sobbing gay men were sitting opposite us holding hands and hanging on to the most enormous drooling, pointed-toothed mastiff called, apparently, Flora. Far from behaving like a child model from a Victorian advertisement for Pears Soap – which the name suggests – you could sense the hostility in her bared teeth, and smell her evil breath from across the room.

Once they'd emerged from the consultation, looking, I was glad to say, happier than when they went in, I took the basket and popped it onto the vet's table. Now the problem was coaxing Pouncer out of the wretched thing. It was like getting tomato ketchup out of a bottle. Eventually the vet put in his hand and hauled him out.

'Kidney problems,' he said, after giving him the once-over. 'Let's see, he's how old . . . yes, fifteen. I'm afraid this does happen to old cats. Is he soiling the house?'

I had to say that indeed he had 'soiled the house', as the vet so delicately put it, a couple of times.

He gave me some pills and told me to return in a month. 'I'm afraid you'll have to resign yourself – this old man is in his autumn years,' he said. I felt very sad, but in a way I've always known Pouncer couldn't last for ever.

As for the pigeon, the vet told me he would probably leave when he'd grown into adulthood – another couple of months, he thought – and then he'd be bursting with testosterone and desperate to find Miss Right and reproduce.

The nurse charged me £120.

When I got back, I was just planting some nicotiana in the front garden and rose from a bending position when a little boy, wearing a round white hat on his head, smiled at me over the wall.

'I didn't see you there!' he said. He was obviously on his way to the local mosque. 'What are you doing?'

'Just planting some plants,' I said. 'And hello to you, too!'

'Is there anything I can help you with?' he asked.

'No, darling, but thank you so much,' I said. I had never seen this boy before in my life.

He ran on, and a few minutes later an elderly Muslim man came shuffling down the street.

'Was that your son?' I asked, pointing.

'No, not son, my . . .'

'Grandson!' I said. 'Well, he's a charmer!' Then I realised he couldn't understand most of what I said. So I made a thumbs-up sign and smiled and blew a kiss after the boy.

'Lovely boy!' I said.

The old man beamed. 'Good boy!' he said, and nodded and went on.

Went indoors smiling, feeling that the area is full of goodness and kindness. How can I possibly be thinking of moving?

May 5

David came up today.

It was lovely to see him, but I was in the middle of ringing up estate agents when he arrived and didn't have much time to say hello. I signalled him to go upstairs and make himself at home and then come down and have a drink, but he insisted on coming over and giving me a huge hug while I was on the phone.

I pushed him away, rather crossly. Honestly, he just doesn't know when to be affectionate and when to keep his distance. Even more maddeningly, he insisted on sitting there listening to my phone call, and of course was horrified when I told him what I was thinking of doing – all of which he'd deduced from listening in.

'But you can't move!' he said. 'Why didn't you tell me? Are you getting a smaller house? Will there be room for me?'

'Of course there'll be room for you, you old idiot,' I said.

He looked a bit sulky, I thought.

'I think that with such a big thing you might have asked me first.'

'God, you don't ask me about your flood defences,' I said.

'Anyway, I'm only putting out feelers. I'm not actually moving. I'm just seeing the lie of the land. Don't worry. I'll probably not go anywhere. Now, where are we going for supper? I'm looking forward to it!' I added, trying to change the mood.

May 6

Oh, God! What an evening!

We'd gone round the corner where a posh restaurant has sprung up next to the mosque, packed with the young lawyers and bankers who are moving into the area, fleeing from the high prices in Notting Hill next door. I know the owner, and we had a nice chat with him about whether the duck breasts were nicer than the lamb shanks.

'I can't tell you how grateful I am to you for getting Sandra out of that dreadful situation, darling,' said David.

'I couldn't have done it without you pulling all those strings at the British High Commission and organising everything,' I said.

'Yes, we make a good team, don't we?'

'We do,' I said, and I leaned over and touched his hand.

'You know I love you, don't you?' he said.

'Of course I do,' I said, but slightly briskly, because to be honest we've been through so much together there's hardly any point in saying it any more. 'And you know I love you too.' And I took a helping of roasted cauliflower with almonds.

'Darling, I've been thinking,' said David, as he poured me out a glass of wine before tucking into his steak. 'You know when you were in India, I missed you so much. And I was wondering. What do you think? I don't know how to put this. But have you ever thought what it might be like to get married again?'

I practically choked on my cauliflower. I've been aware he was getting rather closer to me than I am to him, but I thought it was the usual old sentimental male thing. They're always much more soppy than women in affairs of the heart, I find, when you get down to it. But I wasn't expecting this!

'Get married again!' I heard myself saying, when I'd swallowed the cauliflower. 'You must be joking!'

Not the kindest thing to say, I know, but I was so taken aback and it just popped out.

'I mean, thank you very much, darling, and I take it as a huge compliment, but I don't think we should rock the boat, really, do you? I mean, we've been there, done that, got the T-shirt, and we've been through a lot together. Now we've got a really brilliant situation with seeing each other lots, and at the same time not on top of one another. Surely to get married again would just be like it was before? I don't want to break up with you, sweetie,' I said, trying to be soft. 'And I like things just as they are.'

David looked absolutely crushed. He pushed his plate away from him, and wiped his lips with his napkin rather nervously.

'I thought you might say that,' he said, sighing. 'Well, I don't like things as they are. I don't know where I am.'

It was as if the normal situation – man not wanting to commit, woman desperate to – was reversed.

'Well, I know where you are and you know where you are, really. I mean, you're not planning to run off with anyone, are you?' I asked, knowing the answer would be 'no'.

'Of course not. But all the time you were in India, I kept worrying you might find some gorgeous old maharajah and then I'd lose you, darling, and it was torture . . .' He reached over to hold my hand.

'Oh, tosh,' I said.

'What?' said David.

'I said "tosh"!' I said, loudly, starting to feel irritated. 'Look, for God's sake, get a hearing aid. We can't even have a conversation about getting married or not because you're so deaf!'

When we got back, David said he was going to sleep on the sofa, and I said don't be silly, and he said he didn't feel like making love and I said he was mad and we ended up in bed, but afterwards he got on one elbow and stared at me mournfully and stroked my face.

'Darling,' he said in a very sad voice, and I said, 'Hey, what's all this . . . nothing's changed.' He said, 'Are you sure it hasn't?' Then we went to sleep.

This morning he got up and brought me a cup of tea as usual, and we laughed over the *Daily Rant* headline: 'Cult leader sold his victims' flesh in pies'. But there was still a terrible air of depression hanging around like fog. I felt horribly guilty, and David shuffled around like Pouncer knowing he's got to go to the vet. I had no idea that my reaction would upset him so much. I thought we'd just have another glass of wine and have a good laugh at the idea. But I was really thrown when he hardly kissed me goodbye, just gave me a hug and was off far earlier than usual.

Not sure why I feel so terrible. Probably because I realise I've hurt him so deeply, and yet there is nothing I can do to put it right.

I don't want to get married again. Ever. And that's the truth. I can't pretend I do just to make everything all right for David. But I do hope it doesn't mean I don't see so much of him.

God! Relationships! Why do we have them? Why do we need them? Sometimes I think I'd be happier living as a hermit on a remote island with no one to relate to except the wind and the seagulls. Though no doubt, being me, I'd find a seagull who I'd think didn't like me and I'd get all upset about that.

Talking of which, the poor old pigeon is looking so unhappy and bedraggled in all this rain. I dutifully put out his food, but other pigeons have caught on to this now, and they all crowd round it before my poor pigeon gets a look-in.

May 9

Melanie has just posted this on her Facebook page: 'Expect nothing and then anything you receive is a blessing.' Probably a hint for me to pop over with some more soup. Must check to see how she is.

Later

Rang up some estate agents to get them to come over and give me a valuation. They seemed rather over-eager, some desperate to meet straight away. No doubt they're gagging for a commission.

Later still

Had Penny over to supper and found myself sounding quite indignant as I told her about David and what he'd said.

'God, I'd have said "yes" at once!' she said, as she helped me clear away. 'You're so lucky! A marriage proposal at sixty-nine! You jammy bugger!'

I winced. I always hate that expression. 'Well, it's only jammy if the person who's proposing is someone you want to marry, and one thing I don't want to do is marry David,' I said, rather cruelly. 'It would be asking for trouble. It would be like *Groundhog Day*. We'd then be finding ourselves getting divorced all over again, and it would be just as painful the second time round, if not more so.'

Penny put her arms round me as I realised I was starting to sound tearful. 'Whatever you say. I'm sure you're right,' she said. 'Now, how can we cheer you up? Didn't you say you'd bought a couple of ecstasy tablets from Terry? Wouldn't now be the time to give them a whirl? They're meant to make you happy!'

'Good idea!' I said, jumping to my feet and rushing upstairs to find them – hidden, as they were, at the back of a drawer.

'Are you sure these are safe?' asked Penny nervously as I produced them. She examined them, turning them over after supper. 'Oh, how creepy – they've got a horrible little smiley face printed on the back! You don't think they're poison, do you? Don't we have to drink lots of water?'

'Yes, we've got to keep hydrated,' I said, 'but we mustn't drink too much water or we'll drown. That girl, you know, who died taking ecstasy. She didn't die of the drug itself, she died of drowning because her friends gave her too much water to revive her.'

'Oh God!' said Penny. 'But we don't know how much too much is!'

'Several litres, I imagine,' I said. 'Come on, let's give it a go. Thousands of young people take dozens of these every night. It can't do us any harm. Anyway, not both of us. And I'm sure Terry wouldn't risk giving us something dodgy,' I added.

And I was sure. Terry's been doing quite a bit for me in the last few days, and I'm starting to really like him. He's been most helpful about looking for the market stall for our pop-up shop and he says he thinks he's found somewhere. It's a place that's been boarded up for the last fortnight – it used to sell shoes but the guy's gone back to Angola – and Terry's found out who's letting it out.

'Why don't we take half a pill to start with,' said Penny. 'I feel a bit freaked out by it all, to be honest.'

'Okay,' I said. I got a kitchen knife and sawed away. 'God, I hope Robin doesn't find us. Which half do you want? The bit with the staring eyes or the smile?'

'This is like being a teenager again,' said Penny. 'It reminds me of smoking dope in my bedroom and hoping that my father wouldn't smell it.'

'Though no doubt Robin lives on E,' I said, 'considering how much dope he smokes and how extraordinarily amiable he is.'

'Do you think it would be better to have it on a full stomach?' Penny asked. 'I mean, I know we've had something to eat, but a little more wouldn't hurt, would it?'

'Good idea,' I said. 'I'm sure it's safer when you're not even the teeniest big hungry.'

So we rather nervously chomped our way through a couple of bits of toast, more to delay the awful moment than anything else.

'Okay, it's ten,' I said, looking at my watch. 'We'd better take it now or we'll never get to sleep.'

And we did. We took half a pill each, feeling incredibly frightened. And we waited.

By this time we'd moved into the sitting room. Penny had cleared away the old Sunday papers on the comfortable chair and had made herself at home there, while I put my feet up on the sofa.

'Nothing's happening,' I said after a while.

'I bet it's just chalk. You've paid a tenner for some chalk,' said Penny. Then she started looking at me very oddly. 'Though, actually, I am feeling a bit funny . . .'

And then I started to feel a bit funny too. And to be honest it wasn't nice at all. I thought it was going to make me feel all warm and friendly, but I just felt kind of paralysed and distant. Penny seemed miles away and yet very close all at the same time. It occurred to me that I could read her thoughts and she could read mine. I then had a kind of revelation that the essence of me was the person who was recognising the essence of her recognising the essence of me. It was all terribly complicated but made some kind of sense.

Suddenly I heard myself saying: 'I'm thinking of moving!'

'Where?' said Penny, very slowly.

'Here!' I said. And we both started giggling. 'Because,' I added, and at the time, it seemed extraordinarily significant, 'I am here!'

'And David,' said Penny, 'is there!'

'Exactly!' I said.

'Well, I'm glad we've got that clear,' said Penny, before going off into another zombie-like trance.

May 10

Felt absolutely FRIGHTFUL all today, incredibly depressed and with a hammering headache. Also felt a total chump for even thinking of taking any Es. Penny said she was fine when I rang her, but I'm only just starting to feel normal at six in the evening. Honestly, why people take these things constantly I'll never know. Certainly it had a weird effect on my brain, but it wasn't nice at all. Perhaps Penny and I are too old to enjoy it. Perhaps you have to have young and groovy synapses to respond to it properly and follow the drug to nirvana. Perhaps ours are all shrivelled and wrinkly and there's a traffic jam by the amygdala (always the culprit, if it's not the hippocampus, I discover, from reading about psychology in the *Daily Rant*), meaning older people find it rather scary and distancing. Oh gawd.

Anyway, glad I gave it a go. Nice to know I've not been missing anything all these years.

To make matters worse I had the first of the estate agents round this afternoon, and heaven knows how I managed to get through that encounter.

I opened the door to this incredibly heavily made-up girl with a clipboard wearing one of those strange suits that women wear to work – black jacket, white shirt, very short skirt and high heels. She didn't actually have shoulder pads because shoulder pads are too seventies, but you could see the psychic ones sprouting from her sleeves. She was called Rashmi. And as she walked round the house, she oohed and aahed at every room.

It was only when we sat down later to discuss the price that she came up with her reservations. 'It's lovely, just what everyone's looking for. And once the bathroom is done up – my clients probably would need more than one bathroom, by the way, and of course the kitchen would have to be entirely refurbished – but this house has some of the greatest potential I've seen in a long time,' she said.

Potential? My house has reached its full potential, thank you very much! How could it be any nicer or more charming?

I was of course longing for her to tell me the value of the house, but it was like one of those antiques shows on tele-vision, where the expert examines an object that some poor soul has brought in, and turns it over and marvels at it, points out the entire history and the small chip in the base, and then waffles on some more and finally – by which time you wish you'd never started watching the wretched programme in the first place – he says: 'And I expect you're wondering what it's worth?'

Whereupon the poor punter nods eagerly, practically fainting with suspense.

'Well, without the chip, it would be worth a lot of money,' says the expert, spinning out the agony. 'A lot of money. But I can say that even with the chip there are plenty of people who would be very happy to see this on their mantelpiece. So I would say . . . I would say . . . about ten pounds!'

What Rashmi said, after what seemed like hours of waffling, was that she thought the house might be worth a million quid. And I have to say that my jaw did rather drop since I'd bought it for £15,000 in the seventies. Still, to be fair, I was only earning about £20,000 a year then. All relative, blah blah blah. Anyway, a million quid, eh? Not bad.

I said I'd think about it because I had other agents to see, and she asked who they were. I told her and she said that Furlin were crooks, and Ashton Manana took far too big a percentage, and Brown, Brown and Brown sold properties very quickly but that was only because they undervalued everything. Finally I got her out of the door and as she was leaving, who should pop out of her front door but Melanie – looking slightly less ashen than she had ten days ago.

I was amazed when she did her ghastly Thai bride bow to Rashmi and said: 'Nastase! Oh, Rashmi! What are you doing here?'

Clearly she'd met her before.

'We're old friends,' said Rashmi, turning to me. 'I sold Mrs Fitch-Hughes this house a few years ago! I hope you're happy here!' she added. 'You've certainly got a charming neighbour.'

Melanie looked astonished. 'Mar!' she gasped. 'You're not thinking of moving, are you? Why didn't you tell me? How could you! This is terrible!'

Later

Terrible it may be, but it didn't stop her ringing me that evening and explaining that she had a friend who was dying to move into our street, and that if we did it all privately I wouldn't have to pay a commission. Oh really? I thought. I'm old enough to know that that way madness lies; somehow one's always left with the stamp duty or, because they're friends of friends, no one looks at the deeds properly and it all goes pear-shaped. Worst of all, of course, is that there's no one to blame, and I like having an estate agent as a scapegoat in the negotiations, so I ignored that offer.

I felt a bit depressed, though, as if Melanie had just said to herself: 'The king is dead, long live the king!' I mean, I could have done with a bit more wailing and moaning and tearing of hair before she suggested a pal of hers move in next week.

May 11

Today it was the turn of Brown, Brown and Brown, in the shape of a rather greasy young man bursting out of an over-tight suit, with slicked-down hair and a very white drip-dry shirt, clutching the same old clipboard and standing in the rain outside under an umbrella. Oddly, since Rashmi of James and Tweedsmuir had assured me that Brown, Brown and Brown always undervalued, this guy put an estimate on the house of £1.2 million. When I told him of James and Tweedsmuir's valuation, he chuckled.

'They always undervalue,' he said. 'Anything for a quick buck. Never think of the client. But the client is our main priority at Brown, Brown and Brown.'

And this afternoon, the so-called crook came over from Furlins – and far from being a crook, she turned out to be the friend of a friend who valued the place at £1.3 million. So ethical was the Furlin rep that she refused even to comment on her competitors, saying, discreetly, that they were all in this together and she didn't believe in back-biting.

No doubt tomorrow the Ashton Manana chap will value it at £1.5 million.

May 12

Which, of course, he did. And far from taking a big percentage he assured me that their rates were the lowest in the whole of England. He also told me that he had three people on his books who would snap the place up if I would let him show them around. But, he said, looking up at the roof of the kitchen which the pigeon has been using as his lavatory, 'I would recommend that you get someone to deal with that before we show anyone anything. Doesn't make the place look, well, loved. And as you know, fresh flowers in every room always helps a sale.'

I have to say I rather warmed to the Ashton Manana guy, being, as he was, about twice the age of any of the other estate agents and someone who looked as if he'd been around the block, as they say. And being an estate agent, he probably had been round many blocks, literally, for years on end and probably flogged half of them off to Russian oligarchs.

May 14

'More terrorists than drug dealers on every street in Britain!' (*Daily Rant*)

May 15

Email from James: 'Darling, why on earth do you want to move? Your house is an absolute treasure! I couldn't bear it if you moved! I feel the world would come to an end! Do think again!'

I wrote back: 'Well, darling, you've moved so who are you calling the kettle black? The only reason I want to move is to be nearer Jack. Don't worry, I will reproduce the house exactly down in Brixton, like one of those Thames bridges that are transported to California and sit, high and dry, in the middle of the desert.'

'But what kind of house do you want to live in? Isn't Brixton rather dangerous?' he emailed back.

'Not at all! I want a house that has a lovely garden, three bedrooms, a bathroom, near the shops, nice neighbours, off-street parking, no basement . . .' And as I wrote I realised that apart from the off-street parking (not really a necessity) I was talking about an identical house to the present one.

Wonder: is this madness? We'll see.

May 17

Marion came round very excitedly saying that they've got a short lease on this shop in the market and can start selling stuff from it from the second week in June. But we'll have to get it all prepared first.

Melanie, Marion, Penny and Tim all came for a meeting at my house and we discussed how we'd go about it.

Tim's going to do the leaflets, Terry's going to paint it (I'll pay), Marion's going to organise some photographs of the orphans and get a big banner printed to display outside.

Then we wondered what to call it.

'Let's call it The Orphan Shop,' said Marion.

There was a silence. 'It sounds as if we're selling orphans,' I said. 'And anyway, isn't the word "orphan" rather politically incorrect these days?'

'Why don't we just call it Rescue?' suggested Tim.

'Sounds too much like Cats Rescue,' I said.

'Show Some Humanity!' said Melanie.

'We are showing humanity,' I said crossly. 'We're setting up this shop.'

'Oh, Mar, don't be such a bore. I mean that as the title of the shop! Show Some Humanity!'

'No one in Shepherd's Bush knows the meaning of the word "humanity",' said Tim, tartly.

'Now that is politically incorrect.'

We settled on 'Help for the Lost Children' and then we all had a large drink.

Later

Jack rang and was very enthusiastic about the idea of my moving. No doubt he thinks it will be easier for him to pop in on me when I become old and lame – and it would. And very nice too.

Had a word with Gene, who was very excited about the shop and said he could make a website for it and get me 'online presence'. He'll put it on his Facebook page, and tweet about it, and ask the school if they could make it their Christmas charity.

'But it's not a charity,' I said, touched at the idea. 'You have to get official approval to call it a charity.'

'Don't worry, Gran, I'll fix it,' he said, sounding very competent, rather like the estate agent from Brown, Brown and Brown. 'I'll come over at half-term and we can have a brain dump.'

Brain dump?

Even later

Having not heard from David for a couple of weeks, I rang him rather nervously to let him know the news. I could tell from the beginning of the phone call that he was still in a huff about the marriage thing. He couldn't have sounded less interested as I tried to jolly him along.

'David, for heaven's sake, don't get into a sulk about the other day. I still love you just as much!'

There was an awful silence. 'It's a funny way to show it,' he said, 'refusing my proposal.'

He's obviously been brooding on this for days.

'Oh, darling, don't. I can't bear it. I know you're hurt—'

'I'm not hurt,' said David angrily. 'I'm just confused. It seemed like a sensible plan and you wouldn't even consider it. Anyway, let's put it behind us. I'm glad about the shop but I'm very busy at the moment, so I'll ring you soon, okay?'

'Okay,' I said, helplessly. 'But I do love you!'

'Okay, okay, okay,' he said, giving a grudging laugh, and put the phone down.

Leaving me feeling very mean.

Later still

House seems awash with animals' poo and pee. If it's not Pouncer 'soiling', as the vet puts it, the carpet (with me following him around with a cloth soaked in Dettol and doing masses of scrubbing), it's the wretched pigeon. Must get the roof sorted before any house viewers come round. Will ask Tim if he knows anyone.

May 20

Tim was round today with piles of boxes of stuff he'd collected for the shop, to add to the piles already accumulated from neighbours. Apparently he and Marion went through their house at the weekend and sorted out a whole load of rubbish. I can't believe much of it would be saleable, but as Tim says, 'every penny counts'.

When I asked him if he knew anyone who might be able to remove the pigeon poo from the roof he went outside to have a look. And as we were both peering up, we were amazed to see Melanie tramping up the lawn.

'Mar!' she said. 'Dreadful news! Your garden wall has fallen down!'

'My wall?' I said. 'I thought it was our wall, a party wall. Where?'

So we all trudged down – and there, completely collapsed, was a huge section of the wall.

'Old mortar,' said Tim, picking up a brick and staring at it. 'Very porous. Bound to happen one day. Look, I'll see if I can't sort you out with a roof cleaner and a wall builder at the same time. I've got someone in mind.'

'But I can't show people round the house if the wall has fallen down!' I wailed.

'Showing people round the house? You're not moving, are you?' said Tim, shocked.

'No, I'm just seeing whether anyone's interested. Don't worry,' I said, 'just testing the water.'

May 25

Very gloomy about the wall. Will have to put people off coming for the moment. And I dread having the builders in. Particularly the ones that appeared on the recommendation of Tim. I was hoping for one of the new breed – not the sort who make you put your head between your knees and gasp for cups of hot, strong tea laced with brandy.

The last builders I had were the new sort from Poland and the Ukraine – the East European hordes that the *Daily Rant* had told us would overrun the country and alter our way of life. In my books, altering it for the better. They rang the bell at seven in the morning – the time they'd said they'd arrive, no less! – and clicked their heels on the doorstep and called me 'madam', refusing all offers of cups of tea, and working till the light faded. When I asked if by any chance they could also fix a shelf in the bathroom while they were here, and unscrew that ceiling spotlight that seemed to have stuck, they set to, smilingly. When they left, I wished another bit of my house would collapse so I could welcome them in again.

I'd imagined it was a builder like this that Tim had in mind, but no: these builders appeared to be old-style, dredged up from some fifties rockpool. The moment Mike and Sean shambled into my kitchen with their glazed eyes and unfriendly mumbles of 'He'o, mum' (one appeared to have no teeth), I should have heard alarm bells.

They gave me an estimate, asked for a lot of cash upfront, and disappeared.

'Are you sure these builders are any good?' I asked Tim, when they still hadn't turned up two days later.

'Oh yes, they're lovely blokes,' he replied with confidence.

But here I am, still waiting.

May 28

Today the builders returned. Sean, they explained, had had a bad leg. But now they were here, they said, 'You don't have to worry about a thing, Marilyn. We'll have it done in no time!'

'Marie,' I said.

But half an hour later they disappeared again, and they still haven't come back.

Well, to be fair, it is raining quite hard – but still. I keep ringing them but there's no reply from their mobiles and I feel helpless.

May 29

Today Tim arrived in a hired van to collect half the stuff that had been piling up in the hall. What a nightmare. Still, we managed to unload it at the shop's premises. It's a broken-down affair with bits of wire sticking out of the wall, a corrugated iron roof, and a rusty metal roller blind with a padlock at the front, more like an enormous box than a shop. But Terry, who was on hand, says that given a lick of paint it will soon look amazing.

It was pretty difficult to work with the rain pouring down, hammering on the roof, but we managed to sort it all into piles of old clothes, books and general bric-a-brac. Tim's taking the really revolting offerings to the skip in the van. I must say I'm rather astonished that anyone could imagine that even the poorest people could want shoes that are actually split at the sides, or a burnt saucepan with a cracked handle.

Terry suggested writing the sign in graffiti lettering to make it cooler which everyone seemed to think was a very good idea – although I thought it a bit old hat. But when he said he could teach Gene how to do graffiti art at the same time, of course I changed my view. Wouldn't mind seeing how it's done myself, come to think of it.

Gene's coming over next weekend so we've made a date.

One of the donors had wrapped her bits and pieces in bubble wrap – which, rather sadly, I stuffed in the bin. It reminded me that in the past Gene and I used to spend many a happy moment jumping on bubble wrap to make it pop, but I imagine he'll be past that, now. I'm still up for it, but feel I can't really do it all by myself.

Oh dear, oh dear.

May 30

Woke feeling very stiff after a day spent down at the shop helping Tim and Terry put up shelves and take back stuff for washing, and so on. It's not very pleasant and the other stall-holders don't seem to be particularly friendly. They all appear to be from Pakistan or Syria and speak hardly any English at all. They smile, but look at us with suspicion – and I don't blame them. They've got their own community there, selling suitcases, saris, hats, false flowers, ornate mirrors, shoes and so on, and don't want to be undercut by a lot of middle-class do-gooders who are trying to save the world.

Oh well. We're not going to be doing it for more than a few months so no doubt they can put up with us.

Later

Still no sign of the builders. Rain pouring down. Jack brought Gene over and he seemed be very game to do more leafleting. The prospect of going out in the rain to shove leaflets through doors didn't appeal, but Jack said he'd be fine. I thought nine was a bit young, but Jack said he'd accompany him for the first half-hour and then leave him to come back on his own. Two hours later Gene was back, hair sodden, grinning, saying he'd met Tim who'd given him even more leaflets and they'd finished the streets on the west side of my road together. Wouldn't have minded Tim ringing me since I was, by then, gibbering with anxiety, but clearly Gene had so enjoyed being independent I didn't have the heart to mention it.

May 31

Slightly better weather today. At least the rain's meant that some of the pigeon poo has cleared from the roof – but only, presumably, into the gutters so it can't be very healthy.

'What are you going to do with him?' asked Gene, who has rather taken to 'Pij' as he calls him.

'The vet said he'd soon be off to find a girlfriend,' I said. 'So I hope he'll hurry up.'

'I'll be finding a girlfriend soon,' said Gene, grinning.

Later, when the rain had cleared up, Gene got into his painting clothes that he'd brought with him, and we walked down to the shop to meet Terry, who'd got all his spray cans lined up, and a couple of vast sheets to start making the signs. Gene was immediately taken by Terry. Most odd. He instantly looked up to him as some kind of icon of street cred, and started, rather oddly, calling him 'mate' and giving him high fives. God knows what Terry made of this, but he's a natural with kids – being, himself, barely older than one, at least mentally. But I was touched at how caring he was and how enthusiastic.

'Respect, bruv – that's bare sick,' said Terry, once they'd got the words down. 'Now for the border!'

'Trust, bro,' said Gene. 'This is really peak!'

I had no idea what they were talking about.

When we got back, we were just having tea when who should rap on the kitchen door, from the garden, but Melanie.

'How did she get here?' asked Gene. 'Does she have a ladder?'

'No, darling, but the wall's collapsed and she keeps walking into my garden which is most irritating,' I said, but put on a welcoming face as I unlocked the glass doors to let her in.

'Hello, little man!' said Melanie, sweeping in with a flourish. It was much easier when she'd got dysentery – she wasn't around so much poking her nose into things.

'Not so little,' I said, thinking Gene must feel ghastly being addressed as 'little man'. He, of course, seemed nonplussed, and just grinned.

'Hello, Melanie,' he said, sliding off his chair and putting out his hand. 'How are you?'

'My dear, what manners!' said Melanie, delighted. 'Isn't he sweet!'

'What do you want, Melanie?' I asked.

'I thought I saw a very nice feather boa in your hall a few days ago that someone had donated, and I wondered if you'd yet taken it to the shop, because when I went down I couldn't see it there.'

'No, it's still here, I think,' I said. She went into the corridor and came back with it draped around her neck.

'Perfect!' she said. 'Just my colour! Thanks so much, darling!'

Suddenly Gene piped up. 'How much was it?' he asked.

'How much? Oh, it's organiser's perks, I think, don't you, Mar? First pickings for us, don't you think?'

'I think first pickings ought to go to the people buying so the money can go to the orphans,' said Gene, stoutly, turning over the pages of a football magazine he'd brought with him, and staring intently at a fixtures listing.

Melanie and I looked at each other, stunned. Of course he was right, and I felt relieved I hadn't helped myself to anything in the past, but there's nothing like getting a sermon from someone a quarter if not an eighth your age to make you feel small.

'What do you think, Melanie?' I said. 'A tenner?'

'I've seen them for twenty pounds down in Brixton market,'

said Gene doggedly, turning to examine a picture of some goalie leaping to save a ball.

'Oh, well, twenty pounds it is!' said Melanie, fumbling in her handbag. 'Don't want to let the lovely orphans lose out, do we?'

After she'd gone, Gene looked up at me with an expression of shocked astonishment and said: 'What cheek! But I didn't let her get away with it, did I, Granny?'

'You certainly didn't,' I said.

There was a silence as he absorbed his success. Then he said, out of the blue: 'Do you know what you call someone who's been a lesbian all their life and then gets married to a man?'

'No,' I said, rather alarmed.

'A hasbian,' said Gene seriously.

I couldn't help guffawing with laughter.

I've been worrying about how he'll cope with big school but after today I don't think I need have any fears at all.

JUNE

June 2

Great news! I haven't seen the pigeon for a couple of days now! This is the first time he's gone missing, and I'm absolutely thrilled. Penny is adamant that Pouncer must have finally got him – he's been seen eyeing him suspiciously out of the bathroom window – but I'm afraid that Pouncer isn't up to catching anything at all these days, let alone a pigeon living at the top of a drainpipe.

His fur is totally lifeless – he looks in need of one of those amazing shampoos you see advertised on telly, with women tossing their glossy, bouncing locks in sunlit fields. His nose is dry and he's wide-eyed and frightened. I feel so sorry for him. Even though I spend my life clearing up after him, and I spray everywhere with Lily of the Valley, I'm aware there's a faint smell of cat pee around. What with the pigeon poo on the roof and the smell of wee and the traces of yellow-greenish patches on the carpet, and the piling up of other people's

174

rubbish in the hall, it hardly matters that the builders haven't been back yet because the house is in too poor a condition to show to prospective buyers.

Still, since they've disappeared, along with the pigeon, I ring constantly and leave desperate messages. But apart from one call from Sean three days ago saying they'd definitely be over in twenty-four hours, ha ha, I've not heard a squeak.

Terry is most disapproving and has suggested that he take on the job himself – apparently he did half a bricklaying course a couple of years back – but I feel I ought to give the guys a chance, particularly having, stupidly, parted with so much money upfront.

June 3

'Will you go senile? It's all in your walk' (*Daily Rant*)

Got Robin to film me on my iPhone (naturally he doesn't have one because of the brain-destroying rays), but when we watched it back it seemed as if I was walking okay, according to the article. Of course, having read the piece first, I knew how it was that I was supposed to walk in order to prove myself entirely sane, so perhaps it doesn't count. It is, apparently, not only connected with whether you shuffle or not – I was careful to pick up my feet so I looked like one of those Arabian horses at an equestrian dressage event – but the arm swing is important. So I put quite a lot of energy into that, too. Robin did point out that my resulting antics could have easily been mistaken for one of John Cleese's silly walks in *Monty*

Python, but as long as I'm not going to develop Alzheimer's, I don't mind.

Later

I searched YouTube for a particularly good clip of the Cleese walk, and sent it to David in the hope of getting a jolly response, but so far nothing.

I'm starting to have real difficulty sleeping these days because I keep thinking about David. I hope he means it about putting the marriage thing behind us, and he's not still sulking.

June 4

Builders are back.

'The van broke down,' explained Sean. 'But now we're going to crack on. You'll see, Marion.'

'You won't pull up my plants or destroy my lawn, will you?' I asked, as I filled giant cups of tea and provided huge slices of cake to bribe them to stay a bit longer this time. 'By the way, it's Marie.'

'To be sure,' said Sean. 'We've gardens of our own and we know how precious plants can be. We'll have to cut a bit back, but everything will be right as rain . . . why, talk of the devil! There was a spot, wasn't it, Mike? We can't work in this weather. We'll be back tomorrow. My, that cake was good! See you tomorrow, Martha!'

Mike mumbled his goodbyes.

I would have believed them but when I went out shopping that afternoon I saw their van parked in the next street with the back doors open. They were clearly on another job. Ah well, tomorrow we'll see . . .

June 7

It's midday, the sun is shining and there is no sign of the builders . . . I am incandescent with rage.

No sign of the pigeon, either. Though I did see, on a faraway tree, something that looked a bit like him, sitting looking rather lonely on a branch, but even with my old opera glasses I couldn't really make anything out.

June 9

I picked Gene up this morning from Brixton to bring him back to help with the shop. I now have to pay the chap to visit! Admittedly it's only a tenner, but bribery seems the only way I can get him to come over and stay the night.

Anyway, he was more than helpful. First we visited the shop, where Tim and Terry have hoisted up the enormous sign – Help for the Lost Children – and Gene was very keen to watch Terry put up shelves inside. He made some pretty good suggestions, too – recommending we got some glass fronts for valuable items, so that people couldn't just come in and nick them. When I say valuable, I mean anything small and pocketable over twenty quid. He was quite happy, too, to take the few little bits of jewellery that we'd got to the jeweller on the Green, and have them individually valued, and returned greatly excited with the discovery that two of them were worth about £50 each.

'He said those are real pearls, Granny,' he said. 'I bet the person who gave them to you didn't know that. But I found out, didn't I?'

Melanie, who'd been deputed to get the clothes cleaned, was sorting them out into shirts, skirts, dresses, trousers and so on, and Gene had the job of checking that none of them were too torn or stained to be saleable. He picked out a few blouses with horrible underarm sweat rings and we stuffed them hastily into a black bin bag. He also counted the pieces of a thousand-piece jigsaw of Piccadilly Circus and found there were only 999. He volunteered to bring it back to my house and construct the missing piece until I pointed out that he'd have to do the jigsaw first which would take all day. Still, he insisted on putting it aside to take home with him so he could do it there.

'I mean you could get five pounds for that jigsaw. And that would buy an orphan a toy, wouldn't it? Or two toys, as toys are cheaper in India, aren't they?'

We went back home for lunch. Afterwards we were just about to load the last boxes from the hall into the car to ferry back, when Gene, looking through one, suddenly gave a huge shout: 'Oh, no! Granny! Come here!'

'What is it?'

'I think Pouncer's been using this as his toilet!' he said, holding his nose and backing away.

I looked. And I'm afraid he was right. Some of the clothes had been thoroughly soaked.

'Well, come on,' I said, briskly. 'I'll get you some rubber gloves. We can sort through the stuff that's undamaged and chuck out the rest.'

Which we did, accompanied by loud cries from Gene who kept yelling: 'Oh yuck, oh pooey! Oh, the smell,' accompanied by a lot of coughing. I wasn't sure if this was put on to make himself seem braver, as if he were fighting dragons – but then I remembered an article in the *Daily Rant* which had explained that children weren't fussy about food, it was just that their taste buds were more acute than ours and they genuinely found lots of flavours repulsive. Wonder if it works for smells too? I certainly remember being completely unable to eat cauliflower or bacon fat when I was small without retching. Now, oddly, I can't get enough of them.

Anyway, by the time I'd remembered this we were almost through, and after Gene had practically asphyxiated us with Lily of the Valley spray, we threw away the Pouncer stuff and put the rest into the car.

When we arrived, Tim presented us each with a rota of who is to serve in the shop and when. He'd also done a huge spreadsheet so we can organise the accounts, which is lucky because most of us are pretty hopeless at that kind of thing. Penny, I thought, had had a glass of wine too many at lunchtime, but on the whole she's been better than before, recently, so let's hope her drinking was just a phase.

June 10

Gene was very worried about Pouncer when I told him he wasn't well. He insisted on sitting with him, stroking him and singing Pharrell Williams' 'Happy' to him, quietly. Not sure what Pouncer thought of this, but it's so lovely to see a little boy involved in caring for something smaller than himself when up till now he's almost always been the one being cared for.

Jack flew in to pick him up and didn't stay for coffee, which was sad – but he said he was frantic. I was just about to slump into a post-Gene gloom when I heard Robin coming downstairs.

'Can I come in?' he asked. 'I was just wondering how Pouncer was.' He took a look at him, curled up in the corner, and shook his head. 'I'm worried about two things,' he said. 'First, the water. Do you give him water from the tap to drink? If so, can I recommend you change it? I never drink water from the tap. You know the government is filling our drinking water with drugs – drugs to make us forget the terrible things they are doing to us on a daily basis! You'd be amazed at what they put in without our knowing it. Also, I've noticed a mobile phone mast on the Uxbridge Road. I'm sure it's sending out bad rays. I haven't felt very well recently and I put it down to that, entirely. The moment I move away from its influence I start feeling better and full of energy.'

'Oh dear, I'm so sorry,' I said, worried. 'I hope there's not something in this house that's upsetting you . . . I do get the gas checked every so often so it can't be carbon monoxide poisoning. But I have to admit I'm having terrible trouble sleeping these days, myself.'

'No, no, not at all. I'm sure it's something in these rays. I'm thinking I'll have to move to somewhere in the country, like Wales or even the Shetland Islands . . . but it's very difficult these days to get out of mobile range.'

I suggested that he try to leave his windows open rather than shut (to protect him from the rays) so that the smell of joss sticks could waft out through the windows.

'Joss sticks have always given me a headache,' I said. 'You know I sometimes wonder if something evil isn't put into joss sticks to twist our minds . . .'

At this, Robin looked very nervous. 'I hadn't thought of that,' he said. 'I think you may be right. I'll do that straight away. Good idea.' And he left to go upstairs.

Honestly, sometimes I think I should just set myself up as a healer and guru. I'm sure I could make a good living. I could borrow all Melanie's scarves from next door, bung a turban on my head and then it would just be a matter of talking the talk and raking in the cash.

Later

Am taking Pouncer to the vet tomorrow for a check-up. I must face the prospect of having him put down, sad as it will be. I couldn't bear to think I was prolonging his life unnecessarily and putting him through any pain.

Oh, dear. I wish David were around to help share the burden

of all this. I keep waking up in the night and worrying. Still no word.

June 15

Now that the shop is sorted – we're having a Grand Opening in a few days – I've finally got down to marking up the Indian tree pictures from my sketchpad – which means I've transferred the basics of most of them onto canvases – and suddenly feel energised. I'd forgotten how engrossing it all is. I wake up in the morning just dying to get started and have been painting away like Vincent van Gogh. Now I've got going I don't think it will take me that long to get them finished – I should have them done by the end of August at the latest, if I keep going at this rate.

Later

I've just come back from taking Pouncer to the vet. After feeling him all over – staring at the ceiling all the while, no doubt picturing every single one of his intestines, heart, liver and so on – he put him back in his basket and put on a serious face.

'Mrs Sharp,' he said. 'I think you know what I'm going to say.'

Of course I knew what he was going to say. The truth is that I have had cats before, and although I'm very sad when they die, I do know that they're going to die before me. It's the idea of Pouncer in pain that agonises me, not so much his death. I can't bear the idea of keeping him going just for the sake of it.

'Do you think he should be put down?' I asked. I felt as if I had to help him along.

The vet looked shocked. 'Don't let's jump the gun. He's not ready yet,' he said. 'But I think you ought to prepare yourself for some time in the not too distant future, I'm afraid, when your dear friend will have to be put to sleep.'

'How long in the future?' I said. 'I mean, I don't want him to suffer. If it's today – well, that's fine! I mean, of course it's not fine, it's very sad, but I only want what's best for him.'

'No, not today!' said the vet, shocked. 'No, he's got a while yet. I think we can make him comfortable for the next few weeks, at least – perhaps longer.'

'Look,' I said, putting my cards on the table. 'I don't have a problem with putting my cat to sleep, as you call it. You don't understand. I love my cat very much and he's my only real companion, but if he were to suffer or be in pain, that's what I couldn't forgive myself for, not bumping him off early.'

The vet looked outraged. 'You're very, er, down-to-earth, Mrs Sharp,' he said.

'Well, I come from an age when we killed animals routinely, not "put them to sleep",' I said. 'If a cat was unwanted, we'd take him to the vet and that would be that. I'm not a sentimentalist about animals. They live shorter lives than us, and anyone sensible knows that when they take one on. My duty is to Pouncer, not to myself. However much I might want him to live, I don't want him to live in pain. I owe it to him.'

I don't think the vet had met anyone like me before,

because he'd already got out the box of tissues, imagining I'd break down.

'Well, yours is a very unusual attitude,' he said, rather coldly.

'The reason is,' I said, 'that I was born during the war.' In truth, I was born in one of the last of the air-raids, hardly during the war. But I thought it might help him get the point.

'Bring him in next week and we'll take another look,' he agreed, reluctantly. 'If we feel the time is right, then perhaps we might consider . . .'

The nurse charged me £120 as usual.

Honestly, people nowadays! They think they make things easier by spinning it all out with tissues and 'this might be the beginning of a long process towards thinking of the ending of his time as we know it and starting to consider perhaps that one day he might die', when people of my age find it much easier to cope if they just say: 'Look, he's had a great life, but now it's time to go. Okay?'

Driving poor old Pouncer home I actually felt quite upset, partly of course at the idea of him dying, but mainly at the idea of the vet just dragging it all out.

June 17

To make matters worse, the pigeon returned this morning. He looks as if he's been mugged by a gang of other pigeons – a real possibility, I fear. He's sitting on the pipe again, black and dirty, the little crest on top of his head all askew, and his wings covered in mud. God, I seem to be surrounded by suffering animals. What is it about me? If it's not Chummy, the ghastly dog across the road who I had to rescue from dying of starvation, it's Pouncer and now the pigeon.

I put out some food for him but before he could get a look-in, a whole gang of horrible feral London pigeons came storming along and jostled for the corn, pooing en masse over the roof. Soon no one will know it's glass. It'll be totally covered with this black gunge.

I really have to find a home for him. I can't go on like this.

June 18

Today was the Grand Opening of the shop. We'd put out balloons, dressed up in our best clothes, and invited everyone we knew. There must have been about a hundred people coming and going throughout the day, and the other shop-owners couldn't believe their luck, because after our customers had bought a broken teapot from us, to show support, they explored the rest of the market, oohing and aahing about the wonderful rolls of Indian silk, or offers of two African nightdresses for a pound, or amazing hair accessories, all glitz and bling. They were buying like billy-o.

At first, we'd wondered if we hadn't overstocked, but by the end of the day it was a question of whether we had enough stock left.

Five o'clock came and Penny, who'd arrived with the now rather-too-often-seen bottle of champagne, suggested a toast and kept offering the other stallholders a drink, but they looked extremely disapproving, all being non-drinkers. Not wanting to give offence, I rushed up to a local cafe and bought quantities of mango and lychee juice and plastic cups and offered more acceptable drinks all round.

'We've made over a thousand pounds on our first day!' said Tim, astonished. 'But we've got to keep up the stock. Perhaps we should leaflet further afield.'

James, who'd come up with Owen (leaving the farm in the hands of a neighbour), promised he'd do what he could down in Wiltshire and I wondered whether I could dragoon David into scouring his village for stuff – though he keeps saying he's so busy these days. I've hardly heard a word from him.

James and Owen were staying the night, and as it's the tenth anniversary of Hughie's death, we decided to go out to dinner. I'd booked at a particularly smart new restaurant in Holborn and we all piled off there with Penny in my Fiat 500, only to find, to my horror, it was one of those offal places which only served nose-to-tail stuff, where you're offered lamb shanks and barley for £22.50. Not to mention bone marrow with a special long fork for £9 as a starter.

James was very much up for it but Owen couldn't believe his eyes. 'This is what I used to live on when I was a boy,' he drawled in his Wiltshire accent. He insisted on wearing his hat all through supper. 'Look at the price of pig's liver! And kale! Only horses eat kale. Stuffed swede? No thanks! And couldn't they have peeled the potatoes before serving them up? They're taking the piss, surely!'

Rather difficult explaining the whole metropolitan irony of the thing. But I must say, having tried the bone marrow, I ended up rather on Owen's side. Horrible jelly-like stuff that looked and tasted like some kind of unwanted discharge. Yuck. (Though I'm not sure, now I come to think of it, that any discharge is exactly wanted.)

Much to my embarrassment, Penny became extremely drunk, but luckily it was at the end of the evening. She fell over when she got up from her chair, and needed the two chaps to support her as she tottered towards the door.

Very worrying.

Later

After Owen had gone to bed and Penny had reeled home, James sat up late and we chatted. Gosh, it was nice. Haven't done that for ages.

'I'm so glad to see you've removed your beard at last,' I said, helping him to a glass of wine. It was so lovely and warm that we were sitting in the garden, with a candle on the table, talking in low voices in case Melanie overheard what we were saying. Luckily, all the lights were out in her house so presumably she'd gone to bed. Though you can never tell with her.

'Yes, Owen said it was ruining his complexion,' he said, laughing. 'Anyway, tell me – how are things?'

I told him about Pouncer and he sighed. 'The vets aren't like that in the country,' he said, scornfully. 'God, it's all you can do to stop them coming round and committing whole-sale murder. Any chance to bump something off, they do. It's

187

because you've got a vet in Notting Hill. Probably keeping ailing pets alive with needless operations and pills is how he pays for his golden taps and his holidays abroad.'

At this point, there was a faint 'coo' from above the kitchen roof. Now it was my turn to sigh.

'And there's the pigeon,' I said. 'I was told he'd go away and find a mate when he was ready, but he's been away and I suspect he tried to steal someone else's girl, and all her brothers came and assaulted him. He's more miserable than ever. What on earth am I going to do?'

'Now there I can help you,' said James. But before he continued, he said: 'God, wouldn't it be nice to have a cigarette just now? Remember how we used to just sit in the evening and have a delicious fag?'

'You're welcome,' I said.

'Are you sure?' said James. He felt around in his pockets and produced a small packet. Then he lit one, looking up nervously to make sure Owen, who disapproves, wasn't watching him from the window, and continued. 'If you can possibly persuade the pigeon into your cat basket, bring him down to Somerset and I'll look after him. You'll never believe it but I've just found an old dovecote at the back of the barn, and Owen's mad keen to get a flock of doves, and old Mr Pigeon would fit in nicely, don't you think? There's a guy who used to look after the doves on the neighbouring estate who knows all about them, so once we've got it set up, and the doves settled in, maybe they'll let yours join the gang. How about that?'

'Oh, James, that would be fabulous,' I said. 'What a brilliant idea! But how will I ever persuade him into the cat basket? He won't even fly to the windowsill if I'm around. He's petrified.'

'That, my darling, is up to you. I'm sure you can find a way. Darts with Valium. A very large butterfly net. A wriggling feast of worms placed strategically inside the basket . . . you always win through.'

Then we got on to the subject of Penny.

'Look, that girl's drinking far too much,' said James. 'We've got to do something. I know you've mentioned it, but I haven't seen her completely sober for months. What's the matter with her? It's such a shame. She's not very nice when she's pissed.'

'I know,' I said. 'Why don't you ask her down, and give her lots of fresh air and a talking-to? I can't say any more. She'll just get cross.'

'Doubt if fresh air will have any effect,' said James. 'But okay. I'll get her down as soon as possible and have a proper talk. I mean we are her friends. We can't let her go to the dogs.'

He took a sensual drag of the remains of his fag. 'Delicious!' he said, chucking the stub into the bushes. 'Now tell me – what's going on with you and David? I ran into him at that mega-Tesco near Bath, buying nappies, it seems, for that darling Gangi. He said he hadn't been up for ages. There's not something wrong, is there?'

'Well, yes, there is, actually,' I said, dropping my voice in case Melanie had secreted herself behind a bush and was listening in, but relieved to be able to confide in James. 'He asked if we should get married again and I said what a ghastly idea and he's gone into a huff!'

'Oh dear,' said James. 'He's probably terribly hurt. You know us men. Can't take rejection. Far worse than women. Silly boy! He should never have asked. He should have devised a scheme – always a mistake to ask directly.'

'Thank God he didn't devise a scheme,' I said. 'If he had, I might be married to him by now.'

'And then?'

'And then we'd get back into the same old pattern and get divorced. I'm not going there again!'

'Well, ring him up and tell him you miss him!'

'I've tried that. He said we should put it behind us, but I'm pretty sure he hasn't because he's been really remote these last few weeks. Remote and grumpy.'

'Oh, he'll come round,' said James. 'You'd better get your skates on, though, because he's becoming a doting dad to Gangi these days. If you don't watch out, Sandra will have moved back in – she's there all the time now.'

'Sandra!' I said. 'Surely not! She's another generation and it never worked when they were together.'

'Men get lonely, darling. Give him a bell.'

June 19

After James and Owen had gone, amid promises to come up again soon and invitations to visit them and plans about the pigeon, I nerved myself to ring David to ask him up to stay. It was one of those tasks I had to take a running jump at.

Much to my surprise, Sandra answered the phone. At least she sounded delighted to hear me.

'Marie!' she said. 'How lovely! I'm just here helping Dave sort out his barn! We've found the most amazing things. At the back you'll never guess what we discovered – Jack's old high chair! We're going to do it up for Gangi! It's brilliant, a really old-fashioned one . . .'

I felt a pang. How on earth had it got down there? I'd looked for it all over the place when Gene had been born – and then I remembered I'd asked David to store it ages ago when I had no room for it. I didn't particularly like the idea of Gangi using it as the next generation but I couldn't object.

'Lovely!' I lied. 'Is David there?'

He was, and as usual he sounded in a rush. But at least he agreed to come up next weekend and stay. He said he could combine it with some meeting he's got. Maybe I can sort something out then.

June 20

'Muslim lesbian tortured her eight-year-old daughter to death at behest of her vampire-loving girlfriend because she thought it would "stop the gates from hell opening"' (*Daily Rant*)

Later

Robin returned from work staggering under the weight of an enormous box. He brought it into the kitchen and started unpacking it excitedly.

'Marie, I think I've got the answer to all this trouble we've been having recently! You not being able to sleep, my headaches . . . !' he said. 'Ionisers!'

And he produced masses of smaller boxes which turned out to contain little gadgets you plug into the walls which will remove the negative ions from the atmosphere.

'But what are negative ions?' I asked, nervously. 'Don't we need all the ions we can get?'

'Positive ions, yes, negative ions, no,' said Robin authoritatively. 'Negative ions cause headaches, sluggishness, depression, lethargy and a general sense of being poisoned. Take them out of the atmosphere, and we will be amazed at the effect it has.'

'We'll be full of beans?' I said.

'Exactly. You just see. After twenty-four hours, we'll both be whatever's the opposite of shadows of our former selves.'

He's very sweetly bought one for every room in the house and refused to accept any money.

As they're quite discreet, I plugged them in happily, trusting Robin that they weren't bugging devices. Not that there'd be much to report back to headquarters except me crying, 'Oh gawd! Spare me! Why was I ever born?'

June 21

Actually, I'm not sure they're not working! I had a brilliant night's sleep for the first time in ages, and left Robin an ecstatic note on the stairs, thanking him.

June 22, night

Well, eventually, after a great deal of money had exchanged hands (twice the original estimate), the builders did finish the wall today, but the garden's been left like one of those 1918 battlefields in Verdun painted by Paul Nash. The rambling rose that had threaded its way through the undergrowth until it reached my kitchen doors has been cut back to the roots. The undergrowth through which it had threaded itself lies in ashes after a bonfire. The cement that had been mixed on the lawn when Mike had forgotten their plastic sheet has set into a grey smear. The laburnum, the acanthus – everything has been hacked back to the minimum. A pile of rubble – bricks, old mortar, broken fencing – is lying on top of the hydrangeas.

I swear that no birds sing.

'Goodbye, Maisie!' said Sean as they left this morning. 'Love that cake!' Toothless Mike just mumbled.

David, who finally came up this afternoon, was very scathing when he looked at their work.

'It's rubbish, Marie,' he said. I was acutely aware that he called me 'Marie' and not 'darling' as he has for the last couple of years. 'That wall will be down the next time it rains. Look!' and he gave one of the bricks at the top a bit of a shake; it came away in his hand. 'What have they been using to stick the bricks together? Flour and water?'

I found myself racing around, trying to make him comfort-able and slipping my arm through his when we popped out to the shops together, but he was distinctly unresponsive. Yes,

Sandra was fine. Yes, Gangi was fine. Yes, his flood defences had worked brilliantly during the torrential rain – though one of his farmhands had slipped in one of the ditches and it had been touch and go whether the mound of earth would fall on him or not due to the pressure of the water; luckily he escaped.

And no, he wasn't going to stay more than a night.

However, with the aid of a bottle of wine, and a lot of snuggling up and me making affectionate jokes till I felt like a Mata Hari spy, he finally cracked.

'Okay, okay, darling,' he said, laughing. 'I get the message. You know I'd made a resolution to sleep in the spare bed tonight, don't you?'

'What! And leave me all alone like an orphan?' I said, pitifully. 'You're too cruel.'

'You're a naughty girl,' he said, affectionately. 'And I'm just a weak old lovelorn ex-husband. I'll never be the strong silent type. Well, particularly not with you around, darling.'

Just before we turned out the lights, David noticed the ioniser sitting on the bedside table.

'What's this?' he said. 'It looks very sinister.'

When I explained it was one of the ionisers that Robin had got, he sighed in exasperation.

'Honestly, you'll believe anything that man tells you, Marie! Ionisers have been proven to be rubbish since the 1960s! He'll be persuading you that the earth is flat, next!'

'Well, isn't it, darling?' I said.

'I'll give you flat,' said David. And after he'd turned out the light we melted into each other's arms.

June 23

It's absolutely extraordinary!

David left this morning without saying goodbye! I just can't understand it. He didn't even make me the usual cup of morning tea! It seems so odd. I keep racking my brains to think of anything I could have done wrong. Maybe he just had to get back to Shampton early and didn't want to wake me and he'll ring later.

Buried myself in painting all day and felt much better. The jacaranda is nearly finished and I've marked up the banyan tree, which is going to be the most difficult. Anyway, as long as I keep John Ruskin's ideas about trees in mind, I can't go wrong.

Later

No word from David. I thought of ringing, but felt I couldn't. I hope he hasn't had an accident.

Even later

Even worse, I discovered that David has taken everything with him! He's always left his toothbrush here, at least, and a change of pants and socks and a couple of books he's got on the go, but all trace of him has disappeared!

I can't bear it! This is totally mad. It couldn't have been the ionisers, could it? He couldn't possibly imagine anything was going on between Robin and me, surely?

June 24

Finally rang David, but there was no reply. I even rang Sandra but she didn't pick up either.

Could he have gone back and Sandra persuaded him to stay with her? What on earth is going on?

Later

Ghastly residents' meeting today. Melanie is still banging on about hanging baskets and insists that the spikes sticking out of our lamp-posts were designed by the Victorians to hang flower baskets on. Marion, who has been to lectures at the V & A about everything from coalholes to lamp-posts, swears the spikes were to lean ladders against. We've decided to consult the Victorian Society.

Conversation naturally drifted into discussions about the shop and Tim raised the fact that Penny didn't turn up for her shift until he rang her and then she sold a pair of extremely expensive lined chintz curtains for a tenner. Penny said they were ripped and Tim insisted they weren't.

On the way out, Sheila the Dealer raised an eyebrow at me and muttered: 'Them Es? Tried 'em yet?'

'Yes,' I whispered, 'but to be honest we didn't like them very much. Anyway, jolly good of you to get us some.'

'Not me, 'scuse me,' she replied indignantly. 'It were Terry. 'e'll never learn. Always getting ripped off. I'll try to get you some more stuff. Clean stuff.'

'No, no,' I begged, unable to face the idea of ever taking

another E in my life. 'And don't blame Terry. He's been wonderful in lots of ways, helping with the shop and so on . . .'

Poor Terry.

June 25

Tried David again and even more oddly, when he picked up and heard it was me, he just put the phone down. I simply don't get it. He was so affectionate when he came up. What can be going on? Just shows how dreadful it would be to be married to him – he'd always be going into sulks and moods.

Wonder if he's getting Alzheimer's? I'm going to write him a long email and see if that provokes any response.

Later

Just in the middle of painting when I got a text from Penny asking me to man the shop as she'd overslept and couldn't find the keys anyway. This really isn't good news. I staggered down very irritated because I was in the middle of marking up the eucalyptus, and opened up. Found two bags had actually been left outside the shop for once, which is good news, but all the more reason to get there early before anyone nicks stuff during the early hours. There were some rather nice little ornaments and a couple of rings – hope they're not stolen – and a lovely dress which, when I looked at the label, turned out to be by Ossie Clark. Put it aside because I think that's good enough to be sold on eBay, actually.

Penny turned up with her face all puffy and red, and full of apologies. I could smell the wine on her breath and felt really sad. Finally managed to blurt out: 'You look as if you rather overdid it last night!'

'I did,' said Penny, with endearing honesty. 'But I've been so good, Marie. I've been sticking to two glasses a night for the last week. Promise.'

Two bottles more likely.

We sat in the shop together for the next hour – I got some coffees to perk us up – and listened to an old radio that had been handed in. A terrible programme with Melvyn Bragg called *In Our Time*. There were four professors talking about some Phoenician invasion of 2000 BC or whatever it is they call BC in these politically anxious days. One of them was saying: 'Then the Phoenicians invade from the north and take over the entire town. The place is in a turmoil. The Israelites are advancing on the right flank and Emperor Claudius is pursuing the Etruscans in the West,' or something like that – all in the historic present! In other words, instead of saying, 'The Phoenicians invaded from the north and took over the entire town' they were trying to make the whole deadly affair more exciting by speaking of this historic event in the present tense. Drove me nuts. I mean, if the Etruscans really were invading at this very moment we'd have something to worry about – ancient peoples suddenly rising up from the past to destroy us.

I tried to explain how utterly maddening it was to Penny, who would usually get my point at once, but this morning – because she has a head like cotton wool – she couldn't understand what I was talking about. Suddenly wished David was here. He'd get the point at once. Oh God oh God oh God.

The wall will fall down, I'll never get the pictures finished, the shop will be a disaster, Penny will die of drink, and I'll never see David again. Came home feeling utterly gloomy. I think it's the shop that brings me down. There's something utterly lowering about sitting for hours in a shop that sells only cast-off stuff. Perhaps I need to try one of the ionisers and see if that works. Though actually it would need about ten to purify the air in there, honestly.

June 27

Melanie's written on her Facebook page, underneath a picture of a globe: 'God bless the whole world. No exceptions.'

I could make some exceptions! The creep who bred my poor pigeon. Sean and Mike, the so-called 'builders'. Father Emmanuel for telling his congregation they'll go to hell. Melanie, when she comes sneaking up on me through the garden (though at least Sean and Mike's work has stopped that for now). Oh God, have to go. Someone's knocking on my back door.

Later

I should never have written that. Obviously being punished by God. It was Melanie who had come to tell me that the middle of the wall had fallen down again – so David was right. What do I do now?

Much later

Have finally put something on my Facebook page to coun-teract all those holier-than-thou messages. 'Expectations are merely disappointments under construction.'

Shouldn't think I'll get many smiley faces and 'Like!' responses to that, ho ho.

June 29

Wrote a long email to David begging him to explain what was going on, but don't expect I'll get a reply. Not sure what else I can possibly do.

I'm starting to wonder whether he didn't do this deliber-ately, just to give me a taste of my own medicine, as it were. So I'd know how horrible it was to be rejected. But that doesn't sound very likely. No, something's going on.

Later

In desperation, I texted Terry to see if he knew anyone who might do the wall. Rather unnervingly, he put himself forward as a candidate.

'I told you I done a bitter bricklayin',' he said. 'Did an apprenticeship but stopped 'alfway froo. But I could 'ave a go.'

I was so fed up at this stage that I gave him free rein and was extremely surprised when he arrived the following day with a sheet of polythene to cover what I laughingly call my lawn, a bucket of cement and a proper trowel. It was a wonderful bricklaying day, he assured me, sun shining and everything rosy, and once he'd taken down all the old bricks, brushed off whatever it was that Sean and Mike had used to glue them temporarily together and stacked them in neat piles, I felt much more confident. He actually worked from seven in the morning till eight at night when the light was fading and I can already see that he knows far more about bricklaying than the other two jokers.

He promised he'd come the following day and the next, and that he'd clear the garden of the rubble, and reseed the lawn.

Amazing to think I'm now starting to rely on old Terry, even though he still looks a bit like a mangy fox.

June 30

Looked in the mirror today and who should be peering out at me but Edith Piaf. Blinked several times and slowly a person more like me came into view, but it was a bit of a shock. No wonder David's gone off me.

JULY

July 3

'Romanian planned to smuggle 3ft 2in burglar known only as "The Midget" out of the UK by hiding him in his luggage and flying to their home country' (*Daily Rant*)

July 6

Feel absolutely terrible. I'd just rung Jack to find out when Gene could next come over when Jack revealed that David had been staying with them overnight! David hadn't mentioned anything to me about it or coming to see me. The excuse he'd given to Jack was that I didn't have room for him. The moment Jack told me, I felt utterly sick and rejected.

After I'd put the phone down – not revealing anything to Jack, of course – I sat down at the bottom of the stairs and wept. I couldn't help it. It was like being divorced all over again, only worse because when we were divorced I'd been the one to chuck David out and now I knew how he'd felt.

To make matters worse, Jack told me delightedly that his father had finally got a hearing aid and had perked up no end.

'Sandra persuaded him, apparently! It's great!' he said. 'He's just like the old dad! A changed man!'

I'm afraid to say I just took to my bed – at two in the afternoon, too! But I couldn't sleep. I tossed and turned and when I did finally manage to nod off, it was only a couple of minutes before I woke up and the reality hit me again. How could he be so cruel? He must have known I'd find out.

Wandering down to the kitchen I bumped into Robin, who was making a cup of herbal tea. The moment he asked me how I was, I burst into tears yet again.

He did try to be sympathetic but he's a bloke and therefore can't be totally sympathetic. David's sympathetic, of course, but I can't ring up and moan because he's the cause of my misery.

'Venus is coming into Scorpio,' said Robin. 'Everyone's unhappy. It's a bad time. But once Uranus passes over next month, everything will start looking up.'

Even though I don't believe all that tosh, it was a slightly comforting thought.

Later

Decided that the only thing I can do is paint. I'm just going to paint and paint and paint till I can paint no more. It's the one thing that takes my mind off all this stuff.

Even later

Just struck by a terrible thought. Maybe when I'm eighty years old I'll look back on these days, when I'm reasonably able to get around – i.e. without a walking frame or a stick, and at least able to see – and think: 'Happy days! How lucky I was! Little did I know!'

I was going to ring Penny and ask for her sympathy but can't face talking to someone slightly tiddly, so decided I'd leave it. Penny might say how lonely she feels but no one could feel as alone as I do at this very minute.

Though perhaps I should join Penny and become an alcoholic.

In the end, I decided I couldn't go on any longer without talking to someone, or I'd be carted off by the men in white coats. I thought of ringing the Samaritans but was afraid they would laugh in my face and say: 'Ho! Ho! You think you've got problems!'

So I rang Marion and I have to say she was incredibly sweet. She came over right away and, though she clearly thought I'd been absolutely mad to refuse David's offer of marriage, she didn't rub it in. She put her arm round me and said that she was sure in the end everything would sort itself out.

'It takes men a long time to get over rejections,' she said.

'But I wasn't rejecting him!' I said. 'I just said I loved things as they were!'

'I know, but he sees it as a rejection. It's a big step to ask anyone to marry you – particularly your ex-wife.'

She also suggested she have a word with David. I said I

wouldn't hear of it, but I was incredibly touched that she thought of it.

She stayed for an early bite of supper because Tim was working on the accounts for the shop, and she was so kind and nice and just like the old Marion I used to know before she got all disapproving of my lifestyle. We used to sit next to each other at school and exchange letters with funny drawings in them and she was always coming over to play. But it was the first time we'd had a good heart-to-heart for ages. She pointed out that these tête-à-têtes with girlfriends are very rare for her, because she's married, and she admitted there were some great advantages to being single.

'Oh, you can have cosy chats,' she said, 'though it's not quite the same. I used to think marriage was a bed of roses but, although I do love Tim, I can't pretend that sometimes I don't envy you the single life. And I wish my grandchildren lived nearer, like yours. I hardly ever see them down in Cornwall. I suppose that's why I'm so keen on helping the orphans. You know, this shop is really making me feel life's worth living. We've made over £5,000 so far.'

After supper we settled down in the sitting room with Pouncer.

'Yes, I see what you mean,' she said, wrinkling her nose, 'there is a funny sort of catty smell in here.' And then she said: 'Look, when we've reached the £10,000 mark, let's all go over to India again to hand over the cheque. We'll stay at that nice hotel Brad and Sharmie got us into. It would be fun!'

But I'm not sure I could face going back there. I did think

India was full of suffering and misery and boiling heat. Aren't I awful? Condemning an entire continent. And I'm sure it's not true. It's just that I saw the wrong bits like the car crash and Dilip's miserable quarters and the beggars which just seem to stick in my mind.

Or did I?

July 7

I must have been looking pretty low, because even Melanie noticed when she caught me putting the rubbish out front this morning.

'What's the matter?' she said. 'You look terrible!'

I hesitated about confiding in her, but eventually she wormed it out of me.

'Forget about David!' she declared, confidently. 'I never thought it would work. How could it? You've tried it once, don't try it again. Leopards never change their spots. I knew it was always doomed. Now look. You and I have got to find some new blokes. And I've got just the ticket. I've met this divine man, just divorced. You must meet him. You'd like him. He's a tremendous intellectual and reviews for all kinds of papers, he's an art historian, just up your street, and best of all he's not gay and he's available! You and Hugo would get on like a house on fire. Come on, you and I've got to get ourselves some men! Decent men! David's disappeared, I've got no one . . . I'm going to organise a supper for us, I've got my eye on this chap, he's in telly, you can have Hugo, and I'll set up a foursome . . .'

And before I knew where I was, I'd got out my diary and we'd made a date for dinner next week.

Later

Penny isn't much help. While we were talking on the phone, I told her about Melanie's dating dinner party.

'She's dredged up some frightful intellectual called Hugo and some telly person she's keen on,' I said. 'Can you imagine!'

There was a pause at the other end.

'Not Fabian Rostrum?' she asked. 'I saw him with Melanie the other day in the shop. Oh, dear, you won't like him, Marie. He was wearing red trousers.'

I winced. Whenever I got on the wrong side of Jack, when he was in his twenties, he would always threaten to buy a pair of red trousers. And wear them. Thus, he always got his own way.

'Worse, he said he only wore them at weekends to relax, because he couldn't live them down at what he called "the Beeb",' she added.

'How could I like him, anyway?' I said. 'He's a "meeja" person. Anyone in the "meeja" is a different species.'

Penny seemed about to giggle before she checked herself. 'Perhaps we should remember that each and every one of us can teach us something about ourselves and humanity.'

'Oh for God's sake, Penny. We're talking about telly people! They're not part of humanity!' I said.

She did at least have the grace to put her AA slogans to one side and finally burst out laughing.

'Can't wait to hear about it!' she said. 'I want a blow-by-blow.'

July 13

Tonight's the night of Melanie's bloke-grabbing dinner. I'm dreading it on the whole, but I suppose a bit of me thinks: Hugo . . . sounds interesting. Academic. Art historian. Can't be all bad. But then there's Fabian. Red trousers. What normal man wears red trousers? It sounds like an affectation. You see men with affectations everywhere. Men in vast W.B. Yeats-type hats, men with crazy ties, men with voluminous coats, men with goatee beards, men with bald heads and rings in their ears, men with tattoos, men with one gold front tooth . . . men with bright red trousers.

Later

I put on a really nice dress I'd bought recently at Toast. Though it was a bit hard to do up at the back, I managed it and it looked terrific. It was lemon yellow with bright green stitching, and the skirt was cut on the cross so it hung beautifully.

I rushed round to Mr Patel's for some mints to take to Melanie but unfortunately he didn't have any.

'Finished!' he said, as he always does when his stocks are low, as if mints were a seasonal item. I ended up by getting a very sleazy bunch of flowers that looked as if they had all been dyed garish colours by mistake.

Came back, and saw I was a bit early so I'm writing this. Fingers crossed the evening isn't too ghastly.

Even later

The evening was a total nightmare! Fabian and Hugo argued the whole evening while Melanie and I sat by with nothing to say. We didn't eat till nine thirty, by which time everyone's stomach had shrunk in sensible anticipation of famine, I suppose, and we could barely choke anything down.

I'll enlarge. Even though she must be at least my age, Melanie insists she still suffers from hot flushes. I think it's probably to fool people she's younger than she really is. Surely people are over the menopause by their late sixties? Anyway, there she was, swathed in shawls which, as per, she took off one by one like some pathetic girl in a lap-dancing club. When there was nothing left to take off, she opened the door into the back garden and fanned herself even though by now, even in July, it was quite nippy. The men didn't say anything, of course, because it's considered unmanly for men to be cold, and they just suffered silently.

Poor Fabian, the first to arrive, wasn't even wearing a jacket. He had put on his signature red trousers, and wore a pink shirt with a turquoise green jumper on top. He fancied himself no end, with masses of grey hair sprouting in waves from his head making him look much younger than, I suspect, he really was.

He was amiable enough, I suppose, but, like all telly people, utterly wet and completely out of touch with the real world. He was probably happiest yakking away to his pals in some media hothouse where they discuss ratings and programme costs. Straight out of that telly series, *W1A*.

The tension rose when Hugo arrived, and Melanie and I immediately sensed rivalry. For Hugo was also wearing red trousers, and from then on the men were like two cocks squabbling over who was the leader of the pack.

Hugo had the advantage of having a louder voice. But his disadvantage was that he clearly wanted to be on television so didn't dare go too far with Fabian in case he queered his pitch – a pitch which he proceeded to make at once, with no thought for anyone else in the room.

'I have always thought what's needed on television is a series about how art and literature combine. I see it in twelve parts – I mean, it's high time there was a rival, but a rival with a difference, to old Ken Clark's *Civilisation*, don't you think?'

'Tony suggested this a few weeks ago,' said Fabian. 'But Jo – that's Jo Deacon, head of programmes – she put her foot down. We'd got to the pilot stage, too – shame.'

'But . . .' said Hugo, and then proceeded to outline his proposal, down to the last in the series being about punk music, comics and YBAs, '. . . and ending anticipating Instagram, Twitter and everyone making their own art, art being for the people at last and coming full circle! Back, you see, to cave paintings!' he added with a flourish.

This went on all through supper which, as I say, was not served until nine thirty, and by this time both men were drunk.

Finally Melanie clapped her hands. 'Now stop it, boys!' she said. 'We have a wonderful artist here and you've neither of you addressed more than a word to her!'

I could have shrivelled up and died at this clunky inter-
vention, and graciously nodded for them to continue. But of
course they had to turn to me after that.

'What do you paint?' asked Hugo.

And I could think of nothing to say except, 'Trees, mainly.'

Whereupon he said: 'And nature. The series could, of
course, include nature in its brief. Art, music, literature –
and nature . . .'

'Except, of course,' said Fabian, 'in the sixteenth century
there was no such thing as "nature" per se. The whole idea
of "nature" didn't come in until the seventeenth century and
indeed, the whole concept of art didn't exist until the – what
would you say – late seventeenth?'

'Art has always existed,' argued Hugo, wiping his mouth
with his napkin. 'Ars . . . artis . . . the Greeks were obsessed,
the very word comes from the Greek . . .'

'I think you'll find,' said Fabian, helping himself to more
potatoes, 'that the words "ars" and "artis" come from a word
meaning "skill", not art as we know it in the twenty-first
century.'

Melanie interrupted. 'Why don't you have a woman pre-
senting this programme?' she said, winking at me. 'I'm sure
we're all feminists here!'

'I'm a feminist,' said Fabian, determinedly.

'And I'm a feminist,' said Hugo, angrily. 'I mean, look at the
number of women artists – er, Gwen John . . . Maggi Hambling,
Elisabeth Frink . . . er, that woman in America . . .'

'And Gwen John!' said Fabian.

'I said her!' said Hugo.

'Well, I'm not a feminist,' I said, suddenly getting angry. 'I'm an equalist!'

After which the whole thing turned into a complete bunfight, with Fabian suddenly shouting, above everyone else, 'Grandma Moses!'

I felt more and more ignored and miserable so I left at ten forty-five, the earliest I could get away without appearing rude. Dinner parties are meant to be fun and make one feel connected with other people. After this one I felt as if I'd been actively ignored and sidelined, and the only way I'd succeeded in drawing attention to myself was to be horrible, so I returned home feeling tense and unhappy.

I missed David especially, because it was after such an event that he and I would have the most fun, imitating the other guests and howling with laughter. We would have had a field day after Fabian and Hugo.

Couldn't help ringing Penny, even though it was late, and telling her all about it.

'Sounds ghastly,' she said sympathetically. 'You're describing what they used to call "a pissing match".'

'That's it!' I said. 'Oh dear, I wish David were around. He'd never bang on like that.'

Later still

Just been trying for the last twenty minutes to get out of my dress, but I simply couldn't reach the top of the zip. God knows how I'd done it up in the first place. In desperation I knocked on Robin's door, but he was out, so it was a matter of either sleeping in the thing and waiting till I could ask someone to unzip me the following day (though I didn't fancy the idea of bearding – probably literally – a passing Muslim and asking him to defrock me), or cutting myself out of it.

But I then had a genius idea. I dug out the toolbox and found a pair of pliers. After about ten minutes I managed to secure the tag, and pull the zip down.

Phew! In future I will have to tie a bit of cotton to the tag so I can always get myself out of it.

Don't remember this happening to me when I was young.

July 14

The pictures, at least, are going splendidly. I only have two more to finish, and then I'll leave them for a couple of weeks to see if they need anything more doing to them, get them photographed and send them off to India. I am really thrilled with them, actually. Misery must make me paint better because they all look much more part of a series than the ones I did for Brad and Sharmie before. Much as I hated India there were moments I wished I could go back just to discover a little bit more how the light fell, but Google images were pretty good and showed me a banyan tree in every stage of its wriggling, rooted glory.

But nothing else is going brilliantly, I have to say. The pigeon stays resolutely on his drainpipe, looking more like a mixture of the little match girl, orphan Annie and Oliver

Twist every day. Rather meanly, in order to make him more desperate for food and more willing to be lured into the cat basket, I kept his corn back for one day. The next day I stood like a statue for what seemed like twenty-four hours (probably ten minutes) with some corn in my hand, and at least he flew down from his pipe onto the windowsill near me. He wouldn't peck the food from my hand, but it was the first time I've got that close, and I could see his bright beady eye, and the lovely colours on his feathers – little touches of blue and purple.

Having recovered from his mass pigeon mugging or whatever it was – perhaps he'd been caught by a cat? – he really is a delight to look at. Can't imagine what a breeder could have found wrong with him. No doubt his beak wasn't the right shape or something. Or his feather trousers weren't flared enough.

July 15

This morning I caught Robin on his way out to work and asked him what he thought about the pigeon. Robin thinks he can talk to animals (naturally) and says that in a few days he will have the pigeon completely tamed. He told me he used to have a cat and they could read each other's thoughts. (What are a cat's thoughts, I wonder? Is it wondering if a tree falls in a forest and there's no one else around, it makes a sound? Or perhaps it is considering whether, if you stare long enough into an abyss, the abyss stares back at you? Or is it just thinking, 'I'd quite like some Whiskas now'?) Robin says to catch him all we need to do is to construct a pentangular box to put on the windowsill which will create the right zone for him to feel comfortable in. Pigeons just can't resist pentangles, he says, and he loped upstairs on his long thin legs, and brought down a book of symbols which showed dozens of reproductions of medieval pictures with pentangles and pigeons in them to prove his point.

I said go ahead. If he thinks he can lure the pigeon down with a pentangle, then great.

Later

Hardly know how I can write this. I was busy painting away when I heard the siren of an ambulance and looked out of my window. I could see the lights flashing at the end of the street so naturally, being incredibly nosy, I grabbed my keys and sauntered up the street, avoiding the odd old sofa that had been put out for the bin men, wondering if it had been called out for anyone I knew. As I got towards Tim and Marion's house, I realised that that was exactly where the ambulance was parked. I broke into a run and as I arrived, the front door opened. Tim was in the hall and two ambulance men were hoisting a stretcher down the stairs. The stretcher was covered in a green blanket and, as they got further down, I could see that the person under it was Marion. She was white as a sheet, but managed a weak smile when she saw me, before they lifted her into the back of the ambulance.

'What happened?' I asked Tim, clutching onto his arm. My heart was beating fast.

'She was . . . she . . . I heard her call from the bedroom and when I went upstairs she was lying on the floor. I think she's had an attack of some kind. But at least she's still alive!' he said, in a croaky voice. 'We've been waiting half an hour . . .'

At this point the paramedics approached him with a clipboard and he nodded. Then he climbed into the back of the ambulance. As he strapped himself in, he stared out at me, his eyes full of tears.

'Pray for us, Marie, won't you!' he said.

The engine revved up and the paramedics started to bang the doors shut. I just managed to shout: 'Let me know what happens and if I can do anything . . . lots and lots of love!' before the ambulance drove off, lights flashing and siren whining, before I staggered back to my own house with legs like jelly, utterly breathless with anxiety. I thought of looking in on Penny but I felt first I had to get home and sit down. I felt sick and my head was swimming. Surely not – not Marion! She can't stop banging on to me about eating properly and going for walks. And now, a heart attack! She's always been so healthy!

Even later

After twenty minutes, I rang Penny and told her what had happened.

Penny was speechless. 'It can't be true!' she said. 'Not Marion! She was so fit and well and always walking and eating pulses and all that rubbish and barely drank . . . oh, poor Tim, poor everyone, poor us!'

'What can we do?' I said. 'I feel so helpless!'

'Look, I've got their spare key,' said Penny. 'Why don't you ring Tim and say anything he needs we can just bring over right away, wherever he is.'

So I rang Tim and luckily he'd got his phone on and in a whisper he said she'd been whisked into surgery, but he was sure that she could do with a nightdress when she got out, and maybe some slippers, and a book – and could we bring both their phone chargers. He sounded absolutely stunned.

'We'll look around and bring what we think's right, and you can pick out what you want,' I said.

So Penny and I went round to their house – eerily quiet – and went up to Marion's bedroom. She'd obviously collapsed while she was making the bed. There was such an emptiness in the room, such an enormous 'NO MARION' presence. Penny said, 'It feels awful going through her drawers, as if she's dead!'

There was a cold cup of tea on the bedside table and Marion's shoes lying askew on the floor.

Then we both sat down on the bed with our arms round each other and tried not to cry.

'She's not dead!' I said, firmly. 'She'll be fine!'

Penny gave me a strengthening hug and we got up and carried on.

Bundling everything we could find that we thought she might want, we got into my car and set off for the hospital – the same one where I'd been so often to have my lump tested a few years ago. On the way, Penny had the bright idea of hopping into Pret and getting some smoked salmon sandwiches and a couple of bottles of their bright green Goodness drinks, because Tim would probably be starving. When we got to the hospital, I was an old hand in the car park and knew exactly how to find a space.

We were quiet in the vast lift going up to the ward where Marion was – very conscious that the lifts are only big to accommodate prone bodies – and eventually emerged onto a brightly lit corridor. At the nurses' station we asked the way and they pointed us to the end of a ward, packed, it seemed, with patients on drips, with tubes coming out of them, and all looking terribly ill. Tim was sitting on a metal chair, and a Filipino nurse in a white coat was handing him a cup of tea.

'How is she?' I asked, as we approached, and Tim rose but, unable to stand, fell back down on the chair, supported by the nurse. From his face we could see at once what had happened. He looked completely grey. It was as if someone had punctured him like a balloon and he had just diminished into a piece of putty-coloured rubber.

'She's gone!' he said, with a groan. And then he broke down. 'They couldn't save her! She's died.'

The nurse stroked his back with the knuckles of his hand. 'Very sad, very sad,' he said. 'Doctors did best, but very sad. You friends?'

'Yes, we're friends,' we said.

'Tell me if you need anything. I will get cup of tea. Sugar milk?'

'Anything,' said Penny, pulling up a chair next to Tim and holding his hand. 'You poor, poor darling.'

July 16

I stayed over at Tim's that night in the spare room, to keep him company. Luckily his sister is coming up tomorrow, so she can help with all the paperwork and everything. I gave him a Valium but then found it was my last one so naturally couldn't sleep a wink myself.

We're all going round in a state of complete shock, and even Melanie is doing her stuff, offering to cook meals, and pop in, and endlessly taking round healing oils and visualisation tapes, though quite honestly I don't think Tim's in a condition to visualise anything. He seems utterly broken, though between the moments when he just sits looking rather like Pouncer, unable to take anything in, he has the odd hour when he's manically efficient, sorting out life insurance and death certificates. I do hope he won't crack up.

He sat downstairs on the sofa, eyes wandering vacantly round the room. 'I was the luckiest man in the world,' he kept saying. 'Forty-three years we'd been married. I never looked at another woman, she never looked at another man. When I first met her . . .' and he'd go off down memory lane, recalling their initial date, and when they'd kissed, and what had happened when he'd asked her to marry him. And then, predictably, he'd break down, following it all up with a lot of apologies, typically English, and snuffling into his handkerchief.

I was there when Melanie came round and he suddenly broke down. At this, she went into full drama mode.

'Cry! Cry! Let it all out!' she declaimed, seizing him by the shoulders. 'Don't suppress it! Don't bottle it up! Crying is good for you! We'll all cry together! Let out the pain! Work through the agony!'

But Tim just did his usual harrumphing and, as gently as possible, pushed Melanie away, and I don't blame him. Melanie seems to have some weird idea that grieving should be done her way and that anyone who doesn't wail and gnash their teeth and rend their garments is repressed and no doubt will, eventually, get cancer.

Penny and I were very disapproving. 'Can't she let him suffer in his own way? He's got enough on his plate without being told how to grieve,' said Penny. And I couldn't agree with her more.

July 17

We've not seen a lot of Tim the last few days, because not only has his sister been up but also the famous Angie, Jim, Bella, Perry and Squeaks – his daughter and her husband, the two grandchildren and the dog. They seem to be taking him over, which is a very good thing.

The funeral is on Friday, and Tim's got it into his head that he wants to give Marion a 'progressive' ceremony which, again, we all approve of. There'll be no vicars involved, it'll all be presided over by a Humanist in a jersey, and Marion'll be buried somewhere in a forest. I feel so pleased. It's so easy, when someone's died, to get caught up in the simple way out – let the funeral directors take over – but Tim's very particular that he wants her buried in a recyclable coffin, and that it's to be a very low-key affair.

I'm surprised actually because people like Tim usually go back to their roots and can't resist a church, but perhaps the kids have overridden him.

He's asked us all to contribute photographs for a 'memory board' and I've been rootling around in my old photograph albums to find pictures of Marion at school . . . there's a very touching one of her trying to play tennis.

I have to say I keep thinking about Marion and really can't believe she's gone. It's particularly sad that her death came just after we'd had that chat the other day – although in another way it was good. It means I won't remember her as a 'nagging-me-to-live-on-lentils' person, but the sweet person she really was.

She was my oldest friend. We'd been inseparable at school. Afterwards she went to university and I went to art school, but we still kept in touch, and when she moved near me in the seventies, we took up our friendship again as if we'd never been apart. To be honest, we didn't have that much in common, but we'd known each other so long she was more like a relative than a friend. I always felt completely at ease in her company, totally uncompetitive, able to talk to her about anything.

Penny's a later friend. We have more in common, but

Marion goes – or, rather, went – back such a long way. We even remembered each other's parents – and there are increasingly few people who I can say that about. One thing about her was that she was incredibly kind. I will miss her so much.

God knows how Tim will manage to cope on his own. Though he'll probably be snapped up by someone before he can say Jack Robinson. No doubt Melanie will try to get her hooks into him.

What a thought.

July 20

I ordered flowers for the funeral this morning. I thought Marion would have liked a colourful arrangement rather than simple blues or whites, so I picked the gaudiest bunch I could find. It took hours to organise it, particularly as I did it all online, and in order to pay I needed yet another password (I think I must have about 150 already) and had to press a million buttons. Each page that came up announced something like 'Nearly done!' or 'Almost there!' or 'Just one final thing and we're sorted!' as if the computer actually knew what torture I was going through and could hear me wailing, at my end: 'Oh God, oh God, will this never end?'

This afternoon, slightly panicked, I must admit, by Marion's death, and thinking that unless I got myself more in shape I'd be the next to die, I went for a walk. The trouble is there's nowhere to walk round here. I could go left to the West End, past dozens of pound shops, mobile phone outlets, supermarkets with dismal bits of greengrocery outside, opticians and fast-food joints, along a pavement so covered with bits of old chewing gum you sometimes wonder whether you'll be able to walk at all without becoming glued to a paving stone and being trapped there for the rest of your life. Or I could go right, which is a dreary stretch past masses of modern blocks of flats. Up the road is the patch of green that Penny and I saved from the developers a few years back. But that's awash with drug dealers and dog poo and benches appropriated by East Europeans drinking tiny bottles of vodka – not particularly jolly. Or there's south, past rows and rows of houses until you get to another row of houses and on and on till you get to a motorway.

North leads to the grisly housing estate where Terry lives.

Eventually I hopped into the car and drove up to Holland Park. Much prettier, but even so, as I tramped round the woodland, I rather wondered what I was doing there and kept looking at my watch to see how long I'd been. Luckily I was reminded of the app on my phone which shows how many steps I'd done and I promised myself that after three thousand I'd go home.

Some people love walking. But what is it about it that they love? What do you think about when walking? All I do is think how cold it is – yes, even in July, being the coldest person on the planet – and whether I'm going to trip over an old tree trunk. Walking is so BORING!! If I knew that every step I took I was turning a mill to grind corn to make bread for a starving child or producing electricity I could see the point of it.

Anyway, what's the difference between walking and going about one's house all day, up and down the stairs, into the garden and so on? If that's not walking, what is? Somehow everyone thinks it has be done in the open air. Not much open air around here, what with the traffic fumes from the Uxbridge Road and the rays from the mobile phone masts and the hundreds of other people all breathing out carbon dioxide.

Walking didn't take my mind off poor Marion, either. All I could think of was how much I missed her.

But when I got back, at least I felt virtuous, so I made myself a cup of tea and had a chocolate-covered digestive biccie as a reward.

Later

Just finished talking to Tim about the funeral arrangements and it turns out that David is coming up, with Sandra. For God's sake, has Sandra just moved back in with him again? I must have been mad to help her get back home. I should have just left her to rot in her wretched hovel to fend for herself. No, I'm being too mean – but even if she hasn't moved back, it's clear that she's spending a lot of time at David's and he's taking on the role of granddad to Gangi, if not father.

Oh well. At least I'll see him there and be able to have a chat. I'm determined to get to the bottom of his coldness.

July 21

Penny came over before the funeral, looking rather wonderful in black. Amazingly, she hadn't had a drink. Robin had said he'd meet us there, but Melanie knocked on the door and swept in, begging for a lift, all hat and scarves and bearing huge branches of greenery and flowers.

Naturally they shed stuff all over the car, but I didn't say anything. It took us about an hour to get there. The funeral had been organised somewhere near Oxford in a woodland setting and, though there was a car park, we had to walk for what seemed miles to get to the spot where Marion was being buried.

There were masses of people there – Marion's friends from her Oxford days, and relatives I'd never met and some I had. I felt so sorry for her poor daughter, who looked absolutely devastated.

Tim had ordered something called a 'coffinless shroud' which meant that Marion was actually encased in a kind of hammock woven of bamboo, resting on a bamboo frame. It was covered with flowers and it all looked marvellously natural and quite unlike the normal sinister coffins that remind me of Dracula movies. It was carried along, underarm, by Jim, James and two other men I'd never seen before,

The service was led by a man in a maroon jersey, as I predicted, but he was pleasant enough, and it was all very low-key, no mention of God at all which was a relief, and lots of stuff about nature. One of the grandchildren, presumably Perry, a sweet little chap of about eight, sang 'All Things Bright and Beautiful', substituting the word 'Nature' for 'Lord God', and it was difficult not to feel intensely moved as his piping voice carried through the air, up through the trees to the blue sky above. And in the periods of reflection, the chirping of the birds through the undergrowth seemed so poignant and right, somehow. At one point a blackbird jumped right into the circle where the shroud was. Everyone held their breath as he hopped around and then, finally, flew off.

After it was over, Robin went up to the body, which was resting on a wooden platform, and made a very peculiar sign on it, I noticed, while muttering a few words. Melanie went up to it dramatically and placed her hand on it, trying, as she later explained, to inject bursts of loving energy into it to help Marion on her way. Penny and I just stood at the back, our eyes full of tears.

Afterwards, we wandered around the woodland, and I was rather surprised not to see my flowers arranged against a tree with all the others. Christ, I'll have to get back to the flower website and that'll involve putting in the password, which of course I've forgotten. Felt very fed up but didn't think it was the moment to explain to Tim that I had sent flowers but they hadn't turned up.

Later, we all convened for coffee, drinks and sandwiches at a local village hall. Finally I caught up with James and Owen, who'd driven all the way up from their farm.

'Isn't it terrible?' said James. 'Another leaf off the tree.'

'I know,' I said. 'First Hughie, then Archie and now Marion . . . Who next?'

'We must all be very nice to each other from now on, darling,' said James. 'It might be the last time we ever see each other again.'

'Well, Marion would have wanted us to be nice to each other, I know that,' I said. I could feel her presence around me all the time, and I kept wishing I'd been nicer to her myself, and appreciated her more, and told her how much she'd meant to me, instead of moaning about her disgusting cooking behind her back and getting irritated about her nagging me to do Pilates (though I have to say Pilates didn't get her very far).

I'd been scouring the group for David, and finally spotted him, under a group of trees. As I approached, I noticed that with him was not Sandra but the Widow Bossom. She turned to me gushingly.

'Wasn't that the most moving ceremony you have ever attended?' she asked. She wore an enormous black hat and was encased in a tight black dress. I don't think she'd ever met Marion in her life.

I smiled and nodded and asked if I could have a word with David alone.

'If you have to,' he said, coldly, and stepped aside.

'David, what on earth is going on?' I asked. 'Everything was so happy last month – and now this! You'll hardly speak to me! Is it some kind of punishment? Have I done something wrong?'

'Wrong? Of course not!' said David, icily. 'You're perfectly entitled to do what you like. You're a free woman!'

'What on earth are you talking about?' I asked, confused.

'You should know. You made your feelings quite clear with that message you left on the stairs for your lover.'

'Lover?' I said, incredulously. 'Lover? What on earth do you mean?'

'You wrote a note to your guru friend saying you'd had the best night ever,' said David. 'I don't wish to discuss it any further.'

He turned on his heel and strode away.

Widow Bossom winked at me. 'Oops! He doesn't look too happy!' she said. 'I expect he'll get over it, whatever it is.'

And she hurried off to console him.

I stood there, under the trees, racking my brains. And then, slowly, it dawned. I'd written that note to Robin about the ionisers and left it on the stairs. And as far as I could remember it said something like 'Robin! I had the best night ever! You are incredible! Much love, Marie!'

David must have misinterpreted it and thought I was having an affair with Robin.

I rushed after him to try to explain, but at the same time Melanie came swirling up and put her arm through David's.

'David, darling!' she said, which I thought was a bit much, considering she hardly knows him. (Well, I know they had a one-night stand once but that was about it.) 'How lovely to see you! And how is Sandra and the baby? And the flood defences? You're SO clever to build flood defences. I don't even know how to fix a dripping tap!' And she gave him an adoring look. 'Now, a word of advice, David. I know you and Marie are back together, but you'd better watch out. Because Tim's a free man now and who knows what he'll get up to when you're down in the country!'

While I reeled at her impertinence, I was horrified to hear David reply, rather sourly: 'Oh, I don't think he'll get very far with Marie! I can't think who would penetrate her defences. Except perhaps some new-age quack.'

And Melanie turned to me with a rather surprised look and shook her head, obviously trying to calibrate his response and realising that something was wrong between us.

Luckily, she rallied. 'Well, don't say I didn't warn you!' she said, giving his arm a squeeze. 'Jimbo!' she cried, noticing James. 'Darling!' By which time David had vanished into the crowd and I didn't see him again.

I was left feeling a mixture of misery and fury. How on earth, after such a lovely night, could David have possibly thought I was two-timing him with Robin of all people? He must be going mad. On the one hand I was tempted to prostrate myself and explain, and on the other I felt absolutely sickened and furious to imagine that David could have thought I would behave like that.

And so the afternoon passed. I managed to do absolutely nothing, and remained in a boiling rage until we drove home. Poor tall Robin was squeezed into the back seat, where he had to sit with his knees under his chin until we got back to London, Melanie having appropriated the front seat with all her bags and scarves and bits of woodland still clinging to her.

Penny, having had rather too much champagne at the wake, started singing rather embarrassing songs in the back, which started off being funny and ended up incredibly irritating.

Later

I was just brooding on the afternoon's events, when there was a ring at the bell. The man from across the road stood at the door holding a huge bunch of flowers.

'I took delivery of these for you when you were out,' he said.

'But they can't be for me!' I said. 'No one would send me flowers.'

But there, inside, was the card. 'With deepest sympathy,' it read. 'Lots of love, from your old friend Marie.'

Somehow I'd sent the flowers to myself! God, I could kill those wretched websites! What am I going to do? Felt so upset and pissed off I rang Penny and asked her over and for once I was jolly glad she'd brought a bottle of champagne. We polished it off easily and even glugged through nearly another bottle of wine before she staggered off home and I crawled, drunk, fraught and sad, to bed.

July 23

I'm still unable to understand David's behaviour. I'm going to do nothing until I calm down a bit because I'm too over-wrought to speak to him for the moment. So, as Tim's family have all gone home, I asked him over for dinner. Not to cheer him up, because nothing will cheer him up of course, it's all so recent, but really because I couldn't bear to think of him alone in his house, surrounded by all the emptiness.

He came bearing a bottle of wine, and I explained about the flowers and he said not to worry, he hadn't noticed, and no, he wouldn't take them with him because the house was groaning with flowers but thank you anyway.

He looked extremely tired, and after taking off his chunky Barbour, he slumped into a chair in the sitting room. He seemed completely lost. I'd roasted him a chicken – I always roast chickens when people are feeling low – and we sat together waiting for the potatoes to crisp up a bit.

It's been barely a week since Marion died so obviously I couldn't ask him anything about his future, but it turned out he'd already made a plan. At first I thought it was too soon, but then he's a bloke. He used to be in the army before he became an accountant, so plans are what keep him going.

'Well, one thing's certain,' he said. I noticed his face looked all grey and crumpled, like a tin that's been run over by a car. 'I'm never going to marry again. I've got to resign myself to being alone for the rest of my life. That means taking a cookery course for a start – Marion was a wonderful cook, as you know – learn how to iron my own shirts and change the sheets and clean the house. I'm not going to let these new tasks defeat me, Marie, I can tell you that. Other men can do them, and so can I. And I'm going to devote my life to work – work that Marion would have approved of, work that would have made her happy. And that's why I'm going to throw myself heart, body and soul into making money for those damned orphans. That's what she would have wanted.' And here of course he broke down, snuffling and pretending he'd got a cold and apologising.

I didn't say anything, just waited, feeling a bit like some

231

ghastly psychotherapist, but I was sitting too far away from him to put my arm around him, and sometimes people don't want all that touching, particularly not people like Tim.

Anyway, eventually through the tears and the coughing, he explained that he wanted to bring the shop up to a different level.

'Not just sell old junk, but sell things that people might want. And I've noticed a gap in the market,' he said. 'Aids for the older person.'

Here he shuffled around in his briefcase which, of course, being Tim, he'd brought with him, and produced a couple of catalogues, one of which was the magazine 'Grey Matters' that had been shoved through my letterbox a few weeks ago.

'Now, just have a look at this, Marie,' he said, handing it to me. 'Don't you think that there's a real need for a shop that stocks stuff like that? Everywhere I look there are people on mobility scooters, people with sticks, people who can't see . . . and this catalogue has everything they need. But older people,' he said, 'aren't used to the internet. They need a place where they can come and buy things – a shop! They want to try things out! It would be such a help for them to have a shop like this! I think there's a profitable market in this – and since my pension's okay, all the profits can go to the orphans. What do you think?'

I was in a difficult position. The potatoes were probably getting rather too crisp in the oven but I didn't want to break the flow, so I leafed through the catalogue, imagining I'd find all kinds of advertisements for commodes and huge nappies.

But I was pleasantly surprised to find some genuinely useful things in it.

'Crikey!' I said. 'A special device for helping you open packages! Easy-to-read weighing scales . . . Actually, that's a very good idea,' I found myself adding. 'I'm so short-sighted I can't read my scales when I'm standing on them even with my glasses! Needle-threaders! Vibrating neck-toners!'

Tim seemed pleased that I'd found some things I approved of, and after about a quarter of an hour I was able to steer him into the kitchen.

The potatoes were blackened, the chicken dry and the beans soggy, but still. All in a good cause. And, being Tim and used to Marion's cooking, it didn't seem to make any difference to him.

'If you can be in the shop a bit more,' I said afterwards, as we sipped coffee, thinking I'd kill two birds with one stone by making Tim feel needed and getting me out of sitting around so much in the grim space in the market, 'that would be incredibly useful.'

'Well, I've got a lot to deal with, with probate and insurance and so on, but you know me, I've got most of it sorted already so it won't be long before I can get down to making a real contribution.'

'Even more of a contribution,' I said, kindly. 'Marion would be proud of you.'

And then poor old Tim collapsed in tears again. Oh, I feel so very, very sorry for the poor chap.

July 24

Told Penny about the flowers this morning.

'In the past, doing something silly usually meant one ended up in bed with someone whose name one didn't know,' she said. 'Now it's sending funeral flowers to oneself. Sad really.'

Later

The estate agents had warned me that they'd be showing a couple round the house today, so before they came I did all the usual things. Brewed real coffee (something I never normally do, since I live on Nescafé) and divided Marion's funeral flowers into separate bunches and put them in every room, so when the man from Ashton Manana appeared I was all prepared. I was even dressed, though it was ten thirty in the morning, a time when I'm usually hurtling round in my dressing gown trying to get chores done.

I didn't much like the couple he'd brought along. They were in their thirties, obviously both professional working people; he probably in a bank and she probably – well, probably in a bank as well. She had tight, scraped-back blonde hair and he, shorter than her, had a rather unpleasant strut to his step and an arrogant face, as if he was used to pushing people around.

Obviously I left them to it, but I felt curiously invaded. I was reminded of the feeling I'd had after I'd been burgled, even though I had, as it were, invited them in.

After about a quarter of an hour when I could hear them walking about upstairs, peering into rooms and mumbling, they came down.

'Do you have the key to the garden?' asked the agent.

I produced it and was horrified to hear the man say, when they stepped outside: 'Well, that grass would have to go! I'm not spending my weekend mowing!' And she said: 'We could put down some decking, and have lots of pots and a barbecue.'

'Or AstroTurf,' he suggested.

'And one of those exterior heating lamps,' she said.

'Maybe a couple,' said her husband.

When they came in, I heard a scrabbling on the roof. Looking up, I saw the pigeon doing a poo directly above their heads – straight onto the sparkling roof that Terry had only just cleaned. And as they turned their heads away, there was Pouncer in the middle of the carpet with his back to them, very obviously weeing.

I felt like raising my fist and saying: 'Right on, Pounce, old chap!' But instead I said: 'Oh, I'm so sorry, he's ill. Obviously I'd take the carpets up before you came.' They gave each other wan smiles.

When they'd finished looking, the agent politely said goodbye, and I was astonished that the pair of prospective buyers never even nodded to me as they left. It was as if I'd been some kind of ghastly old fixture or fitting that, when they moved in, they would get rid of at once.

AstroTurf! What vandals some people are! How would my poor worms and beetles breathe if they were trapped under

235

VIRGINIA IRONSIDE

AstroTurf? And how would my blackbirds and robins get food?
Outdoor heaters! More than one! Eco-vandals!

July 25

Just got back from the shop, where I took over from Melanie.
I found her in the middle of selling some used babygros to a
poor pair who'd come in to look around. The girl was heavily
pregnant, and Melanie was asking ten pounds each for them.

'Look, they've only been used a few times, and they're from
Petit Bateau,' she said. 'At Petit Bateau these would cost at
least fifty pounds each. Look at the stitching on them! And
they've got the famous label. Tell you what – I'll sell you three
for twenty quid! It's a bargain!'

And blow me if these poor dumb young marrieds didn't
cough up!

I must say I was astonished at her salesmanship.

Tim looked up from a desk at the back – I'd only just noticed
him. 'She's our best saleswoman, Marie,' he said. 'She's made
more money for those orphans than all of us put together!'

Melanie preened and went over to Tim. She positioned herself behind him and kneaded his shoulders.

'I've told Timmy-wimmy he ought to go home and rest,
but no, he insists on coming in! Now, would you like a cup
of herbal tea?'

Tim looked up gratefully and gave her a glowing smile. 'I'd
love one, Mel,' he said. And then, to me: 'What a woman!'

'How can you bear to be working like this?' I said. 'It's so soon . . . You needn't worry, we can cope without you! Don't feel you have to come in every day!'

But Tim looked up and said: 'No, this is my homage to Marion. When I'm here, I feel close to her. Everyone says I should stay at home and grieve, but I don't want to. I want to be here, close to her, close to her work.'

I felt rather choked up when he said this and thought my previous suggestion had been rather trivial and insensitive.

We're planning to close the shop for August because everyone will be away, but Tim is thinking of working on plans for a complete revamp before Christmas, when he wants to turn it into a proper commercial shop, aimed exclusively at Old People.

Sounds like an excellent idea. As long as I don't have to serve in it.

July 29

I'm afraid I'm going to have to lock Pouncer in the garden when house-viewers come round. It takes me ages to get the stains out of the carpet every time he wees, and honestly, I can't have him showing his disapproval quite so blatantly. And the pigeon doing the same! Both of them are obviously psychic and were trying to express, in their own crude way, exactly what I'd felt about that horrible pair.

Needless to say they haven't made an offer, which is rather a relief.

July 31, night

Absolutely ghastly evening. Penny had suggested we go round the corner to dinner and, because we thought he'd be lonely, we asked Tim, too.

We went to the new posh place, but it started badly because clearly Penny had had too much to drink before she even set foot outside her front door. By the time she arrived at the restaurant she was in a foul mood. She refused to sit at the table we were given, and when we were offered another she said there was a draught. Then she complained that the music was too loud and while she was complaining, she knocked a bottle of red wine off our table and onto the lap of the woman sitting next door.

The woman was quite prepared to be nice about it, until she realised that Penny was drunk. At this point, Tim took charge and said he would pay for the dry cleaning and he was very sorry, while I suggested we all go home before we cause any more damage. But Penny refused to budge and kept insisting she wanted a hamburger.

'But I want it to be well done!' she said emphatically. 'I mean WELL DONE!' she shouted. 'I don't want it to be pink, or even slightly pink, I'm not one of those bloody gourmets who think they know what's what, I want mine WELL DONE! I want my burger COOKED. Properly COOKED! Not seignbloodyant. Not bloody bloody bloody bloody. WELL DONE!'

At this point I got up and had a word with the manager. I was very apologetic and we discussed whether it would be better to serve her or remove her. From the tone of his voice I knew that he wanted her out as soon as possible. Somehow between us Tim and I managed to cajole her to come with us, saying we'd go to a proper burger place and get her a well-cooked burger. Finally we got her out of the door, where she tripped slightly and then began to insist on going straight back into the restaurant.

'Have you seen her like this before?' asked Tim, helplessly, as he guided her down the street. 'I know she's been a bit tipsy recently, but this is ridiculous!'

'I've never seen her quite like this!' I said, truthfully. 'I can't think what's got into her. Maybe she took a pill or something and drank on top of it. This is a nightmare!'

Half pulling and half pushing, we kept her occupied in the street while I went into the local McDonald's and bought her a burger. We thought she ought to have some food before dragging her home. But once we got back, she couldn't find her key because she was too drunk. She constantly put her hand down the side of her coat and screamed with laughter. I took it from her pocket, opened the door and we shoved her upstairs. Once in the bedroom, I almost pushed her onto her bed where, luckily, she fell fast asleep immediately.

Tim and I tiptoed down the stairs, feeling rather guilty.

'You don't think she'll choke on her own vomit and die or anything, do you?' I asked Tim, and then felt awful even mentioning death, but he said, 'No, she's not unconscious, she's just utterly plastered. God, she can't go on like this. What a dreadful evening. Well done, Marie . . .'

'Well done you, darling,' I said. 'We could only have done it together.'

Resolving to check on her in the morning, we parted company and I got back home starving.

There was nothing to eat in the fridge except a raw leek, half a beetroot and a pot of sour cream. By grating up the vegetables and boiling them with a stock cube and then adding the sour cream I managed to make a reasonable kind of borscht and mopped it up with a piece of toast and a boiled egg.

Could have been worse.

AUGUST

August 1

Was woken by the man from Ashton Manana ringing me saying he'd got a special viewing of a house in Brixton because so many people were after it, and I had to go down to see it this afternoon. Reluctantly I agreed. But immediately afterwards I rang Penny to see how she felt, and got extremely worried when she didn't answer the phone. Was convinced she'd choked on her own vomit and it would be all my fault, so I raced round there as quickly as I could and banged on the door. Eventually I heard heavy steps on the stairs, and was relieved when a grey-faced Penny appeared and led me creakily into the kitchen. She was still wearing the clothes from the night before.

'What time is it?' she asked rather crossly.

'Don't worry about what time it is,' I said. 'I was just worried because you didn't pick up the phone.'

Penny used the kitchen table for support as she lowered herself into a chair.

'God, I've got such a headache,' she said. 'Jesus! Did we go out last night?'

'We certainly did,' I said, putting on the kettle and reaching for her coffee. 'Penny, you'd had far, far too much to drink! Don't you remember?'

'I can't remember anything,' said Penny, smiling rather rue-fully. 'Oh, how awful. I must have had a blackout. God, my head!'

'Penny, listen,' I said, as I put her coffee in front of her and sat down myself. 'You can't go on like this. Last night was simply awful. You made a complete spectacle of yourself. We were all chucked out of the restaurant – that's after you'd knocked a bottle of wine all over the next-door table. Tim and I had to pull and push to get you home. I've been so worried, I could hardly sleep! You've got to stop! Not just cut down, Penny, I mean stop. Stop drinking completely.'

Penny looked furiously at me, and then clutched her stomach. 'Oh, God, I'm going to be sick,' she said.

And then, to my horror, she was. She just leant forward and was sick onto the kitchen floor, splattering me and the tablecloth with horrible blobs.

'Oh God, I'm sorry,' she said, bursting into tears. 'Oh, I'll clear it up!'

'Don't be silly,' I said, gritting my teeth. 'You sit there, and I'll do it.'

Seizing a huge handful of kitchen roll, I mopped and mopped and wiped and sloshed, and eventually the sick was all cleared up. I'd got Penny a large bowl – the same priceless Chinese one, now I know where to find it – so that next time she could be sick in that. During all this time, Penny was silent except for the odd moan and garbled apology.

When I'd finished, I said: 'Now, you drink your coffee and lots of water' – I placed a jug and glass beside the coffee – 'and then go upstairs, get changed, have a hot bath, get into your nightdress and go back to bed. Have you got any aspirins?'

She nodded.

'Up you go,' I said, peremptorily. Holding on to the furniture as she went, Penny tottered upstairs and I heard the sound of the bath running. Finally she appeared in her blue silk dressing gown, still looking ashen-faced.

'Now take these,' I said, giving her two aspirin, 'and go to bed and I'll ring you later. And don't forget the water. Drink lots of it!'

She nodded dumbly and staggered back upstairs.

'And remember what I said!' I called after her. 'You've got to stop. You're my friend and I love you! You've got to stop!'

She turned round. 'I will, Marie,' she said, rather pitifully like an obedient child. 'I will. I promise. I really will.'

'Not just promises to keep me happy?' I said.

'No,' she said. 'Promises to keep me happy. I've been so worried about it, particularly recently, but I haven't found any way to stop. I couldn't bear the idea of going to AA because I don't really think I'm an alcoholic. Anyway, those meetings will just be full of down-and-outs and ghastly smelly old piss-artists with no teeth.'

'You are an alcoholic,' I said. 'Or at least you're addicted to drink. And what do you mean about down-and-outs? AA meetings these days are packed with stars and celebrities. You'll probably find Mr Right there! I'll find out where the nearest meetings are and when. You must go.'

'I'd be too frightened to go on my own,' said Penny tearfully. 'I'm sure I can manage to stop drinking now I've had that awful experience.'

'Rubbish! I'll come with you if you want!' I said.

'But you can't come with me,' said Penny tearfully. 'You're not allowed in unless you're an alcoholic. I did ring up and ask last week.'

'I'll pretend I'm an alcoholic,' I said, laughing. 'They'll never know.'

And at this Penny did manage a weak smile though her eyes were full of tears. 'Thanks, Marie,' she said. 'You're a brick. I don't know what I'd do without you. Thanks.'

Now it's just a matter of seeing whether she'll be so keen to go to AA when she wakes up. I absolutely dread going because of course there won't be any stars or celebs and it'll just be, as she says, down-and-outs and ghastly smelly old piss-artists with no teeth.

Had splitting headache all the rest of the morning and don't know how I can face trailing down to Brixton to see this house that Ashton Manana have found for me to look at.

Oh gawd.

Later

I'd tried to get hold of Jack and Chrissie to see if I could pop in and see them and Gene when I was in the area, but it seemed they were tied up with having friends round and Gene was going for a play-date so there wouldn't have been much point, sadly. But before I set off, I wrapped the last of the tree pictures in bubble wrap and brown paper, so they wouldn't be damaged in the post to India. Terry was here, repainting over some of the hairline cracks in the odd wall that, according to the agent, the potential buyers had apparently spotted when they came round, and when he saw me setting off with the parcel he offered to take it to the post office himself. I gladly handed it over because going to the post office these days always involves a ten-hour wait. Terry could probably make a good supplement to his living if he simply offered to take people's parcels there. I bet they'd pay him a quid apiece not to have to make the journey.

I must saying, I'm becoming rather dependent on Terry. He's smartened the house up no end and even fixed the creaking floorboards in the room where I work by taking up the entire carpet and banging them down with nails. The Ashton Manana agent had said the couple he'd shown round had found the creaking particularly unnerving.

I drove down to Brixton, where I found the first problem – there was literally nowhere to park – which won't be very helpful for people coming to visit me. Residents' parking ends quite late so unless I have dinner parties or visitors who are prepared to visit me after my bedtime, like Dracula, I'll never see anyone.

The house was in a grid of streets with names like Chaucer Road, Shakespeare Avenue, Dryden Close – after all the poets.

To be honest, that put me off a bit, too. I don't want to live inside the *Oxford Dictionary of Quotations*. And what really freaked me out was there wasn't a tree or a shop to be seen. At home I rely on the corner shop run by the delightful Mr Patel, and as I'm constantly popping down there in my dressing gown to pick up things I've run out of, I'm not sure what I'd do if I had to get dressed and drive just to buy a pint of milk.

The other odd thing about the street was that not only did there seem to be absolutely no one in it, but the few people I did see in it were white. I felt as if I were walking back into the fifties. Brixton, of course, comprises a brilliant ethnic mix just round the corner, but this curious enclave – well, I wouldn't have been surprised to see the England flag hanging out of every window. I suddenly realised how used I've got to the jolly mix of tribes and nationalities that make up Shepherd's Bush.

The house itself – well! Although the façade was Victorian and much like my own home, someone who thought they were very stylish had ripped out every single old feature and bunged spotlights into the ceilings, flat-screen tellies into almost every room, and as for shelves for storage space, forget it! All the fireplaces had been sealed over, meaning there was no central point to any of the rooms, the walls were white and the floor had been 'poured' white. I felt like one of those people in the graphics at the beginning of a seventies James Bond film.

To make it worse, the stylish somebody had pulled down every interior wall he could see and installed a spiral staircase to the upper floors. I'm afraid the first thing that came into my mind was that I wouldn't be able to fit a stairlift in that when the time came!

Everywhere you looked there were glass-topped tables and white laminate cupboards. The only things on the walls were giant black and white photographs of leaf skeletons in white frames.

No baths, only showers – and about a hundred of them – and a kitchen with a central island – something that always, I feel, gets in the way. As this was also white, it was asking to be bumped into every time you turned round. The only seats were four white barstools.

Feeling awful that I'd given the Ashton Manana man the trouble of showing me around, I feigned interest and said I'd consider it, but all the time was thinking: 'If I don't get out of here soon, I'll become dizzy and faint.'

Recently I met someone who lived in Camberwell – which is just next door. 'You'd love it,' he enthused. 'It's full of writers, artists, painters . . . people just like you. You'd love the Camberwell Society . . . we're all nice and bright . . .'

And then suddenly I could imagine myself, surrounded by all these educated white people, knee deep in delicatessens, community arts festivals and local independent bookshops . . . oh God, the local independent bookshops! The worthiness of them! The smugness of them! The knowledge that deep down of course I really admire them, and would support them to the hilt, but at the same time recoil from their claustrophobic air of moral superiority.

Rang the agent later and said, on second thoughts and after much deliberation, no.

August 2

'Could Wi-Fi be harming YOUR health? That's what a growing number of people believe is triggering their headaches, nausea and crippling pain' (*Daily Rant*)

Wonder if that's what's causing my headaches? I seem to have one the whole time now, despite Robin's ionisers. I expect it's a brain tumour. Usually is. Will go and see doctor if not gone by end of week.

Looked up AA meetings and it seems the place is absolutely teeming with them – they're all around us, like Uber taxis. Rang Penny but luckily, before I could speak she said she'd got the address of one near Shepherd's Bush Green and she asked if I could go with her tonight. I was hoping for an evening with the telly, but of course I had to say yes. She also said she hadn't had a drink at all since two days ago, the evening of the frightful scene; and since she hadn't managed two days without a drink for the last year she seemed very pleased.

As was I.

Later

It was absolutely fascinating! The meeting took place at seven, in an old church hall off the market, and a more grisly place I have rarely seen. The walls were covered with the torn pictures done by primary school kids, the glass in the doors was almost obliterated by old pieces of Sellotape and Blu-Tack. The beige skirting boards were scuffed and half the chairs appeared to be broken. At one side there was a rickety table on which sat an assorted collection of chipped mugs with some boxes of herbal tea beside them, some of which must have been bought in the nineties. An ancient kettle sat steaming beside them and we were encouraged to help ourselves. Weak evening sunlight crept in from a dirty skylight.

'Welcome!' said a middle-aged lady in a frayed Chanel jacket. 'Are you new? You'll soon pick it all up. Do sit down.'

We joined a few others sitting in the circle of chairs – and stared at our hands. When I looked up I could see only one down-and-out drunk; the rest were all ages, all classes, both sexes and all colours. I practically fainted when I recognised, across the room, my own Mr Patel from the corner shop. He looked as astonished to see Penny and me, as I must have looked to see him. I didn't think that Muslim people drank! All most mysterious. There was also a guy of about our age who I was convinced was Mick Jagger and I kept nudging Penny and mouthing: 'Look who's here!' but she seemed too nervous to pay any attention. I couldn't take my eyes off him.

At last the meeting started and some kind of chairperson said we should all introduce ourselves and everyone said, 'Hi! I'm Zara,' or whatever, 'and I'm an alcoholic'. (Mick, of course, was pretending and said, 'Hi, I'm John, and I'm an alcoholic.' Actually, it was then that I started to wonder whether it really was Mick Jagger because he had a rather peculiar voice. Could have been French. Or perhaps Mick was still pretending.)

Dreaded it when it came to me so I just said: 'I'm Marie' and didn't add anything else, whereupon the whole meeting ground to a halt and there was a lot of discussion about whether I should attend because I hadn't said I was an alcoholic.

Whereupon I said I didn't think I was an alcoholic because I didn't drink that much but I certainly drank every day (a complete lie) and usually at least three quarters of a bottle of wine a day (again, lying my head off) and someone said: 'If you spot it you got it' and everyone nodded wisely. Eventually they decided that whatever I was I could stay, even though it wasn't an 'open meeting' (i.e. no non-alcoholics could attend) as long as I realised that 'what we hear here, stays here', and I said of course. Then Penny said: 'I'm Penny and I'm an alcoholic' and burst into tears and everyone said: 'Hi, Penny' as if she'd just said wasn't it a nice day, and finally they moved on to poor old Mr Patel who had to say: 'I'm Rajesh and I'm an alcoholic' in front of two of his customers!

Then everyone had a chance to 'share' – and the stories they told! Sue, the nice lady in the old Chanel jacket, had actually stolen from her own children to get money for booze, and Reg had once woken up in the bottom of a bin about to be tipped into a rubbish cart until he screamed and they saved him just in time. My hair was standing on end. Turned out that Mr Patel – Rajesh – had sneaked down from his flat upstairs and raided the drinks section of his own shop and eventually became so abusive when the police arrived that he was lucky to keep his licence, and the Mick lookalike turned out to have been sleeping on park benches and one evening tried to kill himself with a comb.

In the end we stood up and held hands and said something called the Serenity Prayer: 'God, grant me the serenity to accept the things I cannot change, the courage to change the things I can, and the wisdom to know the difference', and then we all had to chant: 'Keep coming back, it works if you work it!' Finally there was a bit of chat and someone stuffed masses of pamphlets into our hands and said they looked forward to seeing us next time. It was so friendly and lovely. Outside, Reg came up to us and intoned, 'I'm not okay, and you're not okay, but that's okay.' I practically cried, and then we reeled back home.

'"One day at a time",' said Penny, reading from the leaflet as we got stuck into some rather delicious spaghetti Bolognese I'd made, using pork mince as well as ordinary beef mince, which makes all the difference. 'Listen to this. "I'm sick and tired of being sick and tired" – that just how I feel, Marie! What did you think?'

I told the truth and said I thought it was lovely and I'd felt really accepted and almost wanted to become an alcoholic myself so that I could go again, but Penny looked serious and said that wasn't very funny. '"Let go and let God",' she said. 'This is amazing stuff. I'm going to get a sponsor and do the Twelve Steps.'

'Steady on!' I said. 'Try out a few more meetings first!'

'I know this can help me,' said Penny decisively. 'Thanks so much for coming with me. I'm going to change my life. Every day is . . . how does it go?' She scrabbled through the leaflet. 'Ah, yes, "Every day is the first day of my life!" That's me.'

And off she went, radiant with a kind of holy conviction.

Must say I was pretty amazed. Do hope she doesn't start lecturing me about drink in future. I may not be an alcoholic but I certainly wouldn't want anyone putting their hand over my glass when I was pouring myself a fourth helping of Merlot.

August 4

Headache's so bad I went to see my doctor. She's convinced it's an allergy to dust mites – and actually it could well be, considering the amount of rubbish I've had dumped in my corridor since the shop opened. She suggested I spray the house with anti-dust mite stuff and buy some anti-dust mite bedding. All well and good until she turned her computer round to show me an image of a dust mite which looked, on the screen, twice the size of Pouncer, like an enormous brown tortoise with crab-like legs. Luckily, she said they are absolutely minuscule and can't be seen with the human eye. Suddenly the spotless clean all-white house in Brixton seems a more attractive proposition.

As I was getting up to leave, she said she had to ask me a few routine questions. Did I smoke? How much exercise did I take? Did I have five portions of fruit and vegetables a day (of course not)! And, crucially, how much did I drink a day? I was about to go into my AA spiel and say that I had a drink every day and it was never under three-quarters of a bottle, when I realised that this wasn't the right answer for the doctor and scaled everything down to a bare minimum.

August 8

The family are off to Devon for their summer holidays – and to celebrate Gene's birthday while they're down there. They've rented a cottage by the sea near Clovelly and it sounds absolutely gorgeous. I'm going to join them for a few days and then I'll see if I can face looking in on David on my way back.

I'm still fuming and upset, but if my mood's changed and I'm calmer I'll give it a go.

No word from Ashton Manana. When I rang I was told that August is a dead month for house sales and that things should pick up again in September.

August 10

Although Pouncer's not quite as bad as he used to be and now uses a tray I've put out for him – at least most of the time – I thought another visit to the vet was due. Terry was about doing some gardening for me, so it wasn't as difficult as usual. Of course Pouncer had wedged himself under the sofa, but instead of having to get hysterical with a broom to get him out, Terry just leaned down, took him gently by the scruff of the neck and calmly popped him into the cat basket. No yowling, no nothing. Either Terry's got a way with animals or Pouncer's sicker than I thought.

Perhaps Terry's like that horse-whisperer I saw a few years back on telly – a guy dreadfully abused as a child who could just go up to any mad horse, chat away quietly in horse language, and immediately convert it into a serene and spiritual being with a permanently goofy smile on its horsy face.

This time the vet seemed more upbeat. Since I'd been there the last time, he said, there'd been great advances in the world of kidney medicine and there was a chance that they could give Pouncer a transplant.

'A kidney transplant?' I said, my eyes starting out of my head in the style popularised by snails, as P.G. Wodehouse so aptly put it in a book that I'm rereading. 'But then he'll have to be on dialysis six hours a day for the rest of his life!'

The vet laughed smoothly as he popped Pouncer back in his basket. 'No, that's before you have the kidney transplant, not after. No, there's a good chance he'd pull through and we could give him a couple more years. He'd be on permanent medication and there are, of course, risks, but on the whole he's a fit old gentleman and I don't see why it wouldn't be worth giving it a go.'

I wasn't sure I liked this option at all. Not the cost, of course, because I love Pouncer dearly, but I'm really not sure I wanted to put him through a major operation. Most cats are dead by his age. Would it be fair to drag him back into the world of the living when he's so clearly on the way out?

'Er, how much would it cost?' I asked.

'Nothing, if you have pet insurance,' said the vet.

'But I don't have pet insurance.'

'Ah. Well, it's not cheap. I'd say about £5,000,' replied the vet.

The old eyes were now waving around on their stalks. 'Five thousand pounds?' I said. 'Well, I do love him, but honestly, I think that's a bit ridiculous – and he'd have to go through the trauma of the operation – and presumably it might not work.'

'There's always that possibility,' said the vet.

'No, I think the best thing is to make his last days as comfortable as possible,' I said, firmly. So the vet gave me some stronger painkillers and again said to come back in a month.

Nurse charged me £200. The pills, she said, accounted for the rise in price. Still, better than five k, as I think the bankers call it.

August 15

Had a lovely email from Brad and Sharmie, saying they absolutely adore the pictures, which is a huge relief. They're not only planning an exhibition of them in the hall of Brad's office, but they've got a mega-rich Indian client of Brad's interested and he says he'll match all the money raised to relocate the orphans and on top of that will give them ten grand for the whole set of paintings!

I felt so delighted I was almost tearful and faint with joy – a feeling I hadn't experienced since I heard that Chrissie was pregnant. It's a wonderful feeling to know I've done something worthwhile – and that other people really love something I've created. Indeed I was on cloud nine when I found myself in Mr Patel's shop, buying the usual milk and a bottle of wine and it was only when I was paying that I realised I'd last seen him at the AA meeting. However, clearly the maxim 'What you hear here, stays here' worked because he behaved exactly as before. I started to wonder whether I hadn't been hallucinating at the meeting. Perhaps it had no more been him than it had been Mick Jagger.

He even put the bottle of wine into a bag without saying a word – but perhaps that was because he knew that the last thing you do with alcoholics is try to prevent them from drinking. Anyway, I came over all blushing and guilty and slunk out feeling like the worst and most deceitful addict in the world.

Soon perked up again, once I'd reread Brad and Sharmie's flattering email about ten more times, and then, when I heard the letterbox click, went down to find the sweetest little letter from Alice.

'Dear my freind Marie,' she wrote, 'I love your pictures, and mom and dad love them too. I wish I could dror trees like you do. You are very clever. I miss you. Your freind Alice' and of course that made me burst into tears, so it was a day of raging emotions.

August 16

I'm trying to prepare for this trip to Devon to stay with the family, via one night with Sylvie, my darling Archie's daughter. I keep checking the BBC weather on the internet to see whether it'll be boiling hot or freezing cold. Endless lists and sorting with Robin and Terry – who's agreed to clear the roof of pigeon poo yet again and leave it sparkling.

He promises he'll feed Pouncer every day – I don't trust

Robin with his vegetarian diets – and make sure the wretched pigeon is okay. James assured me his dovecote (which he now pronounces 'doocut' – how pretentious can you get?) will be ready in a matter of weeks.

Penny continues to go to AA. 'Ninety meetings in ninety days' is her avowed aim – something they do, apparently. Amazingly, Tim has actually gone along with her to a meeting, an open one, as he didn't like the idea of pretending to be an old boozer. He told her that he really got something out of it and that their way of looking at things is incredibly useful because it's made him think of life in a completely different way. Good for him.

Must dead-head the roses when I get back. They've been astonishing this year and at one point the garden looked like something painted by Monet (not waterlilies obviously), but the blooms are starting to dry up now and unless I cut them they won't bloom again.

August 18

En route to Gene and family, it was the first really hot day of summer.

I was bowling along quite nicely when the traffic started to slow down.

We'd got a little way along a one-way slip road that led from the motorway when we all ground to a halt. Ten minutes passed. We were still revving up our engines in anticipation of being able to make our escape, but nothing happened. The noise of a fire engine whistled behind us, so we drove our cars into the hedgerow. Then, down the empty space in the middle of road, an ambulance came roaring down between us, accompanied by police motorcycles. Engines were turned off. Car doors were opened and people put their feet outside.

About five minutes later some of us got out for a stretch, smiling and shrugging at our fellow drivers, looking ruefully at our watches and asking if anyone knew what was going on. Finally, rumour got round from someone listening to local radio that a bus had burnt itself out near the lights at the top of the road. We were in for the long haul.

I rang Sylvie to say I'd be late. She commiserated and said they'd start lunch without me if I didn't mind. The sun beat down and it was curiously silent. We looked around our new surroundings – rows of stationary cars nestling close to mountains of fading cow parsley. Bees buzzed. Birds sang. A perfect English country afternoon.

The Polish driver of the big truck parked on the opposite side of the road was told by his boss that he could remove his tachometer card from his engine so he didn't have to worry about taking a legal break at the correct time. The Chinese woman behind me remained in her seat and got out her laptop. A very amiable English gent and his wife, wearing expensive country jerkins, wandered up and down until they got too hot and started to unpeel their layers.

Down the centre of the road there walked a mother, with her little girl and a tiny dog. As she processed down the avenue, everyone got out of their cars to greet her. They said hello to the little girl, patted the dog and asked its name.

The amiable English gent was walking down the hedgerow plucking flowers. A couple of giggling young girls who were sitting on the bonnet of their car in front said they only lived three hundred yards away and if we were there for hours they'd miss their party that night. One of them had been eighteen only the day before.

A woman came up and said: 'Well, we may be waiting but at least it wasn't us on that bus,' and we all agreed.

The amiable gent presented his wild flower bouquet gallantly to one of the girls in front. 'A late birthday present,' he said. Then he started pointing and explaining: 'This is meadowsweet, this is dead-nettle, this blue is scabious . . . here is lady's slipper . . .'

Then the traffic started moving again. We all got back into our cars, hooting and waving as we passed each other, never to see each other again.

When I finally got to Sylvie's, long past lunchtime, she and Harry rushed out of the house. 'Poor, poor you!' they said. 'It must have been terrible!'

'Ghastly!' I said.

But actually it was one of the nicest journeys I've ever had.

Later

It was brilliant seeing them again. And even more brilliant, I have to say, seeing my old pal Chummy, the Alsatian we'd rescued a few years back from a dreadful chained-up fate in the garden opposite. He fell on me, and started leaping up and licking me, and even though I'm not one of nature's dog-lovers, I was quite bowled over with pleasure. He looked so happy and fit, nothing like the mangy old piece of scrag he'd been on his arrival at my house.

Having heard about the shop, Sylvie's been absolutely amazing, rounding up the most enormous amount of stuff from friends. As they're her friends, everything she's collected is clean and ironed and wildly expensive. Looking at it all laid out in her sitting room, I felt as if I were in a National Trust gift shop – tasteful tea towels, barely worn Barbours, only slightly frayed shirts from Turnbull and Asser and lots of Peter Jones glasses. Or glassware, as we probably should call it if we're going to sell it to the highest bidder. Will have to stop Melanie trying to get her paws on it all first. There's so much, it would hardly fit into the car, but we managed to cram it in.

August 19

I had so many black bin bags I couldn't see out of my back window so, reluctantly, as I drove through Felbersham I stopped at a charity shop and dumped a few bags there. An old lady tottered out of the back and was extremely grateful and I hoped it was far enough away from Sylvie's friends that they wouldn't find out. Felt awful, but honestly it was either that or I'd have been had up for dangerous driving.

Filling up with petrol at the next garage, I could read the

Rant's headline in a newspaper rack from the moment I stopped the car.

'The World's Going to Hell in a Handcart – Now it's Official!'

Brilliant. That's all I need.

August 23

Just writing this before I set off home. Had absolutely brilliant time with the family in their rented cottage. It was on the cliffs and overlooked the sea. Amazing views and as usual I wished I lived in the country. Even though I know that after three days I'd be begging to get back to London.

But it was slightly odd being treated like a frail old lady. I wasn't allowed to cook, shop or Hoover, and Gene was even deputed to go up every day and make my bed.

'You're here for a rest,' said Jack, decisively, 'and we're going to give you a rest.'

I was able, at least, to take them out to the odd supper, and we had one particularly jolly evening when we went to a posh chippie and on the menu was advertised 'fish escorted by chips'. This prompted Gene to draw a terrific cartoon of a fish and a chip going down the road, and eventually getting married.

'What would their children be like?' asked Chrissie.

'They'd be like this,' said Gene. 'They'd be called Fip and Chish.' And he drew them too, half chip, half fish, in skirts. 'Unfortunately, they don't have any legs,' he said, grinning, 'so they have to hop.'

Felt particularly peculiar when Jack announced they were all going off on a long hike along the cliffs. Have to admit my heart slightly sank when he said it would be an all-day trip because I've never been a hiking person. But I found my dread turning to pique when Jack insisted I stay at home and 'have a rest'.

'To be honest, Mum, we do walk a lot faster than you, and you've never liked walking anyway.'

As I waved them off I felt rather sad, remembering the days when Jack and I used to go camping on Dartmoor and I thought nothing of rigging up a tent in the middle of a storm. And cooking a breakfast of sausages and bacon on a gas primus stove in a howling gale in the morning. Still, I suppose 'those days are over'. It's very difficult getting used to that phrase. But I now realise there are quite a lot of things I'll never do again. Paint a ceiling (thank God); go to Paris (actually not that much of a loss since the last time I went it was like Disneyland, there were so many tourists); dance till dawn; roll down a hill; get married.

Oh, dear.

I was pondering all this rather gloomily, considering whether the reason middle-aged children start treating their ageing parents with such deference is because they want to infantilise them so they feel justified in bunging them into a nursing home sooner rather than later. But my paranoid thoughts were soon driven away when, at about midday, to my great amusement (tinged, of course, with sympathy for them), there was a huge clap of thunder and rain came belting down in grey sheets, racing sideways across the windowpanes.

As they were out and couldn't stop me, I made banana

bread and scones and braved the rain to get some WI straw-berry jam from the village shop.

The wind seemed to howl for hours until about four o'clock when the sun came out again. But it was a sad little bunch who came tottering back just before six.

'Christ! Never again! You would have hated it, Mum!' said Jack, as he wriggled out of his soaking jacket. Chrissie raised her eyebrows at me as she seized a towel from the kitchen and started rubbing her hair. Then she went upstairs to use the hairdryer. Gene was hunched at the bottom of the stairs, trying in vain to undo the sodden laces on his walking boots.

'We had to wait for hours under a tree,' complained Gene. 'Mum, hurry up with the hairdryer,' he called. 'I need it to dry my phone out!'

The home-made tea, however, went down a storm and everyone said, as they always do after a disastrous expedition like this, that 'at least we'll sleep well'.

Later
Oh, God! Just as I was about to set off, I got a text from Sylvie which read: 'So sorry, my friend says she shouldn't have given you cottage teapot! Could you drop it on the way back? SO SO SORRY! Xxxx'

August 24

What a nightmare! Well, even after the family very kindly helped me unpack the car and search every black bin bag for this wretched teapot, there was still no sign of it. Gene was convinced he'd find it but even he had to admit defeat in the end. By now it was midday and the family wanted to get off to the beach, so reluctantly I drove off, hoping against hope that the charity shop in Felbersham would be open today and that I'd find the teapot there and be able to buy the wretched thing back.

But when I arrived, there was a completely different little old lady and she knew nothing about teapots or anything. Very sweetly she let me check through the stuff at the back, but the problem was that I couldn't even recognise which black bin bags were mine, so I had to search through them all. God, if it is dust mites that give me these headaches I'm going to have a cracker soon – the old shoes, the used children's bibs, the sec-ond-hand lavatory brushes . . . everything seemed utterly grisly.

Finding nothing, we came to the conclusion that one Betty must have been the lady who'd been there before – but she wouldn't be in until the next day. We rang her but there was no reply. Nothing for it but to stay the night in a dreadful old pub in Felbersham (£100 a night!) and wait till morning. Was in such a flap, I forgot to ring Jack who'd asked me to text him when I arrived home 'so I know you arrived safely' (I thought it was mums that did that to sons, not the other way round) and got a cross and worried text from him asking if I was okay.

August 25

I was in SUCH an angry mood in the morning, and hung around for ages for Betty because the shop didn't open on

Wednesdays till midday, and when she finally did totter in, it turned out she'd sold the beastly teapot! It was all I could do not to shout 'Fuck! Fuck! Fuck!' at the top of my voice in front of her, but I managed to mind my manners and eventually she remembered the name of the person who'd bought it. I went to the library and looked her up on the electoral roll, tracked her down and, with a mixture of charm, oily explanations and money (I had to pay £30 to get the thing back), I returned to the car with the teapot, chucked it in the boot, and set off for Sylvie's. I was now £130 down on the whole venture. My teeth were ground down to their stumps.

And to top it all, when I arrived at Sylvie's that afternoon, she just took the teapot, saying she hoped it hadn't been too much trouble, as her friend had only wanted it because she thought there was an old letter inside. But when Sylvie looked and there wasn't a trace of a letter, she handed it back saying she hoped I could get a good price for it.

Back in the car, I found myself delivering one of those expletive-filled rants that went on for about twenty minutes. I suppose it's better to do it in the car than impose it on anyone outside, but I felt a bit sorry for my poor old satnav having to listen to all that vitriol.

Not that, of course, he can hear.

Right up until the moment I got to David's turning off the motorway I was in two minds whether to pop in on him or not. I'd decided to drive on, but once I got to the first roundabout I turned and followed the familiar B-road down to his farm.

I felt sad, realising it was so long since I'd been there, and I was touched to see the great earth-mounds piled up, making the building itself like a fortress. There was something so courageous about the sight of them.

I stopped just before the farmhouse and texted him, so he'd have some kind of warning at least, but when I banged on the door, it turned out that there'd been no point. He wasn't in.

The person who opened the door was none other than Sandra, Gangi in her arms, a pram in the hall and toys strewn about everywhere. I thought she'd got a flat in Bath, but from where I was standing it seemed clear that she'd actually moved back in!

She seemed delighted to see me and insisted on making me a cup of tea, so I couldn't exactly turn on my heel, but although she banged on about the flat and how Gangi was loving playgroup there, and how she only came to David on days when it was closed – 'to get a bit of fresh air' – I didn't believe a word of it. I realised that I should never have helped Sandra get back to England because she's simply wormed her way back into David's affections and our lovely relationship is over for ever.

Of course it was a great mistake to think it would ever have worked. Melanie was right, much as I hate to admit it. Once divorced, however you try to rearrange a relationship in the future, it's usually doomed and I should be old enough to know that. David's always had the capacity to hurt me and, though he's doing it a different way this time, it's still just as agonising.

To make matters worse, just as I was leaving I bumped into

Widow Bossom, who was coming up the path bearing a casserole. Her dark glasses were still shoved on top of her head, and I noticed she had a very big but pert bottom, crammed into her tight jeans.

'Little Gangi loves my liquidised coq au vin!' she said. 'What a shame you won't be here to share it!'

Honestly, she never gives up, does she, poor woman!

August 26

Still felt terribly upset and wished I'd never popped in on David. After a couple of glasses of wine, I even wrote David an email – none too friendly – saying that I really thought he should have told me the new situation with Sandra because it would have stopped me looking like a complete idiot, and that I hoped he'd be happy with her. I ended up with the words: 'See you sometime. Best, Marie.'

Felt a bit better after that, and was delighted to see that Terry had, off his own bat, dead-headed all the roses. The pigeon was looking fat and healthy but Pouncer is still very poorly. I will have to take him to the vet yet again and see if I can persuade him either to ease his pain – he spends a lot of time yowling and purring, sure sign that he's feeling dreadful – or put him out of it altogether.

No word from the estate agents, but an enthusiastic email from Tim outlining his plans for the reopening of the shop, half of which will be devoted to second-hand stuff, and the other to his new business selling oldie aids.

Later

Spent the evening feeling utterly miserable and, of course, suddenly wishing I hadn't sent David that email. If only one could suck these things back. I was so stupid. I mean, after all, if I don't want to marry him, why shouldn't he try to settle down with someone else?

Then I started feeling furious again. I'm in such a muddle.

I miss Marion so much, suddenly. She'd be very sympathetic about all this with David, I know. And once you've lost an old friend you can never replace her. You can make new friends but they aren't the same.

I was so desperate that eventually I even tried ringing Melanie, but all I got was her answering machine which told me: 'Hellooo . . . I wish you greetings in this the Chinese new year of the Fox. I am either meditating or out simply experiencing the joy of the now. Remember that yesterday is history, tomorrow is a mystery and today is a gift, and that's why it's called the present. Leave a message. Peace and love, Mel.'

Robin put his head round my door to say how glad he was that I was back, and reassured me a recent eclipse had ensured that everyone was feeling low and heavy (I didn't say they didn't seem very low and heavy down Shampton way where they were all having a bundle of laughs, sod them). In the end I braved ringing Penny, worried, of course, that she might have gone back to drinking, But she came over – bearing a bottle of sparkling elderflower no use to man or beast – and spent much of the time saying that I should make a 'gratitude list' instead of complaining.

'You have a house, lots of friends, enough money to get by, a wonderful talent, your health, a lovely son and grandson,' she said. 'Just think how blessed you are, Marie. I find making a gratitude list really works.'

'I know I've got a lot to be grateful for,' I said, crossly. 'But that doesn't stop me missing having David around.'

'Well, in AA we say: "There are two days that we have no control over – yesterday and tomorrow. Today is the only day we can change",' she intoned. 'What I say is, "Let go and let God".'

'I don't believe in God!' I said. 'How can I let go of him – and that's with a small "h", by the way – if he doesn't exist? Anyway,' I added, sorrowfully, 'I don't want advice, I just want an old friend to understand how I'm feeling and be sympathetic instead of preaching to me!'

At this point, fair play to Penny, she did put her arms round me and say: 'I'm sorry. I'm just sharing this with you because I've been so helped by going to AA myself. And honestly, the way they see things – it's mind-blowing.'

Felt slightly better but still alone and abandoned. Maybe I should just sell up and go and live in Italy. That would show everyone!

SEPTEMBER

September 1

As James and Owen were up from the country for a few days, I naturally asked them to supper with the gang. Having given up on James, Melanie now turned her attention to Owen who – being a bit of a farm boy who has never, believe it or not, even been abroad – was rather nonplussed by Melanie with her embarrassing exuberance, and clearly didn't realise that when she called out 'O!' she was actually referring to him.

'Your O is just a darling,' she said, snuggling up to James on the sofa before supper. 'You're a lucky boy. I wish I could find a lovely strong rugged out-of-doors bloke like him. O! Do you have any straight friends?'

Owen went rather pink and stared at his shoes.

Penny and Tim arrived together, bearing large bottles of cordial and sparkling water, and Robin came down from upstairs looking very cool, wearing an Indian silk scarf. With his long grey hair curling round his neck, he cut a rather glamorous figure.

I was in the kitchen, having opened the door into the garden to let the smell of cooking waft out, when I saw a strange blob on the carpet. Thinking it was some bit of mud or a leaf that had blown in with the wind, I leant down to pick it up, and was most surprised when it leapt up making a horrible screeching sound and disappeared behind Gene's old toy box. Naturally I screamed and soon everyone was assembled with broom handles and saucepans, determined to capture the poor animal to put it back into the garden.

'It was like a huge rat!' I said.

'No, it wouldn't screech like that if it were a rat,' said Owen, knowledgeably. 'That were a toad. Just leave it be,' he added, in his sanguine way. 'He'll find his way out soon enough if you leave the door open.'

Robin insisted that everyone be completely quiet, and said that he would sing to it because he had a way with animals, but after five minutes of a very strange song, there was still no sign of the poor wretch. I noticed Owen looking baffled by all these goings-on.

James had an idea that involved a long tube of cardboard, a glass of water, some wire wool and a dustpan and brush, but unfortunately I didn't have a long tube of cardboard, or wire wool, and eventually Tim simply pulled back the toy chest, reached down, cupped the toad in his hands and carried it gently outside.

Say what you will about Tim, he's certainly a capable man.

It was just the sort of thing, I reflected sadly, that David would have done had he been here. I noticed Penny looking at Tim with a kind of awe and though she didn't actually say: 'My hero!' I could see she was thinking it. Mel actually said it, and clutched at him in an awkward kind of hug.

Escaping from her embrace, Tim approached the sink and washed his hands in a very practical way, and we all carried on as if nothing had happened. But there was no question, we did all look at Tim as if he had rescued a maiden from a dragon. There was a little less of the 'Tim, thick-as-two-short-planks' about our attitude to him, and he definitely earned respect from us all.

I have to say we had a great time and afterwards James and I stayed up – Owen had gone to bed – and had a good old catch-up.

'Golly, it's good to see Penny back to her usual self,' said James, helping himself to the dregs of a left-over bottle of wine. 'She's rather admirable, isn't she? It's not that easy to stop drinking.'

'I think it's partly AA – though I'm getting fed up to the back teeth with her sloganeering. But mainly I think it's Tim, who's been really good to her. He's so lonely after Marion's death and it's great that he's got some projects – not just the shop, but Penny as well.'

'I thought Penny always reckoned Tim was a bit of an old stick,' said James, lounging back on the sofa.

'Well, funnily enough, being a widower has rather been the making of him,' I said, 'though I feel rather bad saying it. He's lost weight because he's so unhappy, of course, spruced up and, because Marion isn't around to do everything for him, he's getting his act together. He seems more confident – he's putting himself body and soul into the shop, and is being a real support to Penny. Funny, isn't it, with married couples? You never really know either of them properly until one of them either leaves or dies. They always exist in relation to the other person. And I think, much as I loved Marion, she did rather infantilise Tim. She wore the trousers.'

'And now he does,' said James. 'Witness the toad scene.'

'Yes, that was a surprise, wasn't it? I thought it would have been Owen who would have played toad hero.'

'Oh no. Like all country people, he's got very little regard for wildlife,' said James. 'It's me who rescues the exhausted bees and helps worms onto the side of the road. Owen just leaves them to get on with it. But now, talking of couples, what's going on with you and David, darling? I haven't heard of him coming up to London recently. Everything okay?'

'No, it's not okay,' I said, rather pitifully. And I told him the whole story about the misunderstanding about the note I'd left for Robin, and also going to visit to find Sandra having practically moved in. 'And now I don't know what to do,' I said. 'I should never have written that email. But I felt so upset and angry.'

'The bitch!' said James. 'You rescue her from India and she just moves in and steals your bloke back! But,' he added reflectively, 'I'm not sure it's quite how you imagine it. I've seen her in Bath quite a bit when I visit there, and I'm pretty sure I'd know if she'd moved back in with him permanently. I do have my ears to the ground. Are you sure?'

'No question,' I said. 'Gangi was crawling about as if he owned the place. I know it's mean of me. If I don't want him, why shouldn't he look for someone else? But I still feel so incredibly sad.'

'I'd stick with it,' said James. 'He wouldn't have asked you to marry him unless he really loved you. You can't stop loving someone just like that. I'd just keep on as if nothing had happened. Email him. Ring him. Send him cards. Just keep your cool.'

'Day at a time,' I said, quoting Penny, ruefully.

'That's my girl,' said James. 'Hold the line. Nothing like it.'

Then he got up, gave me a hug, and we both went upstairs to bed.

Felt much better.

September 2

Spent a whole morning emailing. First, remembering that today Gene starts big school and finding my heart in my mouth, I sent him a text saying: 'Good luck!' and I got a lovely one back saying, 'So far so good. Love you! Xxx Gene' which was very comforting. Presumably it means he's not at this moment cowering in the boys' lavatories being threatened by knife-wielding bullies demanding his lunch money and his phone.

It reminded me of Graham, my ex-lodger, who was reunited with his family after his son, Zac, was so unhappy when I was teaching at Gene's old school. I wrote Graham an email and got back an ecstatic one immediately telling me that Zac was absolutely fine and captain of his year's school cricket team, and that Julie was expecting another baby. Graham promised to come and see me soon with the family, but I know what that means. He'd really like to see me but it's unlikely to happen. But a nice thought, anyway.

Minutes later there was another 'ping' and Graham added that Zac often talks of me affectionately, which is good to know.

Checked Facebook and found Melanie's contribution: 'People who say they've got their shit together are usually standing knee-deep in the stuff themselves – Buddhist saying.' Honestly! How charming, I don't think, as we used to say or, as Gene would say, more succinctly these days, 'not'.

Had an email from James thanking me for having him and Owen to stay and saying that the dovecote is ready! He says they're going to get a swarm of doves tomorrow and he suggests that when they're settled in – his bird man, some friend of Owen's, says that'll be in about three weeks – we can introduce my pigeon into the flock. (Did I write 'swarm' just then? Must be going mad.) Not only did he suggest I send Robin down to see David to explain – 'You've got to make it crystal clear' – but he reminded me to keep in touch with David, so I emailed him, just to tell him the news about the pigeon, Gene's first day at school, a bit of stuff about the shop, and ended in a very friendly way 'Love, M', which I hope he'll see as a kind of olive branch from me to make up for my rather foul email last week.

September 4

No reply at all from David, which is terribly sad-making. I so feel like ringing him and apologising, but James was insistent that I should simply bombard him with normal emails rather than make a big emotional drama, so I'll stick to his advice – for the time being, anyway. But oh, I do miss him! Somehow seeing James and Owen together and now even Penny and Tim getting closer makes me feel very alone. I know I've got the family but it's not the same. David was always, well, there.

Later

Didn't mention it this morning because I thought he'd come back, but he hasn't. Pouncer. He's completely disappeared! I went round to Melanie because he used to have a habit of going there for a bit of TLC, not that he doesn't get quite enough here, but she hadn't seen him either.

I searched the house from top to bottom, calling for him, but there's absolutely no trace.

When he got back this evening, Robin was no help whatsoever. He said that 'they' had probably abducted him, in order to frighten us. He says that 'they', who are part of something called the Bilderberg group (also comprising, apparently, the lizards he so often refers to), are making a concerted attack on individuals, carrying out random and cruel acts to terrify us into submission. The more frightened we are, he says, the more 'they' will feel justified in putting up street cameras and strengthening the police force and that way eventually 'they' will control the world and we will all be their slaves.

I thought it was highly unlikely that members of this creepy elite would bother to spirit Pouncer away, but he said it was all to do with the 'narcissism of small differences' and he'd heard of many other animals in Portobello disappearing recently. He's convinced there's a plot and it's all over the internet.

Be that as it may, he was kind enough to write out about twenty notices – in his immaculate italic handwriting – for me to go and pin to trees tomorrow morning.

Penny's agreed to help me, too. She reassured me with the words 'Everything's going to be all right. And if it's not all right, it will be in the end.' Then she paused. 'I've got that wrong,' she said, and I heard her scrabbling for a leaflet. 'I mean,' she continued, reading, '"Everything will be all right in the end, and if it's not all right, it's not the end."'

I would have brained her if I could but luckily for her she was on the phone.

Even later

Before going to bed, I went out searching the streets with a torch and calling for Pouncer. Sheila the Dealer, who was hurrying back in the dark from some nefarious errand, said he's probably got run over but 'there's no point goin' to the fuzz because they just chuck 'em in the bins vese days. Even if they're chipped.'

It was a warm autumn night and there was a wonderful fresh smell in the air. I felt like a complete idiot wandering the streets calling, 'Pouncer! Pouncer! Pounce! Pounce!' and shining my torch under cars. Several Arab gentlemen, on their way back from the mosque, looked at me as if I were mad.

Mr Patel, still awake and serving in his shop at eleven at night – how does he do it? – was very sympathetic and Sellotaped a notice in his window. And I said, because I couldn't think of anything else: 'What we hear here stays here', and he looked at me as if he had no idea what I was talking about and I'm now having real doubts that it had been Mr Patel at the meeting after all.

Oh, God, I wish I could ring David! He'd be so reassuring and think of all kinds of things to do and he might even come up and help in the hunt.

I've just looked through my diary, and the awful thing is that I can see more clearly how casual I've been with him, always getting irritated by minor things. I'm starting to understand why he might have felt so hurt.

September 6

Took to the streets again, this time with the help of Mel, Penny, Tim and Terry. I photocopied more posters and we drawing-pinned them to the trees, but of course the photograph that I've found of Pouncer doesn't look much like the waif he's turned into in the last couple of months.

Before he left this morning, Robin said: 'I know he's been poisoned. I did Pouncer's tarot reading last night, and came up with the Death card. I'm sorry, Marie, but I just thought I ought to tell you so you don't waste too much time looking for him.'

How can he do Pouncer's tarot for him, when he's not even here? A bit presumptuous. And anyway, I don't believe in all that. Terry was much more optimistic.

'I fink 'e's still alive, Mrs S,' he said. 'And not too far from 'ome either. Are you sure you've looked everywhere in the 'ahse? Cats can 'ide in funny places when they're feeling poorly.'

Oh, God. If only it was the pigeon who'd disappeared, not Pouncer. Instead the poor bird just sits there staring at the wall like some terrified prisoner chained up in a concrete cell. Let's hope he'll soon be having the time of his life in James's 'doocut'.

Later

Screwed up my courage and wrote another email to David, explaining about Pouncer. I even added that I missed him and wished he were here to help with the search. And put two kisses after 'Love, Marie'. What more can I do?

September 8

Still no sign of Pouncer. Last night I lay awake for hours just imagining him, lost, ill, lonely and in pain, wondering why he hadn't been found. Got so carried away with this image that I only just prevented myself from bursting into tears. Pointless, of course, because this misery doesn't help him or me. I wonder why one tortures oneself so?

Later

Went down to do a shift at the shop today and take over from Penny. Found Tim busy converting it into two sections.

'There's one bit for the second-hand stuff,' he said, 'and this bit for elderly aids. What do you think about this? Would you buy it when you became unable to walk?'

And he demonstrated an extraordinary wheelchair which folded up into an object that you could sling over your shoulder.

'But if you can't walk, you surely aren't meant to carry this over your shoulder, are you? I mean, it seems a bit mad to carry your own wheelchair. Why would you need it in the first place?'

'For a start,' said Tim, 'it's not a wheelchair, it's a "transport mobility chair". A "handy transport mobility chair" no less. It's for your friend to carry. You do as much tottering as you can, and then, when you can totter no further, presto! Your companion whips out the handy transport mobility chair and wheels you home! Nifty, eh?'

'Should be called "immobility" chair, not "mobility" chair, surely,' I said.

Tim ignored this. 'We'll have to stock continence pads, of course, though we'd keep them under the counter . . .'

'Surely "incontinence pads" is what they really are?' I said. 'It's very confusing the way they label these things the opposite to what they really are.'

'Hmm,' said Tim. 'And what about this? The Handybar? It's to help you get in and out of cars. It can support up to twenty-five stone, apparently.'

I had to say, it was rather tempting. I can get in and out of my lovely Fiat 500 but if Jack gives me a lift somewhere, I'm embarrassed at having to lever myself out of the passenger seat, particularly if I have to get out onto the rising camber side of the road.

'And I bet you've found it difficult opening those ring-pull cans, haven't you?' added Tim, producing a U-shaped gadget. Indeed I have. Sometimes I've had to resort to getting out the pliers to break into a tin of anchovies. 'Here's your answer!'

I was dead impressed. 'I might take one of those,' I said, fishing out my purse. 'Genius idea.'

'I had an email today, from Brad and Sharmie,' said Tim. 'And they say that it looks as if the orphanage might be able to close down in a couple of months. Nearly all of the children have been rehoused in proper families. I only wish Marion were here to see it all,' he added, and I could see that he was welling up. 'She'd have been so pleased to know that all her work really meant something.'

'It's a memorial to her,' I said, in a heartfelt reply. 'I know you miss her, Tim. And I do, too.'

Tim got out a handkerchief and blew his nose.

When he'd recovered, he said, in a businesslike way: 'Well, better get on with the stocklist. Are you going to sort out that latest stuff that's come in?' He pointed to four bin bags of deliveries that had just arrived. 'Pal of your Terry's brought them. Said they'd been cluttering up his place for months and he wanted to be rid of them.'

I must say I was rather puzzled by what I found in the bags.

281

Three contained the usual rubbish – old clothes, battered toy bikes, broken baby-alarms – but the fourth bag didn't contain that sort of stuff at all. They weren't what you'd expect a friend of Terry's to have. There was a pair of Emma Hope shoes, barely worn, two silver clocks, a brass Indian head, a Wedgwood tea set from the thirties, a Ravilious mug. And, oddest of all, an art nouveau silver jug that I was sure I'd seen before.

'This is exactly like the one that Penny used to have, isn't it?' I said to Tim, holding it up. 'I remember admiring it! Do you think she's given it away?'

'It's not in her bag,' said Tim. 'Those definitely came from Terry's friend, not from Penny.'

'Odd,' I said. 'Do you mind if I take it home so I can ask her? I'll bring it back, of course.'

'Fine,' said Tim. 'But I can take it. I'm seeing Penny tonight. I'll take the bag for good measure. Might be something else of hers in there.'

He looked rather embarrassed and shuffled about keeping his head down. I said nothing. Could they be an item? Or are they just good friends, propping each other up?

Even later

No word from David. It's so out of character. We used to dote on Pouncer together and David always said he was his favourite cat. We'd found him as an abandoned kitten in an area of wasteland near our first flat (in the days when there still was wasteland in London) and taken him home. For about a year, his amusing presence bound us together again before the inevitable final split. Still, for a while he was like a late child in our marriage. Sometimes I thought David was more fond of Pouncer than of me.

Maybe I'll have to ring him. Or write to him again. We surely can't go on like this. It's as if we aren't even friends any more – and that's something I really can't bear.

Still pondering whether it would be a good idea to send Robin down to explain. But seems rather a drastic move.

Later Still

I can't believe it! Penny just rang me – it's eleven o'clock – and she says she's absolutely certain that the jug is hers, and was taken during the robbery!

'Couldn't it be a similar one?' I said. 'There must have been millions made.'

'Unlikely,' she said, 'because I got it at a *vide grenier* twenty years ago in France. I even had it valued once, and the guy who looked at it said he'd never seen anything like it before. I'm sure it's mine! Anyway, there are a couple of other bits in the bag that are mine, so there's no question about it.'

'But that means . . .'

'That Terry's friend is the burglar!' said Penny.

September 10

The most ghastly day. I rang Terry and said I wanted a word with him, and he came over, very chipper and cheerful as usual. But I wasn't buying any of it. Behind the cheery mask I saw a scheming con artist, a friend of burglars and piece of low-life who'd wormed his way into my affections.

'Probs with the pigeon, Mrs S?' he said. 'And 'ow's Pouncer? Any sign? What can I do fer yer?'

I didn't say much, but made him a cup of tea. I tried not to accuse his friend straight away, so I said: 'You know your friend, who brought in the stuff for the shop a couple of days ago?'

'I didn't know 'e'd brought anyfink in,' said Terry, helping himself to three teaspoons of sugar. How he stays so thin is beyond me.

'Well, he did.'

'That's good of 'im. I told 'im that anyfink 'e'd got that 'e could spare, not to chuck it aht, but to bring it along to the shop and it'd 'elp the kids in Inja.'

'Well, Terry,' I said. 'He brought four bags. And three of them were indeed full of stuff that obviously he'd collected locally from his friends. But the other bag,' I added, with a gimlet stare, 'had lots of very unusual stuff in it. Stuff that was stolen,' I added, as a *coup de grâce*. 'There was a jug in there that definitely belonged to Penny. Did you know anything about this? I feel I must report him to the police.'

Terry's face, always ashen, went a kind of grey colour.

'Oh, don't do that, Mrs S,' he said, hurriedly. 'I'm ... I'm sure there's some explination. Let me go an' 'ave a word wiv 'im. I'm, I'm sorry this 'as happened. 'e wasn't meant to ... wo' a bleedin' fool ...' And he rushed from the room in a panic, as if I'd suggested putting the police on to him.

He obviously knows more than he's letting on.

Oh, God, it's all most upsetting. No David, no Pouncer, soon no pigeon and now all this drama with Terry.

September 11

I was making my bed this morning, when there was a ring on the bell. I was still in my dressing gown, but I went down to open the door, expecting the postman. To my surprise, it was Terry, who looked as if he hadn't slept all night. He was stammering and wringing his hands and gasping – in such a state I asked him in and sat him down at the kitchen table.

'Now calm down, Terry,' I said, making him some coffee. 'What's happened?'

'Mrs S!' he cried, choking back tears. 'I let you dahn. I know I carn't make it up to you. I've bin hopin' you wouldn't find out. An' you've been so good to me. I shouldn't of done it. I'm sorry! I'm sorry!' And here he put his head in his arms and started sobbing like a child.

'What have you done, Terry?' I asked. I was about to put my hand on his shoulder but then the truth dawned.

'It was me as wot burgled you all. I didn't wanna. I only did it a few times and then you was so kind, and I said to myself, I won't do it any more. But there was this old stuff, I'd left it round a mate's house mumfs ago, and 'e promised 'e'd sell it at the market, but 'e forgot and 'e got the bags muddled. I shouldn't 'ave done it. My auntie Sheila said I should come and tell you everyfink. It was only a few times. I'm not like that. I didn't want you getting my mate into trouble. I know you won't want to see me again, and I'm sorry. You've been so kind, Mrs S.'

WHAT???

I simply couldn't believe it! I felt a surge of fury rise up in me. I couldn't help bursting out: 'You mean you've been working for me all these months, and you've been . . . I've even given you the keys to my house! I must have been mad – and it was you all along! I simply can't believe it! How dare you!'

He didn't say anything.

I ranted on. 'And what about Penny? I suppose that was you as well – and all the other burglaries in the area! My God, you've got some cheek to think you could worm your way into my house! I thought I was helping you, I thought you were a good person, and now you tell me . . .'

I was almost speechless with rage.

'Get out!' I said. 'I never want you to set foot in this house again! You're lucky I'm not ringing the police right now! In fact, I'm not so sure I won't!'

He got up, still sobbing pathetically.

'And leave the fucking key!' I shouted. 'Or have you made a copy already? I'll have to get the locks changed now!'

He fumbled around in his pockets. Then he spoke, pleadingly. 'I didn't do it on me own. It was me uncle got me involved. 'E's always on the take, and me mum – not that I've got one – said I shouldn't listen to 'im, but I didn't 'ave no money an 'e said it would be easy so we did a few 'ahses but then I got worried, and when I met you and of course I recognised the 'ahse, and you told me abaht all those fings you lost and that photograph, suddenly I fort, well, it's not nice, stealin' fings from people, fings that means somefink and then you were so kind to me . . . I couldn't get back what I'd taken from you cos me uncle 'e'd sold it already but I tried to make up for it.'

'I don't care whether it was you or your entire family! You've completely betrayed me!' I shouted. 'I never want to see you again.'

He crawled out of the door, mumbling apologies.

But what a little creep! And what a complete sucker I've been. I'd given him the keys to my house when I was away, I'd left Pouncer and the pigeon in his care . . . and all the time he'd broken into my house and stolen things that I loved!

Later
Of course I'm now having terrible second thoughts. Oh, God, if only David were around. He'd know what to do. One part of me feels absolutely livid with Terry – I even lifted up the phone and dialled the police but I put it down before they answered. But another part feels sorry for him. What if what he'd said were true? What if he had turned a corner, as they say? What if I've just driven him back into a life of crime?

In desperation, I phoned Penny in tears and she came over.

The first thing she said, on coming through the door, was: 'Don't wallow in self-pity . . . get off the cross, we need the wood.'

'What did you say?' For a start I didn't know what she was

talking about and secondly, I could tell it was some sort of admonition and I didn't like it at all.

'Sorry,' she had the grace to say. 'I've just looked in my book, and there it was. I thought it would be helpful.'

'Well, it wasn't. Now what am I going to do?'

Penny shook her head, and we settled down to a cup of tea in the garden. It was one of those lovely yellow autumn days, the sun still really warm and a feeling of peace and comfort in the air. Well, there would have been a feeling of peace and comfort if my nerves hadn't been jangling from the latest revelation.

'I wonder,' she said. 'I must say I tend to believe him. I know you think that now I've joined AA I've turned all pious but I think there's something in the phrase "Hate the sin and love the sinner". And honestly, Terry's been so brilliant, hasn't he – in the shop, and looking after our houses when we were in India? And remember how sweet he was with Gene . . .'

I stared down the garden, and tried to absorb what she was saying.

'I suppose he could have taken more things when we were away,' I mused, 'though of course we'd have noticed. Anyway, there wasn't much left to take after he'd hoovered up all the nice stuff in his burgling days.'

'I'm tempted to believe him,' said Penny. 'Let's give him another chance. Don't give him a key, obviously, but I think he's basically a decent bloke.'

'But you don't think it would be seen as a sign of weakness?' I said.

'No, it would be a sign of compassion,' said Penny. 'Don't

forgive him right away. Let him stew for a couple of days, and then let's have him over and tell him what the deal is.'

'Which is?'

Penny paused. 'What about, that we won't say anything to anyone else, on condition that he posts back all the things he's got left to their rightful owners with an anonymous note of apology. And that if he does that, we'll let it be. And things can continue as before.'

'But without the keys,' I said firmly.

'Without the keys,' said Penny.

September 13

When Terry came round this morning, both Penny and I were here to welcome him. When he saw Penny, he started gibbering his apologies again, but we soon set out our plan.

'Registered post,' I said. 'You'll have to pay for it yourself. And write a proper letter saying you're sorry.'

'But don't put your name, obviously,' said Penny.

Terry nodded obediently.

'And we won't mention it again,' I said. 'But if we ever find you doing anything else, we'll go straight to the police.'

Terry started grovelling and thanking us so profusely that I had to stop him from practically kissing our feet.

'Remember,' said Penny, 'that today is the first day of the rest of your life.'

'You can go on working for us for the moment,' I said. 'But one step out of line and that's it.'

'You're so kind, Mrs S. You're lovely – you remind me . . . you remind me of that actriss . . . wossername . . . Judi Dench, really kind woman.'

And with that, he tottered out.

As I closed the door, I turned to Penny.

'Judi Dench?' I said, bursting out laughing. 'She's ten years older than me, round as a bun and half my height!'

'And she spells her name with an "i",' said Penny, joining in the laughter.

'Burglary – God, I can forgive him that. But being compared to Judi Dench! The Queen of the Luvvies! National bloody treasure! Thanks a bunch! That comparison really is a criminal offence, if you ask me!'

September 14

I feel rather pleased with myself that I was able to take that decision without needing David to help. But it's no fun making these big decisions on your own. Thank God Penny isn't still drinking.

The agent has just sent me more information about houses, but to be honest, when I look at them they're all horrible. I put the address into Google maps and get the little yellow man out, and roam around the areas, and I find that even if they look nice in the picture, when you actually see the surroundings, they're opposite a horrible modern housing estate, or in the middle of the longest, bleakest road you've ever seen without a person or a shop for miles, or there's no station or bus stop within hiking distance. Just wondering, too, whether Penny and Tim and everyone would ever come and visit me if I moved to Brixton. And, even worse, whether I'd ever visit them back here.

Oh dear, I'm rather going off the idea of moving. And all my things! And the expense! And the upheaval!

Still worrying about Pouncer. He's been missing now for ten days. I've rung every vet and police station and the Cats Rescue League, but nothing.

In the meantime, the pigeon is still living on his pipe. At least he will now peck grain out of my hand, which is a step forward, but how I'm ever going to coax him into the cat basket I have no idea. It'll make getting Pouncer into it seem like a piece of cake.

September 17

'It's official! End of world is nigh!' (*Daily Rant*)

Much brought down by this news over breakfast, I ran my bath, jumped in and pondered. Have to say it really does feel as if the end is nigh, and I'm in two minds now whether it was the right decision to let Terry off the hook. Were his tears of remorse real? Should I trust him still to come into the house to do odd jobs? Since there's very little worth stealing here, I suppose it's okay, but I must keep my handbag out of sight at all times when he's around.

As I was towelling myself dry, I thought I'd change the sheets, a fortnight being quite long enough to sleep in the same ones, so I opened the airing cupboard door – which was ajar – to hoik out a clean batch. I was extremely alarmed to see a black shape on top of them, and for a moment I started back. And then I realised: it was Pouncer!

He lifted his head towards me, looking exceptionally sad and ill, and when I stroked him he was just skin and bone.

My heart was beating as I lifted him out gently, keeping the towel on which he was sitting under him, and carried him downstairs. I was practically weeping with consternation and relief.

'Pouncer!' I said to him, stroking his bony body very gently. He was purring madly and tried to open his mouth to miaow but could only manage a harsh rasp. 'You darling boy! Oh, where have you been?'

Where indeed had he been? He can't have been in the airing cupboard for very long – cats are completely mysterious. I imagine he'd been hiding somewhere and then managed to crawl into the airing cupboard, where he'd probably been for a day or so.

I carried him into the kitchen and gave him some food and water, hoping that no one was looking from next door into my glass roof as my towel had dropped off halfway down the stairs and I was stark naked. Pouncer lapped furiously at the water but only ate about a mouthful of food. Then he hobbled to the cat door and I imagined he wanted to go to the loo, poor chap. I opened the door for him so it would be easier and he made his way painfully slowly behind a bush where he relieved himself. He reappeared and then sat in a patch of autumn sunlight in the middle of the lawn.

His fur was completely lifeless and his eyes looked dead and unfocused. I knew he didn't have long to live. A feeling of rage came over me, directed at the vet. Why hadn't he done something when I'd asked him, so that Pouncer could have been spared all this?

I rang Penny and she came over, all sympathy.

'Oh, the poor darling,' she said, looking at him from the door out to the garden. 'He looks so sad! What are you going to do?'

'I can't bear to take him to the vet again,' I said. 'He'd be so frightened being put into the cat basket and driving and then the vet would only say he should be kept going for another week or so. I'm tempted just to let him die here in peace. As long as it is peace, of course. I so hope he's not in pain.'

Penny shook her head. 'Who knows? But he looks quiet enough. And I bet he's glad you came to find him. I tell you what – why don't you put him back in the airing cupboard when he comes back in? He obviously finds it warm and cosy there, and if you leave the door open, and keep popping in, I'm sure he'd feel safe and secure.'

Which is exactly what I did. I look in on him every hour or so, and I've given him a bit more water and I'm keeping the kitchen door open if he wants to go out – and even put a cat tray in the bathroom so that he doesn't have to come downstairs.

September 29

This morning when I went to look in on Pouncer, who's been getting weaker and weaker, he was still breathing, but he didn't seem able to lift his head. And the next time I went in, the poor chap had died.

I feel so terrible. I feel I should have done more for him, and I can't bear to think of his days of suffering. Poor, poor old thing. I shall miss him so much. I have been bursting into tears all day. I had no idea how much he meant to me. Of course it's partly to do with David, I know. Pouncer represented part of our life together, and now he's died it feels a cruel metaphor for my relationship with David.

And I do feel lonely. Pouncer was always there, sleeping on my bed, curling round my legs when he wanted more food, coming in to give me the odd mouse. He was more than a cat, he was a real friend and I loved him, soppy as it sounds.

I've wrapped him up in the towel he was lying on and put him in a corner of the kitchen. I suppose I should bury him in the garden, but, awful as it sounds, I can't bear to dig a hole and say goodbye to him. Even though he's dead, his physical presence is still some comfort to me.

I emailed David, crying all the time, to tell him the news. But when I did get a reply, it was just a brief: 'Sorry to hear about Pounce. Sadly, they can't live for ever, David.' Which was almost worse than no answer at all.

Maybe it would be worth sending Robin down. I can't make up my mind.

Later

After I'd told Penny, she and Tim came over in the evening to cheer me up. Tim had even brought a bottle of wine with him and Penny, seeing me looking surprised, said: 'Don't worry. I'm not going to drink it! It's for you and Tim!' And then they both looked at Pouncer and became very serious and Tim said: 'Well, you can't keep him in the kitchen.' And Penny said: 'No, he'll go off.'

At that point I burst into tears, and they rallied round. Penny said she was so sorry, she had no idea why she'd said such an insensitive thing.

They insisted on taking me to the new posh restaurant and Tim said he'd come round tomorrow and dig a hole in the garden, and we'd bury him. Then, he said, we should have a memorial service for him.

'Remembrance rituals are very healing, even for cats,' he said, knowledgeably. And he blew his nose again, and Penny put her arm round him.

We had supper and they walked me to the front door. Just as I was saying goodbye, I found myself bursting into tears again. 'When I told David,' I sobbed, 'I just got this horrible cold email back' and before I knew it, Penny was insisting she was going to stay the night.

She's gone to collect her things, and I'm feeling a bit better. Just off to give Pouncer one last kiss and then bed.

OCTOBER

October 1

Tim came round yesterday with a spade and dug a very deep hole and we put poor Pouncer into his grave. I wanted him buried under the laburnum tree but it turned out the roots were too tough, so we had to put him in the middle of a flower bed where the earth was softer. I had thought it best to bury him in a plastic bag, but Tim assured me that this would be most unwise since, as he deteriorated, all kinds of noxious gases would escape and would explode, and far better to put him in just as he was. Rather loopily I said I couldn't bear this, and found an old shoebox which I lined with a reject silk scarf from the shop collection. I then spent ages decorating the box with pictures of Pouncer's favourite things – a tin of Salmon with Herbs in Light Gravy, a catnip mouse, a few birds hopping about and a lovely warm fire.

When Tim arrived he gave it the okay, because cardboard degrades, and we popped his body into that. A tight fit, but still, the poor chap was so incredibly thin when he died, it didn't matter too much. At least he didn't have to have earth all around him.

We put the box in the hole and for a moment I stared down, tears in my eyes, but Tim covered it all up very quickly. He marked it with a stick so we wouldn't forget where he was – and somehow once his body had disappeared and I knew he was safely in the ground, I felt a bit better.

'I'm sorry, Tim, to be so silly. You must think "What's she fussing about? It's only a cat!" particularly after Marion, but I'm afraid I was very close to Pouncer and although I've got lots of lovely friends like you, it was Pouncer who was here day after day, year in year out.'

'I understand completely,' said Tim, who was now pulling off the rubber gloves he'd used to carry out his task. 'I would think in some ways it's especially painful because there's no one else who can remember Pouncer clearly like you do. Marion had so many friends and all their memories and letters gave me such comfort. Still do. I read them and reread them quite often, you know – but you've got no one to share your close memories of Pouncer with.'

'Except David,' I said, feeling incredibly upset, and trying not to show it. 'And he couldn't care less.'

'I'm sure he does care,' said Tim, putting his arm round my shoulders and giving me a squeeze. 'But men are very bad at showing their feelings. It's difficult for them.'

October 2

Thank God! James has finally emailed to say that at last he's ready to take the pigeon! The flock of doves has settled in nicely, apparently, and the birds are batting around as if they owned the place.

'So all you have to do now, my darling, is to catch the damn bird!' he said, when he rang later.

'Well,' I said. 'Robin swears that he can. It's all to do with a three-dimensional pentangle which he says pigeons are automatically drawn to – it's some psycho-geographical stuff. No – magical geometry. Or maybe it's psycho-geometry . . . Anyway, we'll get him over to you somehow.'

'Even if you have to shoot it first,' said James.

'He's not an "it", James,' I said, laughing. 'He's a "he".'

Inside, I felt that that wasn't a very amusing thing for James to say. Despite myself, I've grown to love my pigeon. On days when I feel low, I feel that he's an embodiment of my own situation – sitting lonely on a pipe with no one to care for him. Penny would no doubt come up with that ghastly quote of hers if she thought I was writing this. 'Get off the cross – we need the wood!' The bloody cheek of it!

Anyway, the plan is to catch the pigeon in a couple of days and then drive down to Somerset with him and install him in his new life. So easy to say and so difficult to do.

Later

Waited for the key in the door which meant that Robin was returning from work and dragged him into the sitting room before he could go upstairs. I sat him down and gave him a drink.

'Before you say anything, Marie,' said Robin, 'I want to give you as much notice as I can. I'll be moving. Very soon.'

I was extremely taken aback. 'Golly, it feels as if you've only been here five minutes!' I said. 'I hope there's not a problem?'

'Not at all. I've had the most wonderful time here. It's been a haven of peace and solitude. Shangri-La itself. But I've found somewhere to buy in Acton, and I can afford a mortgage with the rent coming in from the flat in Golborne Road, and I just feel I need somewhere of my own. I'll be off in a month or so, but I wanted to tell you well in advance.'

'I thought you wanted to live in the Shetland Islands or the Orkneys?' I said. 'Surely Acton isn't very eco?'

'Good point,' said Robin. 'But I've discovered this particular triangle in Acton that's surrounded by three ley lines and I know I'll be safe there.'

I was very glad he'd found somewhere, though of course a bit of me felt he was another rat leaving a sinking ship (the sinking ship in question being me).

'And I wondered,' continued Robin, 'whether you'd mind if I got in touch with Terry, because there's quite a bit of work needs doing on the flat. He's a really good lad, that Terry, isn't he? I really like him. He told me about his terrible past the other day. It's amazing the way his life has turned around since he's been helping here. I knew from the moment I met him that he was honest through and through. You look at people like me – I went to Eton and most of my old classmates have turned into bankers. Talk about robbers. Dreadful people. But Terry, whatever his background, no education at all to speak of, and honest and motivated as the day is long. Just shows.'

For a moment I thought I might not be able to resist telling Robin about Terry's 'honest past'. But managed to curb myself and smiled vaguely before giving him Terry's mobile number, saying I was sure he'd be glad of a job.

'I wonder if, before you go, I could ask you a favour, Robin,' I said. 'The pigeon has found new premises, too. And like you, he's ready to go. But it's catching him that's the problem. I remember you saying something about pentangles . . .'

Robin grinned broadly. 'Of course. I was going to make a pentangular box, but I found one in Portobello Road a couple of weeks ago so I bought it in anticipation of the bird's flight, God bless him. Would you like to see it?'

Even later

God knows how we're going to put it on the windowsill! It's huge and made of glass, but Robin swears that with the aid of ropes and pulleys and hooks drilled into the masonry, we can make it secure.

'And then, Marie,' he said, 'I promise you, you'll have no difficulty getting him into it. Just put some food inside, I can always sing him a song, then wait for him to pop in, shut the door, and Bob's your uncle.'

October 3

Robin's rigged up the pentangular pigeon-tempter, but unfortunately it means that we can't now close the bathroom window, so every time I go to have a bath I'm absolutely FREEZING. And no question of setting the burglar alarm for the moment. Still, we tried it out today, and it certainly does seem to attract pigeons. I'd barely withdrawn my hand from the bowl of grain that I placed inside than three pigeons from neighbouring trees came flapping down and flew straight into the pentangle; they finished off all the grub within about five minutes.

My pigeon, however, looked very suspicious, and it was only when I put the bowl outside the pentangle that he fluttered down from his pipe and took nervous pecks at it, constantly flying away between bites as if frightened the pentangle would suck him in and trap him. Robin assures me that it's only a matter of a few days and he'll be in there with the rest of them.

Pentangles, he assured me, are pigeon magnets.

October 4

Today we had a little memorial service for poor Pouncer. Penny and Tim came, of course, and Melanie insisted on attending, too. Since she virtually stole him for about six months a year or so back, I suppose she feels she has a right. I felt very cross, as if I were a wife and my husband's secret lover had insisted on coming and sitting in the front row at his funeral.

But this morning, before we got together, she rang the bell, making the usual grand entrance, bearing a small parcel.

'Now you've got to be honest, darling Mar,' she said. 'And I won't be hurt if you don't like it.'

This was such an unusual departure for her, who normally imposes whatever she wants without so much as a by-your-leave, that I felt more open towards whatever suggestion she might be making.

'You may think it "naff" – your favourite word – but I think it's just darling. And it would be just right for Pouncer's grave.'

At that moment, she unwrapped the parcel and put a statue on the table with a cry of 'Ta daa!'

It was a cast-concrete cat, the sort of thing you find in garden centres everywhere. But naff as it indeed was, it had a certain something. I looked at it from all angles and found that really, and very surprisingly, the original model had obviously been made by someone with an excellent knowledge of animal anatomy. And the expression on the cat's face – well, at the risk of sounding like someone who posts drippy things on Facebook – it was exactly like Pouncer's! It was absolutely sweet. Utterly perfect.

I looked at Melanie incredulously.

But it must have looked like an expression of disgust because, 'You hate it, I know,' she said, about to bundle it back into the bit of paper. 'You're an artist, I forgot. No, the ears aren't right. Or his tail is wrong. Don't worry. I knew you'd find something to criticise. Ah well. But I thought it looked rather like Pouncer . . .'

'Wait a minute!' I said, putting my hand on it before she could snatch it back. 'I haven't said I don't like it! I love it! I think it's just perfect! I adore it! You couldn't have bought anything more appropriate! You really are an angel!' And I meant it. So much, that, using her nickname for the first time in all the years I've known her, I found myself hugging her and saying, 'Thank you so much, Mel!'

I think Melanie was as astonished at my reaction as I was to find that finally she had produced something that really touched me. Something that hit the spot. She started to smile and then she laughed.

'Oh, Mar!' she said. 'I really do think you mean it! I'm thrilled!'

After that I forgave her wanting to come to the memorial, and was really pleased when she read Thomas Gray's 'Ode on the Death of a Favourite Cat' as we gathered round the grave, now adorned with the marvellous stone sculpture. Penny had brought a CD of 'Abide with Me' and it wafted out into the cold garden, as we each took a little bit of earth and threw it onto the grave in homage to old Pouncer. I'd found an old boogie-woogie tune called 'Hep Cat' and when we played that, it cheered the proceedings up a bit.

Even when Penny suddenly intoned, 'We're all here because we're not all there,' it seemed fitting in a peculiar way, though of course it wasn't at all, but I just felt so touched that my friends had taken the trouble to come over and make an effort to contribute to the ceremony.

Afterwards I gave everyone champagne and smoked salmon

and scrambled eggs – I drew the line at offering them Salmon with Herbs in Light Gravy – and Penny toasted Pouncer in elderflower, though how she can bear to chuck so much elderflower down herself is beyond me. Poor girl. These days it seems as if it's the only soft drink option available.

Anyway, I felt it was all a fitting end to Pouncer 's life.

Slight hiccup when Melanie asked if I was getting another cat, and I said: 'What a question! If your husband died, you wouldn't expect me to say, a few days after, "Are you going to marry again?"' and she said: 'But Pouncer wasn't your husband!' and I said she knew what I meant, and then I apologised and said I was sorry for being snappy, it was just grief and we were all friends again.

Another cat! What a question to ask!

October 5

Desperately worried this morning because it was the day of Operation Pigeon. James was waiting in the country with lunch and a carefully prepared little room for the pigeon in the dovecote with its own caged balcony, so he could get used to the surroundings before being completely released.

Robin had promised me faithfully that with his special birdsong and the pentangular trap, he would be able to catch the pigeon. He has been whistling and singing to it for ages so that it gets used to him, and assured me he was making terrific progress, but I had my doubts. Anyway, come eight a.m., after about twenty horrible feral pigeons with black beaks and staring eyes had scrambled into the pentangle thing and scoffed their breakfast, I put more food inside the pentangle for my pigeon, and left Robin to it. What seemed like hours went by, though it must have been about twenty minutes, and finally Robin came out of the bathroom very apologetic.

'I don't know what's happened,' he said. 'Yesterday he came down and even went inside the pentangle, and now he refuses. I can't think what's going on. Unless, of course, it's "them" again.'

'Oh, dear,' I said. 'What shall we do?'

At this point – it was now nine o'clock – the bell rang, and it was Terry wanting to collect some paint I'd got under the stairs because apparently the front of the shop needs touching up.

'You look a bit worried, Mrs S,' he said. 'Anyfink I can 'elp wiv?'

'No, thanks,' I said. 'We're trying to catch the pigeon to take him to James's dovecote in the country, but he refuses to be rescued, even when Robin sings to him.'

Terry laughed. 'Want me to 'ave a go?' he said. 'I've got a way wiv birds. Me dad – well, one of me dads, God bless 'em – used to 'ave pigeons.'

I was rather astonished to discover that, despite what Sheila the D had told me earlier, Terry actually ever had a dad. Let alone several. I'd always rather imagined that he'd been found, fully formed, under an old wheelie bin on a deserted and vandalised housing estate. But I said of course, and we went upstairs to the bathroom. Motioning Robin and me to be silent, Terry leant out of the window and uttered a curious cooing noise.

Robin whispered: 'That won't work – that was what I was doing!' But, watching the bird, I was astonished. At the sound of Terry's chirruping, the pigeon pricked up its ears. Well, I know pigeons don't have ears (at least not ones you can see – they can't be totally deaf), but if it did have ears it would have pricked them up. Then it looked at Terry very intently. As Terry continued, the bird puffed up a bit, and moved shiftily along his pipe, turning occasionally to look at Terry. He flapped his wings and, after a while, suddenly flew down to the windowsill where he stood, looking sharply this way and that, his scaly little feet making a skittering noise on the paintwork.

Robin and I held our breath. Continuing with this chirruping, Terry reached out, put his hand gently but firmly around the pigeon's back and popped him swiftly into the pentangle, letting down the shutter as he did so.

'Gotcha, me old mate!' he said, bursting into a grin. He turned to us, pleased as punch.

'You're a genius, Terry!' I said. And Robin had the decency to marvel as well.

'I've never seen anything like that before except with a shaman in the middle of the Amazonian rainforest,' he said. 'It was back in the nineties when I was doing an ayahuasca ceremony there. Remarkable!'

'Think you'd better cover 'im up before 'e gets too frightened,' said Terry, looking around for a towel. 'They can suffer from shock if they get too many surprises, and 'e ain't goin' to like being driven in the car.'

After we'd removed the box from the wall, Robin and I asked Terry if he'd like to come with us because I felt we needed an expert on hand in case of a pigeon emergency en route, so when Terry had nipped back from delivering the paint to Tim in the market, we all bowled down to Somerset, arriving earlier than we expected. Even though only a few leaves were clinging to the trees, the sun was shining and it was a really golden day. How I wished Gene had been with us too! He would have enjoyed that little scene so much!

When we arrived, James came out of the house to greet us. 'I never thought you'd do it!' he said.

'It was all down to Terry here,' said Robin, generously. 'We'd never have done it without him!'

James introduced us to his bird man, who looks after feathered creatures all over the county, and I noticed he was particularly taken with Terry after he heard the story of his amazing feat.

'There's some as can and some as can't, and those 'oo can 'ave a gift, don't we, me son?' he said. 'Now, you 'elp me get 'im up into the loft . . .' and they disappeared with the covered pentangle into a barn. We followed them and saw their feet disappearing up a ladder.

James, Robin and I went back to the cottage to have a drink.

'I feel rather sad,' I said. 'To think I'll never see him again. I'm sure he won't come out onto his balcony today – he'll be far too frightened.'

But half an hour later there was a call from Terry and the bird man, and we went out, and there, on his little netted balcony, stood my pigeon looking as if he'd died and gone to heaven. His view was not of a brick wall and a pipe, but of trees and distant hills, grass and white doves, flying round and round, all curious to take a look at him. A couple of them landed on the uncovered bit of the balcony and starting strutting and puffing and preening.

'Said it was a boy, didjer?' said the bird man, wiping his hands on his apron. 'That's no boy! It's a pretty little girl!'

And he was right. My pigeon was a girl – judging by the admirers surrounding her.

'She'll be layin' eggs before you can say Jack Robinson,' said the bird man wisely.

'God, it's weird!' I said. I'd always got the pigeon down as a lonely bachelor, and now knowing it was female made me feel even more sorry for her. It all made sense – that time she'd vanished for a while, she'd no doubt been gang-banged by the ferals and that's why she looked so miserable when she returned.

No gang-banging here, clearly, though. She was being courted by lovely snow-white gentlemen with quiffs and fantails and feathered feet, pigeons who only needed a monocle in one eye and they could walk into the Ritz any day.

'By the way,' said James, casually, as we went in to lunch. 'I asked David to come over. You don't mind, do you? He did say he might bring Sandra.'

I felt my heart soar and sink all at the same time, if that were possible. 'Oh, God, James, you didn't!' I blurted out. 'I don't know that I could face it! Does he know I'm going to be here?'

'I didn't say anything, actually, just casually invited him. I'm sure it'll be okay.'

But of course, it wasn't okay. As soon as David came into the room and saw me, his face froze. Particularly as, at that moment, Robin had his arm round my shoulder while he pointed out some curious pattern he'd noticed on a map on the wall.

The first thing David said to James was: 'Look, I'm not going to be able to stay long, meant to tell you, got the hedges to see to this afternoon . . .'

He didn't actually cut me dead, but gave me a rather frosty smile. 'Well, congratulations on sorting out the pigeon!' he said. And that was it.

Sandra, on the other hand, was incredibly friendly. She hugged me and kissed me on both cheeks, and said she was dying to come up to London and have lunch because she wanted to talk to me about a couple of things, and could we make a date. Groaning inside as I got out my diary, because I bet I know what she wants to talk to me about, I agreed.

Meanwhile, David spent the rest of the lunch chatting about farming to Owen and, before coffee, he said he was sorry but they had to leave. He gave me a rather brusque wave, and was gone.

It was all I could do not to burst into tears.

'What was all that about?' said James. 'I must say, I didn't realise it was that bad!'

'Oh, I don't know. I don't think there's any hope we can even be friends now,' I said. 'I do wish you hadn't asked him, James. Not that it wasn't a very kind thought,' I added, because there wasn't much point in berating him. We couldn't put the clock back.

'I'm so sorry!' said James. 'I'll have to have a word with him!'

'No. Sandra, the wretch, has asked herself to lunch next week. I'm ninety-nine per cent certain she wants to tell me that she and David have got back together, and she knows I might be a bit hurt but she wants to be friends, and that she sees me like an lovely auntie and would like me to be a godmother to Gangi . . .'

'You don't know that's what she's going to say,' said James. 'Though I agree, in view of how he behaved just now, it doesn't seem beyond the realms of.'

'I do know,' I said. 'I feel like ringing her up and saying: "Don't bother to come up. I agree to everything. I can read the situation like a book."'

October 14

Got home feeling in a complete muddle but at least Robin was with me – I don't think I could have borne a completely empty house, with no Pouncer to greet me and no pigeon either. The pigeon hadn't been exactly a welcome sight in the past, but he – I mean she – was a relationship, even though it was one that made me feel full of pity and guilt. All that was left, now, was a roof covered yet again with droppings. which I must get Terry to clean off.

At least Terry's still around. I'm glad we gave him a second chance. I don't know what I'd do without him.

Mood not helped by sight of *Daily Rant* headline: 'Quiet

please! Tennis club fury at dominatrix next door and the screams from her dungeon!'

Robin offered to make me a cup of tea and we sat in the garden, staring out in the fading autumn sunshine. The garden was now in shadow and slightly chilly, but it was good to breathe in some air after being in the car for so long.

Robin knew I wasn't feeling my best, and he tried, in his own sweet way, to comfort me.

'Well, the autumn equinox has come and gone,' he said. 'And things should be starting to look up. It's been a bad time for everyone recently, but I'm certain that our astral paths are starting to rebalance. And it'll be particularly good for Capricorns. Remember it is always darkest before the dawn. It's a troubled old world, but I have been consulting the charts, and I know it's a new dawn for all of us. I'm moving into a new flat. And you – well, new things are coming, I promise.'

'I hope they're good things,' I said, sceptically.

'Of course they're good things!' said Robin. 'I feel that soon you will be very happy.'

I felt mildly cheered until, on my way upstairs, I saw, sticking out of a crack in the skirting board, one of Pouncer's whiskers. It was, I'm afraid, my undoing.

I went upstairs to bed and pulled the covers over my head.

October 19

It's not a good moment to move house. I've finally realised this. I just feel under too much stress right now, so I'll put it off. Perhaps I'll think of it again in the New Year. Who knows? There's hardly anything on the market anyway, and the few people who've looked round my house, although some of them profess to be enchanted with it, haven't been enchanted enough to make an offer.

October 25

Rather dreading Christmas. Oh, I know it's far too early to think about, but I've just been on the phone to Jack, organising when Gene can come over this half-term, and he said that they're all going down to David's this year. Naturally enough, I haven't been invited.

Can I really face seeing Sandra next week? I suppose I've got to go through with it.

October 26

Gene came over. We had an excellent day together. First we went to a wonderful exhibition of shell art, just the sort of thing I love, and naturally the minute we got back I got out my old bag of shells – one that I've kept since I was a child when I used to pick up them up on beach holidays in Tenby – and we nipped round to Mr Patel's to buy some Turkish Delight, because it comes in lovely round boxes, emptied out the sweets and starting gluing the shells on to the sides, making brilliant patterns.

Sometimes I'm so grateful to my younger self; this time

for the child that collected all those shells so painstakingly, who didn't have a clue that one day they'd be used to have an excellent afternoon with her own grandson.

Then we went round the corner for a posh burger, and Gene had a tutti-frutti to finish up. Afterwards we came back and varnished the shell box, which looked fantastic. One of the great things about being a painter is that I've got all the kit already here – the ceramic glue, the tools for cleaning out the excess, the varnish and so on.

Before he went home we sorted out Gene's toy box, something I've wanted to do for ages. Half the things in it are really childish and he'll never want to play with them again: the giant plastic Lego-like building bricks; the farm animals and the broken farm fences; the jigsaw puzzles consisting of about six huge pieces; the colouring books.

They can all go to the shop. However, I did notice Gene removing the shark from the farm pieces – an amusing addition known as 'Sharkie' which, when we used to assemble the farm, always lived in a bowl of water safely outside the farm gates.

'I like Sharkie, Granny,' he said. 'Let's keep him till next time.'

Delighted to keep Sharkie. But of course I still feel sad when I look back on those never-to-be-recreated days when I used to collect conkers for Gene, and we'd stick pins in them for legs and turn them into strange animals. And I remember trying desperately to keep the half-shells of walnuts intact to make little boats, weighted with plasticine and with matchsticks for masts – and gathering acorns to use the cups as a goblin's tea set.

Later

Penny popped over with part of a gooseberry fool she'd made, knowing I love the stuff.

'How's it going?' I said. 'I saw you and Tim in the street yesterday actually holding hands! Not that I'm spying on you, mind.'

She laughed. 'I feel so awful at the way we used to giggle at Tim when he was married to Marion,' she said. 'Because, you know, he's actually one of the kindest men I've ever met.'

'Kindness – it's all that matters, isn't it?' I said. 'Isn't it awful how we used to think that kindness was so uncool when we were young? For "kind" we used to read "wet".'

She tried to cheer me up about David, and said I couldn't read Sandra's mind, but it didn't help.

Went out and bought some lunch for Sandra. Thinking she might like a walk down memory lane, I popped into the Indian supermarket for all kinds of spices and Basmati rice, and even some Indian sweets which are rather delish. I can't imagine she gets a whole pile of curries or ras malais in Shampton. Or Bath. Or wherever she's living these days.

October 27

Well! What a day it's been! I spent all yesterday evening making curries for Sandra – took me AGES to get everything done and I only made three little dishes, it's all that sprinkling and roasting of spices that's so time-consuming. She arrived on the dot of twelve wearing an enormous overcoat that I recognised as one of David's, and bearing a huge bunch of flowers. I bustled her inside – it had turned bitterly cold – and she came in all kissy-kissy and sweet. I played along with it, but I couldn't help being fractionally distant. I didn't want to be unpleasant, but I couldn't exactly throw my hat in the air with joy at the prospect of having her as a rival wife to David.

She was all smiles and laughter and in one way I was touched, now I could get a good look at her, to see how much she'd blossomed since the days when we'd found her in India. Partly motherhood, I thought sourly, partly being in love with David again.

She took off her coat, sat down and had a large drink. She insisted I look at endless photographs of Gangi, on her phone. Lots of tiny videos of him speaking his first lisping words, and others of him being held by David, David chasing Sandra round the garden, with Gangi in her arms, and David and he making faces at each other.

I feigned delight at seeing what a great little chap he'd grown into even in the last few months. Then she showed me another video, this time of the Widow Bossom holding Gangi up, for all the world as if he were her own grandson.

'Oh, is she still hanging around?' I said, slightly peeved. 'Surely in the circumstances she must realise that she's barking up the wrong tree.'

Sandra looked at me rather oddly, but I didn't think anything of it. We went into the kitchen to have lunch which, though I say it myself, was totally delicious.

'Marie, you're so incredibly sweet to go to all this trouble for me!' said Sandra, as we relaxed afterwards in the sitting room with cups of coffee. 'I know from my days as a skivvy with Ali's mum in the kitchen what an incredible drag it is to make curry. But now,' she went on, 'before we go any further, there are two things I want to ask you.'

Here we go, I thought. I fixed a rictus smile on my face.

'I hope you won't mind, but we're having Gangi christened in a couple of months, and we wanted to ask if you'd be Gangi's godmother.'

'We!' Presumably her and David. But still it was flattering. What could I say? I tried to wriggle out of it by saying I didn't believe in God, but she wouldn't have any of it.

'Oh, no one believes in God, even we don't, but we'd love to have a christening and you're such a lovely person . . . I mean, I know you're a spiritual person anyway,' she said.

'No, I'm not very spiritual,' I said, slightly tartly. 'Whatever "spiritual" means. I don't talk to trees, sadly, or, rather, I do but they never reply, and I don't ever feel at one with the universe.'

'Oh, nonsense,' said Sandra. 'It honestly doesn't matter. We want you to be Gangi's godmother because we love you, and that's good enough for us. I mean, if you hadn't come to see us in India, we'd never have been here, and Gangi would be being brought up as a Muslim in Goa! You've got to be godmother! Please say yes!'

Sandra looked so utterly endearing that I couldn't resist. No wonder David's enchanted by her, I thought. She's young, she's pretty, and even though she might have a few draughts wafting through her brain, you can't doubt her sincerity.

'And now the other thing I want to talk to you about,' she said . . . but at that moment there was a knock on the door and Robin walked in.

'I'm so sorry to bother you,' he said, 'but I just came back to collect a couple of things and wondered what you wanted me to do with the sheets, Marie. Shall I bring them down? Oh . . . Sandra!' he said, looking delighted to see her. 'And where's the gorgeous Gangi, might I ask?'

Sandra looked up at him, confused. 'Oh, I thought you lived here!' she said. 'Are you moving out?'

'Oh, yes, I moved out officially last week, but have been rather sneakily hanging on just for a few days while Terry redecorates my new flat.'

'New flat?' said Sandra. Then she looked at me. 'Oh, I rather thought . . .'

'God, no!' I heard myself saying, perhaps rather overemphatically. 'I love Robin to pieces but we're not an . . . an . . .'

As I couldn't bear to use the word 'item' I was relieved when Sandra filled in for me. 'Item,' she said firmly. Oddly, I could sense a slight change in atmosphere as she said it, and she turned towards Robin with renewed interest.

'Well, you must let us know where you're going to be living,' she said. 'It would be a shame to lose touch. You must come and stay one day! The place is teeming with ley lines!'

Robin positively blushed. 'Of course, I'll give you my new address,' he said and, fumbling for a piece of paper, wrote it down.

After a bit of chat, he finally went and I prepared myself for the worst.

'Isn't he gorgeous?' said Sandra. 'Awful, isn't it – I've got a thing about older men. Always have.'

'Oh well, you're lucky to have got one,' I said, trying to rush the conversation on.

At this Sandra looked at me in a puzzled way. 'Got one?' she said. 'What do you mean?'

'Well, it's obvious that you and David have got back together and are now an, um . . .'

'Item?' she asked, obviously surprised. 'God, no!' She laughed. 'That was over years ago. No, he's been such a love, he's a gorgeous man as you know, but I wouldn't go there again. And nor would he. No, I just wanted to say, oh, it's so difficult, but I DO so wish you and David could get back together again. He's so unhappy on his own, you know. And I'm really worried about Widow Bossom. She's been on the warpath for months and I'm starting to think she might be making some headway. She's always round with little dishes and doing errands for David, and to be honest, well, I know she's a friend of yours, but . . .'

'Friend of mine!' I said. 'She's no friend of mine! I think she's ghastly!'

Sandra burst out laughing. 'Well, so do I, actually. And she's not very nice with Gangi. Whenever she comes round she's always telling him off even though he's not yet a year old, and saying he should be in bed and so on. I even caught her pinching him to make him cry the other day. Can you imagine! She said it was tit for tat because he'd tried to hit her, but she'd been teasing him and he doesn't understand, so he can't be blamed, can he? She's got very old-fashioned ideas. On the surface she seems nice, but David doesn't seem to realise that she's not so nice underneath. Ever since . . . well, he did tell me that he asked you to remarry him and you turned him down . . . he's been so miserable. And he was sure you've been having an . . . well, that you and Robin were an . . .'

'Item,' I said, automatically. But I was staring at her. And eventually, I put my hand out to her, and clutched it. 'I can't believe what you're telling me,' I said. 'I've been trying to get back with David, but he won't have any of it!'

'He says you're the only woman he's ever loved.'

'Rubbish,' I said, but secretly I was rather pleased. 'But if so, why won't he make friends again?'

'He doesn't want to be friends! It's marriage he's after!' said Sandra. 'You know what men are like. They can't cope with loose arrangements. And David, much as I love him, is a terrible old stick-in-the-mud. To be honest, I don't think he'd mind continuing the way you were, but he just feels marriage would make him feel more secure. And he's so hurt he's been rejected. He was crying the day he got back when you turned him down. It was awful. Couldn't you think about changing your mind? It'd be so nice if you and David got back together! Then you could be like Gangi's granny and granddad!'

I slightly winced at this, but my head was still swimming. And I knew it was swimming with a kind of joy.

'Well, I'll have to think about it,' I said. 'I really don't want to get married – we did it once . . .'

'Well, you'd better think about it pretty quickly,' said Sandra, looking at her watch and rising to her feet. 'Oh, my God, I'll miss my train. But thank you so much for being so lovely, and the delicious lunch, and I can't wait to see you at the christening. And,' she added, as she pulled on her coat, 'remember the Widow Bossom waiting in the wings. Watch out!'

I couldn't help myself. I stood up and embraced her in a huge hug. Suddenly I felt she was like a daughter to me, even though I've never had one.

'Goodbye, darling,' I said, in a rush of warmth for her. 'You've been such an angel. Thank you so much for coming. I really will think about what you've said.' And I gave her a big kiss on the cheek.

I spent the rest of the afternoon clearing up, almost unable to grasp what she'd told me.

NOVEMBER

November 1

In films everyone wakes in the same way. They turn over languorously, stretching their arms out and sighing: 'Aaa-aagh.' Then they might murmur: 'Mmmmm.' They snuggle back down into their pillows and wait a bit. Then they yawn, reach out slowly to turn the clock's face towards them and, finally, after rubbing their eyes and wriggling a bit, they slowly manoeuvre themselves into a sitting position and smile at the prospect of the day ahead, exhaling peacefully as they do so.

Does anyone do this in real life, I wonder? I don't, certainly. Well, not recently, anyway. This morning I woke with a start, terror clutching at my heart, rigid with anticipation of some fearful event. Then the memory of what Sandra had said came back to me with a roar and I racked my brains for what would be the best thing to do.

I'd tried emailing, I'd tried ringing and the last time I'd bumped into David he was pretty chilly.

I made breakfast but even a good dose of the *Daily Rant* ('"Outstanding" doctor jailed for supplying meow meow and date-rape drug GHB to university polo club president with foot fetish who choked to death when he accidentally swallowed a sock') didn't clear my head.

Though of course it certainly puts my own problems into perspective.

Eventually I rang Penny and told her what had happened.

'How romantic!' she said. 'Isn't that just what you wanted to hear?'

'Well, sort of – but what do I do now? I mean, he just doesn't want to see me, and even if I appear on the scene he turns away as if I were some piece of old fish he'd left out of the fridge for days.'

'First of all,' said Penny sensibly, 'you've got to decide what you want out of this. Do you want to marry him or not?'

'Of course not!' I said. 'Oh, no, I'm sticking to my guns!'

'You might as well not bother, then,' said Penny, practically. 'But I think you're a complete chump. Look how miserable you've been over the last few months! It's only a bit of paper! Getting married doesn't mean you have to live together twenty-four hours a day! He's not expecting you to go back to the cosy old domestic routine, surely? He just wants to get married to put his mind at rest. And I bet it would make more sense as far as wills go, and financially as far as Jack is concerned.'

'I suppose so,' I said. But still my heart thumped fearfully at the prospect.

'And if it'll help Jack, it will, in the long term, help Gene, too.'

She certainly knew my weak spots.

'It's just like jumping into a cold swimming pool,' she added. 'It's like we always say – "Let go and let God".'

'Oh, please!' I said.

'Okay, let's stick with the swimming pool idea. It'll be lovely once you're in. David's not a monster. You do love him. You don't want to live alone for ever. I mean, it's not as if there's someone else on the horizon, is there?'

'Certainly not!' I said, thinking of Robin, Fabian and Hugo, all no doubt decent blokes in their own weird ways, despite their propensities towards red trousers, but certainly not husband material in my book.

'And,' said Penny, warming to her theme, 'remember you're both so old! I never thought I'd be saying this, but you're neither of you going to be here for ever. Surely you could just manage to stagger through marriage for another ten or so years? That's not as long as you were married last time – you got through fifteen years together then and they weren't all miserable by any means.'

'Hmm,' I said.

'And time goes quicker now you're older,' she added. 'You're always saying that. It'll go in a wonderful flash!'

'You think I ought just to bowl down and say I'm prepared to marry him?' I said, feeling my back was to the wall.

'Yes, I do!' said Penny. 'Stop farting around! Stop being so silly! It's not every day you find a lovely single man who happens also to be the father of your only child who also wants to marry you!'

'I suppose if we had an agreement that we wouldn't spend more than three days a week together,' I said, doubtfully.

'Stop making conditions! You can sort all that out later!' said Penny. She was getting exasperated now. 'You're behaving like one of those young men we keep reading about these days, the sort who can't "commit"! Just go down and ask him to marry you. "Keep it simple, stupid" as we say. Oh, sorry, but you know what I mean.'

'I'm not stupid,' I said crossly.

'I hate to say it, my darling, but you're not usually at all stupid. But on this subject, speaking as your best friend, I do think you are being just the teensiest weensiest,' said Penny, laughing.

'I'm not stupid,' I said resolutely. 'I'm just petrified.'

'"Fear is the darkroom where negatives are developed",' Penny quoted solemnly.

'We could always get divorced again, at a pinch,' I said, dubiously.

'Exactly. You know, Marie, you really do love him. You can't keep denying it. Denial is a river in Egypt, anyway. Go for it! Seize the day!'

'But I don't know,' I said.

'Well, I know,' said Penny. 'You'd be mad not to. You and David were made for each other. You've got Jack and Gene, you love each other to bits – what's not to like?'

I'll sleep on it.

November 3

Melanie's Facebook page today features this: '"Whereof we know nothing thereof we must remain silent" – Wittgenstein.' Underneath the quote is a picture of a teddy bear in a mortar board holding a paw to his mouth as if to say 'shush'!

That's not much help. But I'm starting to think that perhaps Penny's right. I'm making a tentative plan to go down to see David next week. I really have nothing to lose. Except my freedom.

Oh dear, I mustn't think like that.

I have retaliated to Melanie's quote by putting on my Facebook page the words: '"We are all but dead people waiting to take up our posts" – Proust.'

Hope you 'like' that, all you 'guys' out there!

November 6

Could hardly sleep last night for the fireworks – though actually they've been going off sporadically since the beginning of the week. England's become like a third world country over the last few years – fireworks popping off all the time, for any old reason. I remember the nights with Brad and Sharmie in India – the silence not only punctured by the howling of the packs of wretched dogs in the streets, and the continual honking of horns, even in the early hours, but the continuous bangs and whooshes of fireworks throughout.

Another odd thing. Poppies have appeared on sale in the

streets, but while they were once sold by charming ladies in hats, or Chelsea Pensioners in their lovely red uniforms, they're now being sold by young men and women in full army kit. I've always thought of Armistice Day as when we remember the dead of previous wars, and hope there won't be another one – a mournful, sorrowful and peaceful memorial. Instead the poppies are being shoved in our faces by young guys with bulging muscles who look as if there's nothing they'd like more than to yomp down to the battlefield and slaughter a few enemies. Doesn't seem right, somehow.

As a result, this year's the first time I'm not going to buy one.

Or maybe it's just because I've turned into an old grouch. Sometimes I think that life is rather brilliantly organised because, as we get nearer to death, we become, despite ourselves, old miseries. It's not just the *Daily Rant*. I've heard so many moans recently I can't keep up with them.

I think this mood change is like the urge to have sex, or children. It comes over us at a certain age, so we can, if not look forward to death, at least believe it when we say: 'Well, thank God I won't be alive to see the day when . . .'

November 10

I'm going down to see David tomorrow. I'm not going to tell him. I'll just appear. I don't want to risk him either going out, or barricading himself into his farm with Widow Bossom. I'm still not sure what I'm going to say. But perhaps we could reach some compromise. Surely it should be possible?

In the meantime, I'm trying to think about a contingency plan. Perhaps I could get back to painting again – despite my resolutions, I've left it rather a long time, what with the pigeon, Pouncer and the shop and everything.

To stop myself feeling too anxious and to pass the time, I did pop down to the shop to see how Tim was getting on, and found he's made it look really nice.

He's taken on the lease, and is refitting the place. The second-hand stuff is now in one tiny corner, and he's got Terry to build a proper counter from where he can sell the oldie items, like nose hair and eyebrow trimmers, neck toners and, rather a brilliant idea, long-handled toenail clippers. I'm starting to be unable to reach my toes these days so considered buying them until I realised that unless I hoik my feet pretty near my eyes I can't even see my toenails with my glasses on.

There were some pill dispensers and those plastic boxes where you can put all your pills in compartments at the beginning of the week ready for each day. And he'd got some amazing jigsaw puzzle boards, which you can roll up safely and put away till next time when you've been driven nuts trying to find the last bit of sky. He'd made a compilation CD of old Sixties hits and I felt unnervingly at home there, surrounded by all these kindly ancient aids.

Later
Spent the afternoon clearing leaves from the garden. Have to say that if ever there was a job that needed two people this is it. It's impossible to hold the bag open and stuff the leaves in

at the same time. If David were here, of course, we could do it together. Got myself thoroughly cold and wet and wherever I go in the house I leave a trail of blackened soggy leaves.

Replanted my window box with winter pansies and thought of doing a painting of them, but I feel so on edge I can't really do anything.

Spent the rest of the day polishing the silver. I say 'silver'. There's not much about except a few plated spoons, a couple of christening mugs and a sugar bowl of my mother's. But it's the sort of thing I do when I'm desperately anxious. Curiously soothing. Cleaning the tops of the skirting boards is another batty activity that keeps me from going completely mad.

I just couldn't stop thinking about Robin and David and Sandra and the Widow Bossom, and each time my heart started pounding as I imagined the Widow pottering around the farm.

'Don't worry about a thing – leave it to me, David,' she'd be saying. 'I'll do the shopping and we'll have a wonderful dinner. You won't have to lift a finger. Oh, I do declare you've run out of toilet paper! I'll add that to my list. Is there anything else I can get when I'm out? Razor blades? Of course. And don't forget to give me your sheets this week and I'll put fresh ones on the bed . . . and if you see me tomorrow afternoon with my trowel, it's just that I've realised your herbaceous border is getting a bit straggly and is badly in need of a good weed . . .'

How could I ever compete with that? I'm just not that kind of person.

November 11

God, what a day!

I drove down to Somerset, feeling sick with anxiety. I kept imagining David would refuse to speak to me, or that Widow Bossom would come out of the farmhouse with a blunderbuss like something out of an old Western film, and then we'd have a terrible catfight, corsets snapping, buttons flying (though come to think of it, it's unlikely that either of us would be wearing corsets).

But when, after a couple of hours of driving, I approached the farm, it was peculiarly silent. The curtains were drawn and the doors were all shut and locked.

Oh, God, I thought. They're probably on their honeymoon and they hadn't told me! At this very moment they were lying on the deck of an ocean liner in deckchairs, drinking cocktails and staring at each other with goofy eyes.

I got out of the car and walked around, but there was no sound except the crunch of my feet on the gravel and the sound of the wind through the trees. I was just about to text David when I bumped into Reg, one of the farmhands, who was coming up from the field with a couple of buckets in his hands.

'Oh, so you've heard, have you?' he said. He was a ruddy-faced chap, one of David's longest-serving employees.

'Heard about what?' I said.

'The accident, missus,' he said. 'Oh yes, Mr Sharp's been taken to arspital. We're all awful worried about him. Mrs

Bossom said she'd be in touch with the farmily, so I knew you'd be down sooner or later.'

'What on earth are you talking about?' I said. 'I haven't heard a word from her! What's going on!'

'Earthworks,' said Reg. 'We allus said they were dangerous after that accident a while back, but 'e wouldn't listen. Obsessed, 'e is. 'e's lucky to be aloive.'

'But what happened?'

'Same as Alf,' he replied. ''e were walking along on them planks between them earthworks, and 'e slipped and fell. 'e were unconscious, 'e were. Lucky to be aloive, loike I say.'

'But where is Mr Sharp now, Reg?' I asked. 'Which hospital?'

He told me, and I ran to the car and headed straight off.

By now, all thoughts of Widow Bossom and marriage had vanished from my mind. All I wanted was to see David and make sure he was all right. The light was starting to fade, and by the time I got to the hospital, it turned out visiting hours were going to be over in five minutes.

'His wife's in there at the moment, so I don't think you should go in,' said the friendly nurse at the desk. 'But you can come back tomorrow morning if you'd like.'

'Wife?' I said, my hair practically standing on end. 'What do you mean, "wife"? I'm his wife!'

'Oh, er . . .' She looked rather embarrassed. 'Well, we thought she was his wife. Perhaps his partner, I mean, a friend, let's see . . .' She looked down at her notes. 'Do you know her? A very nice woman. Most concerned.'

'But I must see him!' I said. 'You can't keep me out. He's the father of our son! I love him!'

'I'm sorry,' said the nurse. 'But you are very welcome to come back tomorrow. Visiting starts at nine a.m. till eleven.'

'But is he all right?' I said. 'Is he paralysed? What happened?'

'It seems he's cracked a couple of ribs – no problem there – but he keeps drifting in and out of consciousness.'

'I'm sorry!' I said firmly. 'I may only have five minutes but I absolutely insist on seeing him now. If you don't let me in I shall complain to the hospital board. I have every right . . .'

The nurse hesitated, but I seized the clipboard from her and looked down at it. David Sharp. Room 7. Looking around wildly, I set off down the corridor, found David's room and barged in.

There, staring down at the apparently unconscious David, was Edwina Bossom.

'What the hell are you doing here?' I shouted.

'Shh!' she said, putting a finger to her lips. 'He's asleep!'

I immediately pulled up a chair and sat down, taking David's hand in mine.

'Why didn't you let us know, Edwina?' I said. 'You didn't even tell Jack! And the hospital seems to think you're his wife!'

'Oh, that's a bit premature,' said the Widow, smoothly. 'But the reason that I didn't let you know straight away was of course because I didn't want to worry you. I wanted to be able to ring you when he was out of the woods.'

'I want to know when he's *in* the woods, not out of them,' I practically shrieked. 'He might have died and we couldn't have said goodbye! I want to worry about him! I love him, do you get it? He's my husband!'

'Well, I wouldn't say that, exactly,' said Widow Bossom, taken aback. 'He said that you'd turned him—'

'I'm his wife!' I heard myself saying, 'I was his wife, I am his wife and I always will be his wife! Understand?'

The Widow looked extremely taken aback.

'Well, if you're going to be like that,' she said, and in a gesture of defiance pulled the dark glasses down from the top of her head and glared at me. 'I was only doing my best!' With that, she walked out.

Shaking, I turned to David. He looked so pale and wretched that I couldn't help but put my hand out and stroke his cheek. Then I leaned down to kiss him.

'You must get better, darling,' I said. 'I'm sorry, I'm sorry, I'm sorry. I love you. Please, please get well.'

There was a knock on the door, and the nurse looked in. 'Visiting hours are over,' she said, looking at her watch.

'I'll be out in a minute,' I said, looking up at her.

But when I looked back at David, I saw, to my amazement, that his eyes were open.

'What on earth was all that about?' he said.

'Oh, she wants to chuck me out – something about visiting hours,' I said.

'No, not that. I mean all that stuff with Edwina, all that wife stuff.'

'What do you mean? Look, David, you're meant to be ill!'

'Well, I was trying to sleep,' he said, hitching himself up

on his pillows, wincing with pain. 'But I couldn't sleep with all that racket going on. Here I am minding my own business, having a rest, and suddenly you and Edwina are having a screaming match. What's going on? Anyway,' he said, in a puzzled way, 'why are you here if Edwina didn't ring you? How did you find out?'

At this point I couldn't help bursting into tears.

'I came down to say I was sorry, and if you want . . . I've made a mistake, and forget what I said about marriage, it's not such a bad idea at all, I mean, really not such a bad idea, in fact I think it's quite a good idea, actually, it's a great idea . . . oh, I've missed you so much, and I've been so silly . . .'

David leaned over and looked at his watch, which was lying on his bedside table.

He leaned back on the pillow and there was long silence.

Then, 'Get me a glass of water, darling, would you?'

And at that word, 'darling', I started to think I might be in with a chance. I got up, filled his glass and put it down beside him. Then, overcome with emotion, I couldn't help it. I leant down and put my head on his shoulder.

'Ouch!' he said.

'Sorry,' I said, starting up.

'No, it's not that bad. I'll suffer. Come on, back you come, old girl.'

And there we lay, for what seemed to be ages, with David stroking my hair, until the nurse finally appeared with another nurse, clearly deputed to throw me out if there was any trouble.

Reluctantly, I rose to my feet.

'I'll be back tomorrow,' I said, kissing him.

David smiled, weakly. 'That's my girl,' he said. 'Stay the night at the farm. You know where the key is. Love you.'

'Love you too,' I said. 'Lots.'

As I got to the door, watched beadily by the two nurses, David spoke again.

'I've been stupid, too, you know,' he said. 'Not just you.'

Later

David was right. I did know where the key was. I found it under a flower pot, let myself in and made myself at home.

Without Sandra or Gangi around – though there was a spare pushchair in the hall – the place looked suspiciously neat. Almost sterile. No wonder the poor man was lonely, I thought. I couldn't help wondering if Widow Bossom hadn't had a hand in keeping everything so pristine. There were several plastic boxes with labels on in the fridge – no doubt meals provided by the Bossom – and a bunch of rather ghastly orange daisies in a vase on the shelf by the sink. Copies of *Country Life* were fanned out on the sitting room coffee tables as if it were a Harley Street doctor's waiting room.

At least David's desk retained some humanity, covered with papers, and his computer was still on – the only way I've been able to write all this and, rather brilliantly, email it to myself.

Much to my surprise, I found, on the mantelpiece over-looking his desk, a photograph of David and me getting married first time around. It was only at a registry office, and we both looked fairly scruffy, but very happy, too. How odd, I thought. Even though I'd behaved so unkindly, he still keeps that photograph up. There was also a picture of Jack, Chrissie and Gene and, next to it, a picture of Sandra and Gangi. But no picture, I was glad to see, of the Widow.

I rang Jack, Penny and James, just to let them know about the accident, but left the Bossom details out for the time being. You never know. She might be burrowing a tunnel under the hospital and be standing in David's room leaning on a spade, dirty but triumphant, when I appear tomorrow.

November 12

When I returned to the hospital the next day, the nurse looked slightly more pleased to see me.

'Well, I have to say that Mr Sharp had a very good night last night. The doctor came this morning and said he was very pleased with his progress. He's cracked a couple of ribs, of course, but the results of the brain scan have been fine, and it looks as if he might be discharged in a couple of days!'

'Thank you!' I said. 'And I'm sorry if I was a bit overwrought yesterday. I was just upset.'

'We understand,' said the nurse, giving me a knowing smile as if she'd got the picture. 'But go in now. There's no one else there.'

David was sitting up in bed looking much more relaxed. Some colour had come back into his cheeks and he was reading the paper.

'Not the *Daily Rant*?' I said.

David turned the paper to me so I could see the headline,

and pointed, silently. 'Surrogate mum: I'll never give up Burger King baby to his gay dads!' I read.

David smiled, and put the paper down.

'I'd laugh but it hurts a bit,' he said.

'Well, I'll do the laughing for you,' I said, and I went over to his bedside and sat down, holding his hand in mine.

'Now, Marie, you and I have got to have a proper talk,' said David. 'I mean this marriage stuff. It's all very well, but don't let's do anything hasty. I know it's all very dramatic, with me being ill, but we mustn't rush into anything.'

'I don't feel remotely rushed!' I said. 'You asked me to marry you months ago! I've had ages to think about it.'

'But I haven't,' said David. 'You forget, I was just getting used to the idea of being single for the rest of my life!'

'You wouldn't have stayed single long with the Bossom around!' I said, indignantly.

'She's not my cup of tea,' said David. 'You know that. And when I heard she hadn't even told Jack I'd had an accident – that did upset me!'

'I've told him,' I said, feeling like the only schoolgirl who remembered her homework. 'He's coming down tomorrow.'

'So, when you said you wanted us to get married, what exactly did you mean?' said David.

'I meant just that,' I said. 'I want to get married. David, there's nothing I'd like more than to be married to you. The idea of losing you is completely unbearable.'

'We could continue as we were before, if you like,' said David. 'Not being in each other's pockets all the time. But it's just that I'd like to be married to someone.'

'Well, I hope I'll do as "someone",' I said, pretending to take offence.

David narrowed his eyes and appraised me.

'You'll do,' he said. Then he smiled. 'So, what do you think, darling? Could you bear to toddle down the aisle again?'

'We never did any aisle-toddling,' I said, looking back. 'As far as I remember, we got married in a registry office. Or perhaps that was somebody else.'

'Okay, then what about an aisle this time? As a first? Maybe that's what we did wrong the first time round,' said David, laughing. 'Ouch. Maybe it was all about the aisle. Nothing about me drinking or you getting all controlling . . . if we'd just started off our marriage down the aisle, all would have been fine.'

'We could always give it go.'

'I think we should, don't you?' he said. 'Now I can't get down on one knee but imagine I'm down there, kneeling on that horrible scrubbed hospital floor, looking up at you and saying: "Marie, will you marry me?"'

'And imagine me, staring down at you from this revolting plastic hospital chair, saying: "Yes, darling, there's nothing I'd like better".'

David pulled me to him, and we kissed.

November 16

I left Jack in Somerset, and he's staying a few days so he'll look after David for a while.

Jack, of course, had been typically dry when I told him.

'Well, as long as you know what you're doing, Mum,' he said. 'Don't blame me if it goes wrong. But on the face of it, it sounds an excellent idea. And it'll make everything a lot easier when it comes to the wills. And of course it'll be a great relief for us if you've got Dad to look after you when you get old and ill – and vice-versa.'

Jack has a down-to-earth streak which takes my breath away sometimes, but at least he always tells the truth.

When I got back home, I rang Penny.

'I feel personally responsible for this wedding,' she said. 'I really don't believe you'd have gone down if I hadn't nagged you!'

'You're quite right,' I had to admit.

'So goodbye Bossom?' said Penny. 'I'd like to see her face! So when is it to be? Can I be matron of honour? I've never been a matron. It sounds so stable and secure.'

Later

This on Melanie's Facebook page: '"The possession of knowledge does not kill the sense of wonder and mystery. There is always more mystery." Anaïs Nin.'

Fancy having 'Nin' as a surname.

In a fit of pique I responded with a quote I recently saw on a birthday card: 'Eat right, exercise regularly, die anyway.'

Seems a bit more realistic.

DECEMBER

December 7

I've become a woman obsessed. Even the *Daily Rant*'s latest headline can't bring me down ('High on cocaine and date-rape drug "G", NHS children's brain doctor . . . ON CALL!')

I seem to spend all my time organising the wedding. David and I have decided not to wait, and to get married as soon as possible. As we never go to church, and as we don't know any vicars or believe in God, thank God – if you get my drift – I suggested asking Father Emmanuel if he would conduct a ceremony in his church at the end of the road.

I'd gone back down to Shampton, making plans around the old kitchen table beside the Aga. David's still walking with a stick, but it's only because of a hip strain, and his ribs will heal in time. Apart from being a bit shocked and tired, he seems just the same old David. My same old David.

David laughed. 'Do you think he'd do it? Surely he'd damn

us to eternal flames when he knew we'd been married before, even if it was to each other.'

'He's a nice enough old stick underneath,' I said. 'It would be good fun. We could have a gospel choir.'

'Now you're talking. An aisle and a gospel choir. What could go wrong? And Gene could be a pageboy,' said David. 'It'd be charming. Come on, let's push the boat out! And we could have a wedding party in your house with food from the Nepalese across the road.'

'And kill all the guests? No thanks!' I said, remembering the unspeakable evening earlier this year. 'Anyway, it's our house, not my house. But I'd love Zac to be a pageboy as well,' I said, thinking of my ex-lodger Graham's son, who I got so close to a couple of years ago. 'Do you remember him? And Mr Patel could do the drinks . . . And Melanie could do the flowers, and Penny can be the matron . . . and what about having Sandra as chief bridesmaid . . . and maybe Alice, Brad and Sharmie's little girl, too, if we could persuade them to come over from India?'

'And Jack can be best man!' said David.

There was a pause.

'Do you think we could make Robin an usher?' I asked. 'And maybe Terry as well? I'm fond of the lad, despite everything.'

'Despite what?' said David.

I remembered I'd not told him about Terry's past, but I thought that – as by now Terry has proved his worth, since he's still working for James – it wouldn't matter if I told David his history.

'Yes, let's make him an usher,' said David, when I'd explained. 'By the way, I'm going to forget everything you've just told me. Best, I think, don't you?'

'I didn't tell you anyfink, guv,' I said. And we left it at that.

We decided that Chrissie could do my make-up and James could sort out the printing of the invitations.

'And Gene could do the DJ'ing as well as be the pageboy,' I suggested.

'Dancing? I hadn't thought that through,' said David. 'But we always cut a mean caper on the dance floor, didn't we, old girl? As they say down on the street these days.'

December 13

The only disappointment is that Gene doesn't want to be a pageboy.

'Look, Mum, he's ten years old, and he's got a reputation to live up to,' said Jack. 'It's the sort of thing you can get someone to do when they're small, but I think Gene feels a bit embarrassed by the idea. He thinks it's all rather soppy, and he knows everyone would stare at him and say "How sweet". I do see his point. He'll be doing the DJ'ing afterwards, anyway, and you've got Gangi and Zac. It's all getting a bit Richard Curtis, having Gene as bridesmaid as well – I mean, whatever it is that boys are.'

'I quite understand,' I said. And of course, with one bit of me I do understand. And with another bit I just wish Gene were that little bit younger and more biddable. Because I know

341

that when he grows up he'd absolutely love to be able to say he'd been a pageboy at his granny and grandpa's wedding. Still, there's nothing I can do, so I've let it go.

I say I've let it go. Of course in reality I know it'll be gnawing away at me all night, and even now I keep having a pang, thinking that having Gene as pageboy would be the icing on the cake, but I've pretended I've let it go, at least.

December 14

This on Melanie's Facebook page: 'When I follow what I love, what I love follows me.'

Of course it made my flesh crawl, and particularly so because of course it does rather apply to me. So I'm in what's known as a 'conflicted situation'. Part of me thinks it's a load of tosh, and part of me is dabbing my eyes with a hankie, thinking, 'How true!'

The actual wedding is next week, on the shortest day – which is, of course, the Winter Solstice, so I'm sure Robin approves of that. And Tim's been an absolute brick in sorting everything out. He keeps saying things like: 'You must let the DVLA and the tax people know about your change of status. And I bet the insurance needs to know . . . Though as you've always kept your married name, thank goodness, you shouldn't have a problem with that.'

'It's really kind of you,' I said. 'I should be doing all this. Or David.'

'No, it's a pleasure. My little contribution. Anyway, it's interesting to find out about what's involved in getting married again. I was wondering how it would work.'

'Why? Surely you're not thinking of taking the plunge?' I said, jokingly.

'You never know!' he said. And although there was a twinkle in his eye, I thought he said it a little more seriously than I was expecting. Looks as if I might have been right about him and Penny. I do hope so.

December 27

After the wedding we had a quiet Christmas chez David, with the family. Now they've all gone home, it's the first chance I've had to write about how it all went. David's out, trying to deal with some trees that fell over in last night's storm, and I'm tidying up and getting our supper for tonight. Sandra and Gangi are coming over and, believe it or not, Widow Bossom. Yes, I've decided to forgive her, not just because now she's no threat but because the moment she realised David was no longer a potential Mr Bossom, she got off his case and got herself a new boyfriend, a pleasant enough old retired CEO called Gerald, a man who worships her.

Though I'll be really glad to get home and have a bit of time by myself, I'm thoroughly enjoying being here. And being Mrs David Sharp all over again! Weird!

The wedding – well, it was fabulous, and how could it not be? The family came over in the morning, Chrissie with her make-up kit to get me looking 'even better than usual' as she tactfully put it. I'd bought the most wonderful second-hand Vivienne Westwood dress on eBay, which, amazingly, fitted me – it was all black with a tight skirt and frills at the back . . . it would have been too cheesy to have got married in white.

Penny and I had our hair done at an incredibly expensive salon in Bond Street – she had hers put up and it looked fabulous. And all morning she was wandering around the house tweaking bits and peering at the endless trays of exotic food covered with cling film that were being delivered by gorgeous Arab men coming in and out of the house – we'd decided to go with the Middle Eastern restaurant up the road. David stayed at Jack's after a kind of stag night with James and Owen the night before, which must have been a pretty tame affair considering they're both gay and David wasn't likely to go clubbing with them till the early hours.

Brad and Sharmie and Alice had come over and were staying with Melanie – Sharmie horrified, of course, by the hippiness of it all, and Alice enchanted. But after a couple of nights they were looking for a hotel. I think it was all just a bit too Indian for them. I think they're getting a bit fed up with Delhi.

'I just want to be somewhere that's clean!' said Sharmie.

Father Emmanuel promised Tim not to say anything too godly – at least nothing about hell – and managed somehow to keep his mouth shut. Actually, he was so pleased about everything and kept giving us big hugs, I wouldn't have minded what he'd said in the end.

It was funny getting married again. I couldn't really feel as excited as I would have done the first time round – I wasn't anxious that David wouldn't turn up, and of course none of our parents was around, fussing, and it all seemed incredibly relaxed. After the service Penny and Melanie insisted on throwing rose petals all over us, and I made sure that Penny caught my bouquet. We'd practised beforehand, and I noticed her, on catching the flowers, looking into Tim's eyes with a knowing smile.

And the party went on till – well, not dawn, but after midnight. Everyone was there – Ben, Jack's old doctor friend who'd been so kind to me over the cancer scare a couple of years ago, with his wife; Ned, the tree man, and my old lodger Michelle; Graham, Zac's dad and his wife, Julie, and even a couple of the teachers from Gene's school, the head and the dozy old art mistress. Sylvie and Harry were there, with Mrs Evans, the housekeeper – and they'd brought Chummy along, who was extremely excited to be back in the old house (though rather disappointed that Pouncer wasn't there to be chased). James was a superb best man, watched, proudly, by Owen, and we'd even asked Sheila the Dealer, who appeared looking far more presentable than usual, with Terry, actually wearing some lipstick (Sheila, that is, not Terry).

Robin arrived with Sandra – there's clearly something going on there – and the Widow Bossom appeared with a very generous present of some weird kind of vegetable steamer, even though we'd specifically said no presents.

But best of all was the service itself. As I was waiting in the aisle on Jack's arm, with the bridesmaids and pageboys all gathered, who should appear out of the shadows but Gene, looking rather sheepish in a grey suit and crisp white shirt.

He came up to me and gave me a hug.

'I changed my mind, Gran,' he said. 'I'll be a pageboy – and don't worry about the other two. I'll look after them.'

And look after them he did. Turning, ever so slightly, and seeing him coming after me, holding Zac by one hand, alongside Sandra, holding Gangi, my eyes filled up with tears. He looked so manly – almost like a little father – and suddenly I could see exactly the chap he'd be when he grew up.

The gospel choir reached its peak, and as they did, Gene's and my eyes met. He smiled, gave me a big wink, and mouthed: 'Love you, Granny.'

And then the organ burst forth, and David and I were up at the altar. Saying 'I do'. And knowing that this time, at least, we'd be happy ever after.